BOOKS B

MW00654437

CAVALIERED TO DEATH

A BARKVIEW MYSTERY

C.B. WILSON

Copyright 2021 by C.B.Wilson

eBook ISBN: 978-1-7374393-1-8

Paperback ISBN: 978-1-7374393-4-9

All rights reserved. The unauthorized reproduction or distribution of the
copyrighted work is illegal and forbidden without the written permission of the
author and publisher; exceptions are made for brief excerpts used in published
reviews.

This is a work of fiction. Names, characters, institutions, events or locales in this
novel are the product of the authors imagination or used fictitiously.

To Dad
You were right
No goal is unrealistic, just the time frame

CONTENTS

Dolphin Training Center

Fishtails Seaside Cafe

DOG PATH

1. Bow Wow Boutique
2. Posh Puppies
3. Bichon Bisquets
4. Beg-als Shoppe
5. Muttropolis
6. Woofing Best Coffe

7. Urban Pup
8. Snooty Pooch
9. Fluff & Buff
10. Fiesta Chihuahua

11. Bank
12. Gem's Palace
13. Blooming Tails
14. Taj Ma Hound

Cat's Town House

Homes

2nd

Oldman home
(circa 1900-1925)

3rd

4th

Red Door Speakeasy
(circa 1920-1925)

K9 Fine Wine Bar

1st

Graveyard & Ghost — Hounds Hardware

Frosty Pup

1   2   3   4

6   7   8   9

5   10   11   12

Chateau Chien

Salty Dog Seafood

Doodle Pad

13   14

Mutt Hutt
Do

15. Hot Dog Stand
16. Bone Garden Salad
17. Attorney
18. Escrow
19. Hair Salon

KDOG Studio

15
16

Farmer's Market

17

B

18
19

A Lifeguard Tower

Dolce

Ciao Bella

Bark Rock

A

Dog House

B Old Barkview Inn

WOOF

DOG PATH

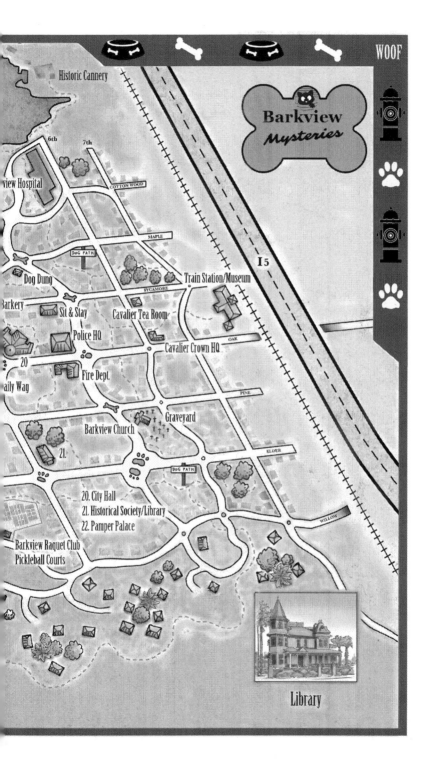

WOOF

Barkview Mysteries

Historic Cannery

6th 7th

view Hospital

COTTON WOOD

MAPLE

DOG PATH

SYCAMORE

Train Station/Museum

Dog Dung

Barkery Sit & Stay Cavalier Tea Room

Police HQ Cavalier Crown HQ

OAK

20 Fire Dept.

aily Wag PINE

Barkview Church Graveyard

21. ELDER

DOG PATH

20. City Hall
21. Historical Society/Library
22. Pamper Palace

WILLOW

Barkview Raquet Club
Pickleball Courts

I 5

Library

CHARACTERS HUMAN

Barklay, Celeste: Founder Barkview in 1890

Barklay, Charlotte (Aunt Char): Dog Psychiatrist on *Throw Him a Bone*. Renny, a champion King Charles Spaniel, is her dog

Barklay, JB: Aunt Char's late husband

Casey Ann: Graveyard Dispatcher

Castro, Tomas: Leader Pit Bull fighting ring. Diseco and Crusher were his henchmen

Castro, Tomas Jr: Tomas Castro's son

Cathaway, Bart: British attorney. Duke, a champion Cavalier King Charles Spaniel, is his dog

Duncan, Franklin: concierge at the Old Barkview Inn

Ford: Sandy's boyfriend

Hawl, Russ: FBI consultant. Works for Blue Diamond Security

Jose and Ria: Barklay Kennel employees

Le Fleur, Michelle: owns Fluff and Buff Salon. Fifi, a black standard Poodle, is her dog

Looc, Howard: Owns Petronics. Bolt, a Border Collie is his dog

Martinez, Ricky: technical Director at KDOG

Moore, Jennifer: Crown Committee Chairwoman. Owns two ruby Cavaliers

Oldeman, Will: elevator operator at the Old Barkview Inn

Papas, Ariana and Chris: owners of Gem's Palace Jewelry. Gem, a German Shepherd, is their dog

Richards, Richie: police officer

Riley, Sean: J. Tracker's president. JRu, a Jack Russell Terrier, is his dog

Sandy: Cat's assistant and computer wiz. Jack, a Jack Russell Terrier, is her dog

Schmidt, Gregory (Uncle G): Chief of Police. Max and Maxine, German Shepherds, are his dogs

Smythe, Linda: Mayor's wife. Lady Mag is her champion Cavalier King Charles Spaniel

Tuner, Gabby: owner of Daily Wag coffee shop. Sal, a Saluki, is her dog

Whitman, Nell: Owner Sit and Stay Café. Blur, a black lab, is her dog

Worth-Austin, Olivia: Married to Richard Worth a developer. Somerset is her champion Cavalier

Wright, Catalina "Cat": Producer/investigative reporter at KDOG. A cat person living in Barkview

CHARACTERS CANINE

🐾Bolt: Howard Looc's Border Collie

🐾Duke: Bart Cathaway's champion King Charles Spaniel

🐾Fifi: Michelle Le Fleur's black standard Poodle

🐾Gem: Ariana and Chris's German Shepherd

🐾Jack: Sandy's Jack Russell Terrier

🐾JRu: Sean Riley's Jack Russel Terrier

🐾Lady Margret: Lynda Smythe's champion King Charles Spaniel

🐾Matata: Russ's mother's Portuguese Water Dog

🐾Renny: Aunt Char's champion Cavalier King Charles Spaniel

🐾Penny: Renny in disguise

🐾Somerset: Olivia Austin-Worth's champion Cavalier King Charles Spaniel

🐾Sal: Gabby Turner's Saluki

CHAPTER 1

I don't hate dogs. I simply prefer sleek, independent, litter-box-trained cats. That makes me the most unpopular person in Barkview, the dog-friendliest city in America. Every freeway welcome sign touts it in big, bone-shaped letters. I kid you not. From designated leash lanes to hound playgrounds, this town is all about dogs.

My name is Catalina Wright, Cat for short, a bona fide cuss word in this canine-crazed community. Fortunately, over the past ten years, I've developed a survivalist's sense of political correctness. I have one of those dream jobs coveted by leash lovers everywhere. I produce my aunt, dog psychiatrist Dr. Charlotte Barklay's talk show, *Throw Him a Bone*, KDOG's nationally syndicated look at life from Fido's perspective. Did I mention the show is live? Yup, every Monday through Friday at seven p.m. Pacific Standard Time I get another gray hair.

So, the moment our teetotaling mayor's wife, Lynda Smythe, DUI-staggered onto my broadcast set, I should've just faded to commercial.

"Gimme M-mag." The slur distorting Lynda's lilting

Southern belle accent made coherency challenging. Her lunge toward me added to my confusion. If not protected by the phone booth we called a studio control room, she'd have been at my throat. I jerked backward, hip-bumping Ricky Martinez, my ponytailed technical director, away from the control panel as Lynda's shoulder pinballed off the glass.

"Holy... This has to be a publicity stunt. Right?" Trust my tow-headed production assistant to verbalize my thoughts. Perched to Ricky's left at the call-in switchboard, Sandy Wynne had a nose for entertainment and a college enthusiasm that reminded me of myself too many years ago. That we'd met over Jan Douglas' murder did cross my mind.

Sure, I wanted to believe this was about publicity. With the coveted Old Barkview Cavalier Club's top King Charles competition just over a week away, every contender angled for an advantage. But this seemed too far even for uber-competitive Lynda.

Naturally, we were on air with six minutes until our hard time out. I keyed up a commercial, but paused. My aunt had defused worse situations.

Poised on a claw foot, Victorian sofa with her own Blenheim champion, Renaissance (Renny to those she allowed), draped in true majestic form across her lap, my Aunt Char might as well be a reigning Nordic monarch.

"Lynda, are you all right?" Aunt Char's ultra-calm reassured me. She'd risen, displacing Renny, but remained in camera.

My hand hovered mid-center on the Star Trek-inspired panel as Lynda pivoted toward Aunt Char.

"Where's she?" Lynda slurred.

"Who?" Aunt Char asked.

"Lady M-mag."

2

Had I heard right? Lady Margaret, Lynda's champion Cavalier King Charles, was missing?

"Y'all nabbed her to win the Crown." Lynda's vehemence astounded me. Aunt Char kidnap a dog to win a trophy? Preposterous, insane. Executive decision made, I pressed the go-to-commercial button. The public had seen more than enough.

"Lynda," Aunt Char insisted. "You need to let me help you."

Panic erupted in Lynda's suddenly clear tones. "No! The FBI will find 'er."

It's true. Life's crises happen in super-clear slow motion. Lynda jerked out whatever had been weighing down her jacket. Renny growled and lunged with Jack Russell agility off the couch. Lynda stumbled backward shrieking. Her arms flayed in perfect unison with Renny's plumed-tail swing. OMG! Had Renny just bit Lynda? No. Something metallic hung from the dog's mouth. A gun!

Furballs! I stood there like an acrophobic in a tree until the clank of metal hitting the wood floor shattered the freeze-frame. Dior flew as both women nosedived for the weapon. Watch out, reality TV. Barkview's catfight raised the bar. A single, deafening gunshot ended it all. My paralysis must've broken because the next thing I knew I stood on stage with Ricky breathing down my neck.

"Aunt Char!"

"I'm not hurt." With a single head toss, her elegant coiffure fell back into place.

I believed her. Renny licked her paw in job-done indifference.

Aunt Char handed the weapon to Ricky. "Secure this until the police arrive." Her signature composure didn't work for me or Ricky, who handled the handgun with the authority of a guy who'd just pulled a piping-hot bowl out of the microwave.

Aunt Char kneeled above Lynda's prone body. "Call 911. I'll check her injuries. Everyone stay where you are."

"Is she...?" My words stuck like a hairball in my throat. That wasn't marinara sauce pooling beside Lynda's ear. Spaghetti-legged, I swallowed hard as Renny bumped my shin, nearly toppling me.

I got a grip as Aunt Char did a cursory evaluation of Lynda's condition. "Lynda's posterior contusion is not from a gunshot graze. The injury is a slow bleed out. It likely happened some time ago."

That explained Lynda's impaired motor skills and speech. "A car accident?" It made perfect sense. My aunt's noncommittal shrug bothered me. "Explains why she was talking crazy."

I knew I was rambling. So did Renny. I swear the dog shot me the evil eye. Now, I was losing it. Cowed by a fourteen-pound fluff mutt with a pedigree that outclassed my mixed-up European heritage. In my defense, this kind of thing didn't happen in picture-perfect Barkview. I smoothed the tawny escapees back into my no-nonsense ponytail. "Talk about free publicity for Lady Mag."

"Lynda had a genuine shot at the Cavalier Crown." The ever-so-slight quiver in Aunt Char's voice struck a nerve.

"Had?" A someone-walked-on-your-grave chill shivered down my spine.

"Cat, you need to get out of here before the police lock us down," Aunt Char said.

"Lock us ... what?" Was I stuck in a B-movie skit? "You said Lynda was hurt before she got here."

"She was, but a shot was fired. The police will investigate."

"Yes, but..." Leave? I was the producer. Captains went down with their ships.

Aunt Char's unwavering sapphire stare kicked my butt into action. "The best medicine for Lynda will be to find Lady Mag."

"How do you know she's even missing? Lynda said a lot of wild things."

Aunt Char's shrug spoke volumes.

"Sandy, call J. Tracker. Have them activate Lady Mag's GPS tracker collar." As if they didn't already know. Gossip traveled at light speed in this town.

I pulled a pink Post-it from my pocket, bummed a pen from Ricky and prepared to take notes. Okay, I admit it. I am eternally indebted to the Post-it king, Art Fry. Without those three-by-three multicolored slips of paper reminding me who, what, where, and when, I'd be a wreck.

"Dog's at Lynda's house." Sandy's voice came over the loudspeaker. "Sending the link to your phone."

We all breathed easier until Aunt Char crossed her arms. "I doubt Lynda's injury is related to a car accident. You need to confirm Lady Mag is there."

"You doubt the locator?" My gaze met Aunt Char's over Renny's identical crazy-expensive jeweled collar. The same collar that inspired my Wright Dog Insanity (WDI) scale, a one to ten over-the-topness rating of the dog devotees hereabouts.

"Lynda would never pass up an opportunity to get Lady Mag on air."

Far be it from me to argue with Aunt Char's uncanny understanding of human nature.

Something was off. Lynda's accusations would also play like a matador's cape to the bull with the oh-so competitive Barkfest coming up. "This could be a serious PR nightmare," I said.

"Among other things. The FBI will be in on this."

"No way. Not for a d…"

Aunt Char cut me off. "Careful, Cat. That kind of talk is treason in this town."

I had the tickets to prove it. A citation for failure to yield the sidewalk to an on-coming Pekinese and another for inciting a pack when I meowed in public on a double-dog-dare.

"By legal definition, Lady Mag is property. The FBI doesn't investigate local missing property crimes." I'd learned that one the hard way. The puncture scar, strategically hidden beneath my signature neck scarf, tingled its reminder.

Aunt Char's frown indicated more. "Lynda's brother-in-law is a big-wig at the FBI."

Find me one person who didn't know. The FBI still had specific and very public operating guidelines.

"I know your plate is full, but your experience..." Aunt Char trailed off.

I bit my lip. "I report fluff now. I haven't worked a real investigation in ten years."

"The reporting you did to put those heathens out of business is intuitive," she said far too reasonably.

Heathens hardly described that vicious dogfighting ring I exposed my rookie year reporting for the LA Journal, a lifetime ago. Aunt Char knew the details all too well. She'd nursed me through four hundred stitches, three surgeries and years of her special blend of developing strength through adversity. Personally, I subscribe to avoidance. Even a TV Pit Bull triggered a channel change.

Her vote of confidence gave me strength. Like I had a choice. Watching out for Aunt Char put me smack in the middle of this one. "What do you think is going on?"

"Whatever it is, I am going to be the main suspect."

No argument. The subjective nature of dog show judging made winning the Crown primarily about politics. And my aunt knew how to campaign, especially when winning solidified her late husband's vision for the Barklay Kennel. If finding Lady Mag cleared her, I'd deal with my insecurities.

"I trust you'll handle this as delicately as possible," Aunt Char cautioned.

"Delicately?" I'd find the dog. "Don't tell me that you're seriously angling for the mayor's job in November?"

"Don't be silly." Her little half smile said otherwise. Mayor Charlotte Barklay. Too bad following rules didn't exactly run in my DNA.

CHAPTER 2

Escape priority one, I slipped out the emergency exit as Barkview's finest burst into the studio. I backed my Jag SUV out of my reserved parking spot and exited onto 2nd Street. No sense advertising my getaway to the gossips loitering outside the main entrance.

Barkview's business district, locally called the Village, occupied seven square blocks, the buildings all iconic Victorians. Some were restored and some built to look old. Charming cobblestone streets illuminated by retrofitted turn-of-the-nineteenth-century gas lamps cast a warm, comforting glow.

I made two quick left turns and headed south toward the twisty-turny, tree-lined road accessing the Terraces. Located due south from the Village, the hillside homes enjoyed expansive sunset views of the Pacific, cool breezes, and privacy not often found in Southern California. Barkview's elite resided there. The higher up the hill, the more exclusive and thicker the marine layer.

Tonight proved true to form. Halfway up the hill, I switched on my fog lights and white-knuckled it the rest of the way to the Smythes' Spanish colonial-style home. Built by a Barklay ancestor in the 1940s, the five-acre garden estate featured a five-horse barn, a caretaker's cottage, and an unobstructed view of Bark Rock when the clouds allowed.

Normally, twinkle lights illuminated the circular cobblestone drive. This evening, high noon spilled from every window. Void of the usual nocturnal critters' chorus, the eerie silence set my teeth on edge. The pancaked petunia bed and gaping front door completed the unnerving scene. I reached into my glove box and removed a six-inch, weapon-quality flashlight. Lady Mag's location signal still read fifty feet straight ahead.

I took a deep breath as I closed the car door and brandished the flashlight like the club it was. "L-lady Mag?" The stutter just came out. Concern did that to a person. "Come here, girl." No luck. Not even a growl or take-cover nail scurry across the marble floor broke the heavy silence. Lynda's accusation suddenly seemed all too possible.

Fear, peppered with reason, said to take cover and wait for the police. What if I caught someone here or worse, disturbed a crime scene? But what if Lady Mag was injured and needed help?

I even half-believed my logic as I crept past the enormous pink and white rose-filled vase in the foyer. To the right, candles flickered on the Botticino marble mantle beneath the formal portrait of a Blenheim Cavalier regally posed on Lynda's lap. My WDI Scale tipped twelve. A shrine to a dog? Really?

I followed the tracking signal down the dark paneled hall to the spic-and-span monochromatic kitchen where gadget envy promptly swamped me. What I could do with a six-burner stove and stainless-steel oven combo and warming tray...

I looked to my left. Bordered in dark wood, the picture

windows offered an expansive view of the mist-shrouded patio. With every light on in the house, the shadowed patio just felt wrong.

I flipped the light switch at the door. Up. Down. Nothing. I stilled instant heart palpitations. The bulb could be out. I turned on my flashlight and opened the porch door. A sparkling flash caught my eye too late. I jack-rabbited, barely dodging Lady Mag's pavé diamond GPS collar dead center on the Travertine, bashed my big toe on a garden statue, and tripped with Laurel-and-Hardy grace into the recently manured coleus.

Ugh. I shook the dirt and crumpled leaves off my hands and inspected the offending sculpture beside me. Naturally, it wasn't a cherub, but a bronze Cavalier, the same regally poised one my aunt had in her garden. Tripped up by a dog. Story of my life.

I tossed the statue into the dirt and attempted to brush the mud-pie mess off my not-so-white capris as I studied the collar arranged in a perfect letter "C" with what appeared to be a paw print epicenter. "C" as in "Cat" or "Charlotte" or just plain coincidence? What other shape would a dropped collar look like?

Suddenly, a bright light blinded me. At the same time, a familiar, deep baritone voice ordered, "Freeze. Police."

"It's me, Uncle G." He should've recognized my voice, but I still surrendered my hands high. Although I called the police chief uncle, he wasn't a blood relative, but rather my aunt's second husband's brother-in-law.

Flanked by his pair of iron gray German Shepherds that matched his neatly clipped beard and full head of hair, the chief of police proved my theory that masters choose physically similar canine companions.

My heart rate spiked as I eyed the dogs' attack-ready

stances. "H-how did you get here so fast?" I mentally counted to ten, squelching my sudden irrational fear. I'd bottle-fed both of those dogs. They weren't going to bite me.

"Lynda called me."

I could tell by his sharp uniform creases he'd just dressed for the visit. Aunt Char had been right about connections. Even Uncle G jumped when the mayor's wife called.

"Who's at the studio?" I asked.

"Officer Richardson is in charge."

I felt better already. Aunt Char could handle All-American Richie Richardson. "Mind if I get up?"

"Mind telling me what you're doing here?"

I retrieved my flashlight and grasped his tree trunk forearm for a hand up. "Looking for Lady Mag. Have you seen her?"

"No. I'm looking for her too."

"Did you see the collar?" I asked.

"Yeah." His gaze scanned the scene with investigative precision.

"Think it's a letter C?"

"An unlatched round collar would naturally fall in that position."

"True. But the paw print suggests this was planned." No response, just the bob of Uncle G's after-dinner toothpick between his teeth. "Is that Lady Mag's paw print?"

"Paw prints are not individual markers like human fingerprints."

A blur in the print caught my eye. I crouched. "Can I have your cheaters a sec?"

Uncle G handed over his black rimmed reading glasses.

"This is Lady Mag's print." I returned the glasses. "See the line in the paw pad? That's the scar from the vase incident."

Uncle G stroked his beard. "Unlikely the dog got out of her collar, left her paw print, and ran off on her own."

You think? "A dognapper with an agenda?" It sounded insane. How do you ink a paw anyway? Good luck getting Renny to step on wet grass, never mind a squishy ink pad.

I pulled a Post-it from my pocket and patted my pants. "Can I borrow a pen?"

"Not a chance. You haven't returned the last five."

Okay, so maybe I was a pen thief. "Fine. I'll buy you a box."

Clearly, he wasn't taking any chances. He handed me a stubby No. 2 pencil. I shined my light on my Post-it, wrote my note, and crammed it into my pocket.

Uncle G pulled on rubber gloves and retrieved a gold disk nestled inside the collar circumference. The button shone beneath his police flashlight.

"Dior," I mumbled, more than a little concerned. The whole town knew Aunt Char preferred Dior. "Lynda wore a Dior suit tonight." I couldn't remember if a button had been missing. I made another note to check.

No comment from Uncle G. Just quiet contemplation that could mean anything.

"Is there a database on dognappings?" I asked.

"I'll check. Missing dogs are filed under theft."

I massaged my temples. "What exactly do we have here legally?" His raised brow got my attention. "Hey, the front door was wide open when I arrived."

"Assuming what you say is true, a dognapping would plead to misdemeanor trespassing or grand theft."

"Grand theft dog?" I choked on my chuckle.

Amusement softened the corners of his frown. "First offense would likely plead to a fine."

"Lynda's going to love this." Get ready for a new town ordinance.

"Lynda has other issues. She hit the Oak Street dogwood," Uncle G said.

Stone benches and a green belt protected the iconic Barkview tree. Lynda had to have been drag racing to hit that tree in her land-yacht sedan. "Was anyone else hurt?"

"Minor cuts and a sprain." Uncle G checked his phone. "Lynda's blood alcohol level was zero."

"No way." My furballs meter ticked up a notch. I retreated from Uncle G's glare behind the marginally smaller female Shepherd. Not that I'd have any better luck fighting her off if she suddenly decided I'd make good kibble. Like her sire, Maxine intimidated with a single shake of her majestic head. "How's the mayor holding up?"

"Left his knife in his Wednesday night rib-eye."

No question who ruled that household. "Aunt Char said Lynda had a head injury."

"She was right." Uncle G referred to his phone. "A concussion and cerebral hemorrhage. Lynda's in surgery."

A strange stillness came over me. Clarity really. Aunt Char had said Lynda's wound had been a slow bleeder. "What if Lynda caught the dognapper in the act?"

"She reported Lady Mag kidnapped at 5:05 p.m."

"What time did she hit the tree?"

"6:25 p.m."

"She arrived at the studio at 6:37." Allowing a twenty-minute drive time to the Village... "What did she do between 5:05 and 6:05?"

"That is the question." He pointed to the shadowed camera above the door. "The security camera's disconnected."

I squelched a ridiculous shiver. "Lynda was scheduled to be at KDOG at 5:00 p.m. to prep for the Crown interview."

"Her no-show didn't strike you as significant?"

My turn to glare. Crosstown rivals played together better than Aunt Char and Lynda.

"Never mind," Uncle G replied.

"What does Lynda's cellphone records say?"

"Cat..."

I cut him off. "Don't Cat me. Whatever is going on, Aunt Char and I are dead center."

"Exactly why you need to let me do my job."

His don't-you-trust-me frown didn't work for me. Uncle G had a town to protect. Aunt Char was my priority. "Are you going to dust for prints?"

He crossed his arms. "Think I'll find any other than yours?"

Okay. I'd been first on the scene, but... "I didn't touch anything. I swear."

"Except the door handle..."

"I told you the front door was open," I insisted.

"The porch..." He motioned me to enter the well-lit kitchen.

"Oh, no." A newbie mistake.

His frown cut deep. "Makes me wonder if this was pure stupidity on your part or if you're covering for someone."

"Oh, please. Aunt Char couldn't possibly have done this. She was on set. A hundred thousand-plus witnesses will corroborate." Might as well get to the heart of it right away.

"What time did she get in?" Uncle G asked.

"Fourish."

Uncle G's uh-huh did not bode well. "You're corroborating her alibi? Your office is directly across the hall from hers."

I had to admit. "I was in the broadcast booth from 3 p.m. on."

"So, you didn't see her." Veteran military police investigative scrutiny fixed on me, questioning me better than any polygraph.

"Renny came in for a head scratch around 4:30."

"4:30 exactly?"

I took great pleasure crushing his skepticism. "Yes. Ricky

14

had just left for our preproduction coffee run. Renny sat in his chair. And you know…"

"Where Renny goes, Charlotte is close by," Uncle G said. "That's a relief. I don't want to think my ladies were not being completely forthcoming with me." He jotted something in his notes. "Impeding a police investigation is a felony."

With more jail time than the crime itself. I had to ask. "What's the penalty for entrapment?"

His grin didn't fool me. "I don't like this any more than you do, Cat, but I have to investigate every reported crime."

"I'm a suspect?"

His silence confirmed. "You aren't a dog person and are associated with the Barklay Kennel."

"I don't wear Dior." Except when my aunt insisted. "None of this will hold up in court anyway." His eye roll pretty much summed it up. Barkview was a world unto itself. "My alibi is solid." Sandy could verify my presence. Aunt Char was another story. "It just doesn't make any sense that Aunt Char would…"

"For the Cavalier Crown? Winning is a dirty business."

"You can't honestly believe that Aunt Char would dognap her competition to win the Crown."

"Personally, no. Officially, Charlotte Barklay does not let anything stand in the way of what she wants. Renny is a successive champion. A three-peat would be historic and establish Barklay Kennel's brand for years."

"Fair and square."

"Maybe. All is fair in love and war, remember?"

In retrospect maybe not the best choice of words, but Aunt Char had shamed the refuse-to-budge Sacramento bureaucrats into approving the funding for Barkview's progressive dog shelter. I pointed to the garden wall. "Can't picture Aunt Char vaulting over a six-foot wall in her pencil skirt and stilettos. What about you?"

15

Uncle G's chuckle lightened the mood. "A shoo-in for *America's Funniest Home Videos.*"

"The whole idea of Aunt Char cheating to win is absurd."

"You and I both know it, but people like Lynda blame others for their misfortunes."

Uncle G knew the score. I suddenly got why he shunned retirement. "What about the other Cavalier contenders? Olivia Austin-Worth is a Dior regular."

"On my list."

"Anyone else come to mind with a grudge against the Cavalier dog show?" I asked.

"Slighted cat people."

"Not around here. You've run them all out of town."

"Not all of them." Uncle G's pointed stare hurt.

Silence seemed prudent. The proverbial stone wall still loomed in front of me. "Now what?"

"We wait for Lynda to tell us."

If she could. More than ever, I hoped Aunt Char had been incorrect about Lynda's injuries. "Maybe someone saw something. We'll open the *On-The-Scent* tip line in the morning for you."

"No. Panic is our enemy. Although likely the dog hasn't run off, I'll assign a few folks to look around for Lady Mag. If a dognapper is in town, I'll find him. Every criminal makes a mistake."

"It better be fast. You'll never keep this quiet with Lynda involved. Where do you...?" Uncle G's growl cut me off.

CHAPTER 3

I pivoted, my gaze following his over my shoulder. A clean-cut, dark-haired man strode through the kitchen. He had to be a Fed. Who else wore button down shirts and shoulder-hugging suits in Southern California? Quick work even for Lynda's top-shelf FBI contacts.

We all met at the granite counter. "Chief Schmidt?" The man paused until Uncle G nodded. "Russ Hawl, Blue Diamond Security. I support CARD. The remainder of my team will arrive within the hour."

Uncle G's lack of enthusiasm registered in a perfunctory handshake. I sensed a definite turf war in the making.

"CARD?" I asked.

"Child Abduction Rapid Deployment team. We coordinate government resources on child abduction cases."

"The FBI outsources investigations?" What next?

"Blue Diamond is both a contractor and consultant to CARD."

And didn't strictly fall under government scrutiny rules.

Aunt Char had called this one. Lynda's FBI connections had maneuvered around the Freedom of Information Act.

"Jurisdiction—" Russ said.

"Jurisdiction remains in Barkview!" Uncle G's exclamation point drew that proverbial line in the sand.

"With all due respect." Had to give points to Russ for political correctness.

Unfortunately, when Uncle G became Gibraltar, no one won. Lady Mag needed to be found. I extended my hand to Russ. "Cat Wright."

All six-foot-two inches of him towered over me as he firmly shook my hand. "Russ." The sweep of his dark hair emphasized startling, baby blue eyes, the hard planes of his face, and a strong jaw. Mid-thirties with no telltale left hand ring or tan band, I noticed. Talk about a fantasy swimmer waistline to go with those shoulders.

"Excuse me, I...ahh-choo."

I couldn't help but be encouraged. "Allergic to dogs?" He'd picked the wrong town.

"Y-yes. I am." He evil-eyed Max and Maxine. The dogs shook their regal heads with dander-spreading perfection. Russ sneezed more violently this time. "Excuse me."

This was going south fast. I looked from Russ's frown to Uncle G's scowl. "First aid kit in the glove box, Chief?"

I took off at his nod and returned a few minutes later. The tension hadn't eased any. I handed Russ two blister-packed tablets and a water bottle from the dog's stash. "These are a traditional Barkview allergy herbal compound."

Russ sneezed again, more violently than last and swallowed the tablets. "How long before..."

"Fifteen minutes or so. So, where were we?" I asked.

"Hawl was telling me that I have, uh, failed to execute proper protocol on the Margaret Smythe disappearance." That the toothpick hadn't snapped under Uncle G's teeth gnashing surprised me.

"Lady—."

Uncle G's raised brow glare shut me right up. I knew the drill and leaned against the counter while his lazy drawl set the big city boy straight.

"Who exactly did you piss off, Russ? You don't mind if I call you Russ, do you?" Uncle G played the good old boy far too well.

Russ wasn't buying any of it. "I am here at the request of the director."

He flipped the cover off what appeared to be a lined electronic notepad. I patted the Post-it collection bulging in my hip pocket. I'd tried my share of market tablets, but forefinger typing and autocorrect didn't exactly make for accuracy. Voice translation required might-as-well-type-it-myself proofreading. My should've-been-a-surgeon scrawl didn't exactly fit the stylus pen revolution. Only Sandy transposed my notes with accuracy. "No pen?"

Russ smiled. "No." His forefinger scribble made a three-year-old's meandering crayon more readable, yet the words *Margaret Smythe* showed clearly on the computer screen.

I could do that. "Can I try?" He towered over my shoulder, his fresh, mountain-hiking scent swamping me, as he placed the screen not much bigger than a grade school notebook in my screaming-for-a-manicure hands. Now, I got why Aunt Char lectured me on preparedness. Who would've guessed Mr. Hottie would come my way today? I should've worn that ice blue, plunging top everyone always told me made my eyes look bluer and my boobs bigger. A little mascara wouldn't have hurt either.

Lost in that dip between his earlobe and smoothly shaven jaw, my attention wandered.

"Earth to Cat." Uncle G's chide did me in. "Don't expect Margaret to reappear on her own."

What was it with me and stupid moves around men? I thrust the computer back at him and tried to put out the four-alarm fire burning on my cheeks. Russ didn't say a word. What could he say? I'd opened that chasm. The awkward silence stretched a mile long between us with Uncle G on the sidelines grinning like a simpleton.

Much as I'd liked to disappear into the tile floor, I had no choice. I filed yet another embarrassing moment away and shook it off. Maybe I just wanted to believe it, but I swear Russ had lost focus, too.

"Where did you get this?" Critical reminders still needed to be addressed, but a pen-free world just might be possible.

"I'll send you the link."

"Russ, what do you know about Margaret Smythe?" Uncle G asked.

"Four years old. Twenty-four inches long. Auburn and white hair, brown eyes. That can't be right. Taken between five and five fifteen from her home..."

Uncle G jumped on the relentless trail. "What does your report say she was wearing?"

Russ scrolled through a document. "Nothing listed." It didn't take a PhD to figure out that something wasn't adding up and Russ was no dummy.

Time to close the deal. "Although your info is technically accurate, I'm afraid you've been misled. That is Margaret Smythe." Russ's gaze followed my finger to a photo of Lady Mag on the counter.

To Russ's credit, he merely blinked. "That's a dog."

"A Cavalier King Charles to be exact. Lady Margaret is a four-time BIS winner. That's Best in Show winner in layman's terms. She's ranked number two in the US," I said.

"Welcome to Barkview, Russ. Dogs are family here. In fact, by city ordinance, a dog in the vehicle qualifies for HOV privileges."

"You don't have HOV lanes in this town," he remarked.

My point exactly. "You're welcome to bring that up to the City Council."

"CARD doesn't track domestic animals."

"You'd better check with Director Smythe before you pack up, son. Barkviewians think otherwise. Heck, Lady Mag has a platinum Amex card," Uncle G explained.

"They turned her down for black." Despite my best efforts, I couldn't keep the dryness out of my voice.

"Not a dog lover, Ms.—"

"Just Cat. Not a dog worshiper." As if on cue, Max and Maxine stood on all fours, their bicuspids gleaming. I swallowed the sudden lump in my throat. "Cute, Uncle G."

"Uncle?" Mr. Suspicion himself asked.

"Related through marriage," Uncle G said.

"Two husbands ago," I added quickly. "Not mine. My aunt's." Russ didn't need to know that Uncle G had introduced Aunt Char to Jonathan JB Barklay. Actually, his dog, Max, had, but no one disputed Uncle G's role. It had been love at first bite.

"Cat produces *Throw Him a Bone*," Uncle G explained.

"On KDOG," Russ said. "My mother loves that show."

"Where does she live?" I'd been introduced to every woman with an eligible son in a fifty-mile radius.

"Southeast San Diego. Mom swears your barking advice saved her neighbor's dog."

"There is a never-ending supply of barking dogs." The irony did get to me at times.

"Don't sell yourself short. There is an audience for practical information. Especially for loyal dog nuts like my mom."

"Not you?" Considering his sneezing and itching eyes, had I found someone I could relate to?

"I travel too much," Russ said.

"Your allergies..."

"Mom has a Portuguese water dog,"

No allergy issues there. I'd learned all about the hair versus fur breeds while researching my Sneeze Free Snoopy story a couple of years ago.

"Matata and I are buds."

He hadn't said best buds. Dog maniacs topped my dating dump 'em list.

"Cat Wright. I know the name." A pondering Russ looked so much like Rodin's Thinker I had to stare. Okay, maybe it wasn't just the posture.

"*LA Journal.*" Uncle G took great pleasure in supplying that tidbit. "She nabbed the..."

"Dogfighting ring. I remember. I worked in gang enforcement back then. Great job by the way. Nasty crowd. Figured you'd moved on to international. What are you doing producing an, uh...?"

"Gutless, fluff show," added Uncle G with his usual flare. "Trust me. I ask that every day. It's a waste for a natural-born investigator."

I crossed my arms. "Nancy Drew-trained, you mean."

"Max's backside. Those boys you put away won't see the light of day for ten more years with good behavior."

"I got lucky." I'd lived to tell about it. That was enough.

"Ask her about it over dinner." Uncle G's conspiratorial wink ended Russ's next question.

"Uncle G." Naturally, he ignored me, instead sharing that embarrassing moment of male cockiness with Russ.

"I just might do that, Chief."

"Wait one minute. I never said..." The blush returned with a vengeance.

While Russ's full attention about knocked me over, he seemed unaffected. "Let's get back to business. I apologize, Chief. Care to share the details of Lady Mag's disappearance? I can wait for your detective if you prefer."

"My detective is on medical leave. I will be heading this investigation."

Russ stroked his jaw. "I might be able to help. The line between runaway, lost, and stolen dogs can be subjective though."

"Not in Barkview." I had to interject that tidbit. Any dog dumb enough to run away from Barkview should be taken out of the gene pool anyway.

"How many dogs are missing?" Russ asked.

"One," I replied.

"No ransom. What makes you think it's more than a simple runaway?" He didn't argue, didn't chide. He remained on point. I liked that about him.

Uncle G's monstrous flashlight directed him to the collar on the patio.

"The owner's in the hospital." I pointed to the security camera. "Offline."

"Checking others in the area," Uncle G said.

Russ circled the collar. "Do show dogs normally carry insurance policies?"

"Some do. I'll check on abductions they've paid out." I couldn't help but be impressed.

"We'll dust for prints. I'm not optimistic." Uncle G's gaze cut into mine. "Don't have much to go on here."

"Where do we even start?" I yawned, setting off the chain reaction.

Max and Maxine sat in uniform attention, their heads

cocked in the same angle as Uncle G's. "Go home, Cat. You'll grill me better in the morning."

Like I stood a chance against him anyway. I wasn't about to argue.

"You sticking around, Russ?" Uncle G asked.

Russ checked his watch. "Too late to head back to LA tonight."

Now that was a shame. "I'll meet you at your office around ten. You should have something by then," I said.

As if on cue, Uncle G's cell phone rang. His cryptic words confirmed my read on the scowl. It wasn't good news.

"Lynda?" I asked.

"She didn't make it." The toothpick snapped between his teeth. "This is now a murder investigation."

That changed everything. I collapsed into the nearest chair, too many feelings I thought I had long buried churning inside me.

"Blunt force trauma," Uncle G explained.

A horizontal strike about four inches long, Aunt Char had said. "OMG. The garden statue," I bolted onto the patio. Uncle G's flashlight illuminated the trampled flowerbed as I stepped into the loose dirt. "It's right..."

"Don't touch it." They spoke in theater Sensurround.

"Too late. I handled it when I tripped over it earlier."

Russ snapped on rubber gloves anyway and held it up to the light. Loose dirt clung to one end. "Blood." His words sounded deeper, less nasal. The allergy pills were starting to work. "Where did you trip over it?"

I pointed to the path, near the collar. "It was on its side. No way it fell there on its own." The whole scene had been staged, begging the question. "Was Lynda the target after all or Lady Mag and Lynda got in the way?"

No response. Uncle G dialed his phone. "Go home, Cat."

"No way. I'm...."

"Go home," he said wearily. "Not a word about the button to anyone. Especially your aunt. This is a crime scene."

And I wasn't a professional. He didn't have to say it. No chance he'd bend the rules with Russ onsite. In a town where three dogs congregating in a crosswalk caused a traffic jam, one dog mysteriously missing and a dead owner constituted a calamity with a capital C.

CHAPTER 4

Good news before the morning sun peeked through the crack in my vertical blinds? Not a chance. When my caller ID identified Casey Anne, the graveyard police dispatcher, I knew the fur had really hit the fan. "I'm afraid to ask."

"You think you have issues? I should've been outta here three hours ago." Casey Anne's scratchy-tin voice woke me right up.

I stretched and yawned. Who needed sleep anyway? I must have managed a sympathetic *hummm*, because Casey Anne spit out her news in a gush. "Another dog's missing from the Fluff and Buff."

My bare feet hit the cold tile floor running. Renny visited that salon every Wednesday at seven a.m. "W-who?" I couldn't breathe.

"Somerset. Odds-on it's a fiasco. You know Michelle Le Fleur."

The whole town knew the grooming shop owner who handled dogs with a whisperer touch had won the Halloween screech award when confronted by a field mouse. Could she have made a mistake? All Blenheim Cavaliers looked the same.

I needed to see for myself. The headline teaser for Aunt Char's show *Double Dare Dognappings* came to mind. So did the question, had the second dognapping been planned or designed to deflect the real motive for Lynda's murder, or was Lynda's murder a consequence of the original dognapping? The possibilities stressed my not-yet-caffeinated mind.

"Better bring treats." Casey Anne hung up before I could probe deeper. Not that it mattered. I traded my flannels for comfy jeans and a KDOG oxford, brushed my teeth and poured my caffeine fix in a no-spill mug in a record seven minutes thirty-six seconds. I alerted Sandy as I drove the two-mile stretch from my Shores townhouse to the Village.

Chaos prevailed as I turned onto Maple Street. Three black and white patrol cars and Uncle G's K-9 SUV barricaded the entrance. Uncle G, the dogs, and Russ milled near the entrance. So, Russ hadn't left yet. I patted my flyaway bangs, now wishing I'd done more than run a brush through my hair and jam it into a ponytail. A little makeup would've been helpful.

I parked in the Hounds Hardware loading zone and wove through the thirty or so curiosity seekers on the sidewalk nursing steaming Joes. Their furry counterparts were dressed with purpose in sleek workout attire or be-seen glitter, all sporting sunglasses. I mean, heaven knew pooches had to worry about squint lines.

A breathless Sandy and her jumping-bean Jack Russell Terrier, Jack, met me at the police-taped barricade. She balanced a four-cup Woofing Best coffee tray and a paper bag bulging with treats in one hand and her twenty-something pound camera like a titanium tennis racquet in the other. For once, I wish she wasn't so efficient or freaking cute in her short-short running shorts and form-fitting tank top. Russ would notice her tight body and forever legs. Everyone did.

"Sorry I had to bring Jack. Ford had early rounds at the hospital. We were running by the studio when you called. I grabbed my camera and came right over. Figured we needed bribes."

Bad luck Sandy's boyfriend wasn't around to watch the dog. What more could I say? She had dropped everything to be here. "It's fine."

Good thing I took the coffee tray and treats because Jack suddenly darted beneath the tape, barking with Napoleonic fervor. Sandy hurdled the fluorescent tape, shouting. "Quiet, you terrorist." Jack kept going, silencing only when she scooped his squirmy body running-back style beneath her arm. "I'm really sorry, Chief."

I wasn't. We'd gotten past the barricade. I handed Uncle G the treats. "Figure you rushed breakfast." Or missed it alto-gether the way he chomped on his toothpick.

"You must be the Fed," Sandy said.

Russ caught my smile. What did he expect dressed in another suit and power tie? "Russ Hawl. I'm not a Fed."

"Apparently, the FBI uses independent contractors," I explained.

"Oh. Sorry. Easy mistake. The Chantilly Scone is a Barkview must try." Sandy pointed to the bag I'd given to Uncle G.

"Thank you for the coffee and recommendation."

I even almost came up with an appropriate response until Uncle G ended further discussion. "You coming, Russ?"

He raised his electronic pad in a high-five acknowledgment.

"Hey. Wait for me." I wasn't about to be left behind. "I can help."

"This is a murder investigation," Uncle G said.

"Don't you mean alleged dognapping here? Unless you've already positively connected the crimes…" The pinwheel spin of Uncle G's toothpick said that he strongly suspected it. Ugh. Not another life-altering murder investigation.

"Off the record," Uncle G stated.

"First amendment."

"Crime scene," he fired back.

No time for a Supreme Court ruling either. "Come on. I'm in TV."

"Don't you mean a paper-pushing administrator?"

Ouch. I stretched my neck just to be sure my jugular remained untouched. In the background, Michelle Le Fleur's high-pitched screech gave me another idea. "You need me."

Another Michelle shriek sealed the deal and he gestured I follow. "Camera stays at the door and no specifics."

"I know the drill. Have I ever let you down?" Okay, wrong door to open. I closed it before he could verbalize that list. "Forget it. I get it."

"Ramos, take the dog to KDOG." A freckle-faced officer led Jack away.

Sandy and I exhaled in unison. Jack let loose at a crime scene promised to be a disaster. We dutifully followed the chief.

"EOMS," Sandy said.

"Ears open, mouth shut," I translated for Russ who walked beside me.

"Good advice," he said.

The leave-the-job-to-the-professionals comment was coming. I just knew it. Fortunately, Michelle Le Fleur whooshed past both men to air-kiss me European style. Parisian born, Michelle's Champs-Elysees flair had graced the Barkfest five years ago, beginning her battle with immigration. Today her gold-logoed black Fluff & Buff smock covered basic black pants and a cap sleeve top. A matching beret dipped smartly to the right on her poodle-poofed hair.

"*Chat, mon cherie*, this cannot be happening. *C'est un* nightmare." Her left hand quivered as she stroked Fifi, her jet-black, standard French poodle look-alike.

"I agree." What else could I say? "Where's Renny?" My aunt's Cavalier bemoaned a delayed dinner in true Spaniel fashion. This commotion had to have her entirely on edge.

"Madame Barklay canceled her appointment last night."

Instant relief coursed through me. I couldn't help it. Renny wasn't here.

"Madame Austin-Worth took the open appointment for Somerset. *C'est* my fault. I never should have called her."

So, Michelle had filled the appointment. Coincidence or bad luck that another Blenheim Cavalier had replaced Renny? "Doesn't Somerset usually come in on Thursdays?"

"At ten. Madame wanted a Wednesday cut this week. Better for next week's show schedule."

I didn't ask what difference a day would make, but my show primping expertise could be measured on a pin tip.

"*C'est impossible*," Michelle moaned with vaudeville flair.

I swear Max and Maxine rolled their eyes in sync with their owner. I hugged Michelle close. "It's not your fault. How could you have known?"

"*Mon Dieu*, I..." Michelle blotted her smoky lined eyes. "You are right. I..."

Uncle G cleared his throat as Max nosed between us. "Tell me what happened."

Sandy handed me a pen as I pulled a Post-it pad from my pocket. Ready.

"*Mais oui*. Somerset was air drying *en Le Jardin*."

"Air drying?" Stylus in hand, Russ was all business. I hid

my amusement behind my Post-it pad. Ready or not, here comes Dog Grooming for Dummies.

"*Oui*, blow drying is too harsh for *le petit* Somerset. The ends frizz like electric shock." Both of Michelle's hands quivered in a high voltage demonstration.

Now that was a picture.

"Dog frizz?" Russ's straight face paid tribute to years of training.

"*Exactamente. Non bien.* You understand." Michelle fluttered her lashes at Russ. "The sun nourishes. Makes the ruby richer."

"Vitamin D," I added in mock seriousness. Who knew I'd ever need that bit of kennel trivia?

"*Absolutement.*" Michelle's brief smile reached ear to ear.

"Except there's no sun," Russ said matter-of-factly.

A valid point. June gloom encroached into July today.

Michelle's brow drew into a mono. Caught or confused? I wasn't sure and noted it. "The fresh air is... Come, you see."

The German Shepherds came to their feet with Uncle G's first step.

I admired Russ's nonchalance as she led us through the opulent Louis XVI inspired salon. Set up with individual mirrored stations exactly like a high-end hair salon, the elegance raised the bar in the Barkview coiffure scene. Ornate tables in front of gilt mirrors replaced swivel chairs and private gold trimmed sinks took the place of washbasins. When we passed beneath another archway labeled *Sanctuarie*, I was intrigued. I had never been invited into this rumored canine nirvana. The Versailles-style garden stunned me speechless. Surrounded by a thick seven-foot hedge, the slate patio looked suspiciously like a throne room, the way a half dozen plush blue and white striped cushions adorned various-level platforms, all facing a babbling water fountain.

My WDI scale just hit a new plateau. "Kill me if I ever get this," I whispered for Russ's ears only. He neither agreed nor disagreed. He simply made another note.

Michelle's model-perfect hand motion drew our attention to the hedged perimeter. "*C'est* secure area."

We circled the diamond and garnet J. Tracker collar. The letter C framed the paw print dominating the doorway. The location had to be significant. I snapped a smart phone photo.

I followed Russ as he walked the lush border, kneeling at a hedge indentation on the far side. He pressed into the greenery. "How do your gardeners get back here?"

Good question. Maintaining this precision manicured landscape had to require a crew of horticultural artisans.

Michelle's brow furrowed. "They work at night. No bother my clients. They have a key to the gate." She pointed toward the evergreen hedge.

Russ disappeared into the thicket. He emerged five feet to the right. "No sign of forced entry."

Russ held the branches aside. Sure enough, a basic key access lock hung drunkenly on the wood gate's latch. No footprints in the mulch either. So much for security. I made a note on my stick figure crime scene Post-it drawing while Uncle G took more photos.

Michelle peeked over my shoulder. "*Non possible.*" Surprise or guilt? She'd rented the space four years ago.

Russ shaded his eyes and pivoted a three-sixty. "Security camera at four o'clock."

Uncle G radioed an officer to gather the footage. Russ had good instincts. I had to give him that.

"Which, uh, pillow was Somerset on?" I asked.

Michelle pointed to a royal blue velvet cushion. Uncle G motioned Max and Maxine to track. The dogs sniffed the pillow, dropped their noses to the ground and headed directly to the gate. Russ pushed it open. We followed the two dogs down the alley to Sycamore Street where they tracked about a hundred yards further east then sat at the curb. Trail gone. A car had been waiting.

Russ studied the corner. "Traffic cams?"

I cleared my throat rather than laugh. "No outdoor ATMs either by city ordinance." Quaintness did have an unexpected price. "Ring and private security footage only."

We retraced our steps to the patio. From the outside, the gate blended perfectly into the fence. Had to be someone familiar with the property. Prior to Michelle moving in, the building had housed a ritzy French restaurant, designed by J. Tracker's owner, Sean Riley's, grandfather. In fact, like so many other village properties, Aunt Char had purchased this building during the real estate meltdown.

"When did you notice Somerset missing?" Russ asked.

"I come to check and discover collar *ici*." Michelle pointed to the collar set up at the entry. "No Somerset. I call the chief *immédiatement*."

"How long was she out here?" Russ's rapid-fire questions kept Michelle focused.

She displayed a digital stopwatch. "Twenty-two *minutes*."

We had an abduction window. An announcement on our show would surely get calls to the *On-the-Scent* tip line. Curious that her accent improved rather than thickened under duress.

"Did you hear Somerset bark?" Russ asked.

"*Non, Monsieur.*"

"Did you have other dogs inside?"

"*Oui.*" Momentarily confused, she caught on quickly. "*Tout les* dog have a unique voice. I would have heard her."

My eyes rolled this time. Every one of Aunt Char's prized Cavaliers barked the same annoying yap. Granted, larger dogs barked in deeper tones. Unlike cats' meows, which were all different.

"She *non* bark. She was *très* relaxed, *Monsieur. Moi très spécial* chamomile biscuits and massage."

"Chamomile biscuits?" Sandy's interest perked.

"*Oui. Mon recipe.* Very relaxing. I also use..."

Sandy ignored Uncle G's foot tap. I knew exactly where she was going. With Ford's Betty Crocker touch, this could be a perfect late-night snack for Jack. "Will you text me the recipe?" Sandy handed Michelle her card.

"Focus, ladies." Uncle G's impatience got through that time.

"We talk later." Michelle patted Sandy's hand.

"You mentioned that you gave the dog a massage?" Russ asked.

"The paws. Much stress there." Michelle's thumb circled in demonstration.

Too much information for me. Russ couldn't quite believe it either, I could tell as he scribbled.

"Unless the dog was muzzled, she should've barked."

I agreed with Russ. "Who doesn't growl and fuss when they're woken up?" I covered my mouth. Had I just confessed to my not-so-ladylike morning routine? Ugh. Sandy and Michelle's gapes and Uncle G's chuckle bothered less than Russ's speculative look. Recovery my objective, I took the infra-red glasses, blue light, and spray from Uncle G and coated the pillow. No sign of blood. The only piece of good news so far.

"Where were you last night at five?" Uncle G asked.

"Here. Madame Collins dropped Ling-ling for a bath." The wife of our town's sanitation czar, Brooke's obsession with clean made for amusing gossip. "I called 911 when Madame Smythe hit the tree."

Michelle had witnessed Lynda's accident. Post-it ready, I asked, "What happened?"

"I heard a crash. Ran outside. Madame Smythe was very distressed when I tried to help her." Michelle's hand movement drew my eye to an artfully concealed dark mark beneath her eye.

Politically suave Lynda struck Michelle? How was that even possible? Lynda could barely stand up when I'd seen her minutes later.

"Ah, *le mayor*. So sad." Michelle dabbed a tear in emphasis.

Uncle G cut off my questioning. "Thank you for your help, Michelle. Officer Richardson will take the rest of your statement."

The All-American escorted Michelle inside. I didn't argue. A private conversation with Michelle would net better results. That left the four of us and the dogs alone at a crime scene Hollywood couldn't even sell.

"So, what's your take, Russ?" Uncle G asked.

"The collar connects the cases. Motive unclear. I'd say, the dognapper walks among us," he said simply.

"No way." Sandy verbalized my thoughts.

"Doggie-doo happens in Mayberry, too," Russ shot back.

Agreeing felt wrong, but insider information seemed the common denominator. Suspect-wise, Michelle knew both dogs, was familiar with removing the J. Tracker collar and had been in proximity of Lynda and Somerset. She was also a newbie by Barkview standards. What did we know about her prior to arriving in town? I needed to dig deeper.

"Any witnesses on the street?" Russ asked.

Uncle G radioed his officers taking statements. His scowling *uh-huhs* answered that one. "The Barklay Jeep was parked at the bank right before Somerset went missing."

"No way. 8 a.m. is...."

Uncle G's evil eye shut me right up. He'd noted the timing as well. "Camera across the street hasn't been operational since '14."

Russ's 'I see' demanded a response. "Low crime rate in Barkview," I said.

"Not any longer." His dry remark got to me. He continued before I could retort. "How can someone walk on a busy street carrying a twenty-pound, comatose dog and no one notice?"

A true outsider question. Sandy filled him in. "Toto."

"Who?" Russ asked.

"Not who. A tote. It's called a Toto. You know, a bag that you carry your dog around in," she explained. "They sell them all over town. It's for smaller dogs. Jack's size. Except he squirms too much."

Russ held up his hand. "I got it. A drugged Cavalier would fit."

Was he starting to see just how insane this town was?

"Or overdosed on chamomile." Neither man appreciated my humor.

Russ sniffed around the pillow. "No odor. No obvious paraphernalia either."

"Drugged would suggest someone with medical skills and access to sedatives," Uncle G said.

Which included just about everyone these days. Even I had opioids in my medicine cabinet from a root canal. "They'd have to medicate without causing the dog to panic."

"A medical doctor or a nurse could also. Ford gave Jack a shot after his paw surgery last month," Sandy stated.

Ugh! In addition to four vets and almost two hundred vet students who were enrolled at Bark U, our world-renowned veterinary school, concierge doctors and trained medical personnel could be involved.

No comment from the men. Not that I expected it. They'd

36

crouched in front of the collar and paw print in that good-old-boy huddle.

Russ blew open a pair of rubber gloves and slipped his hands inside. He examined the titanium collar. "Another GPS collar?"

Uncle G donned a pair of gloves. "Locator is in the tubing."

"I see. Who manufactures and sells them?" Russ asked.

"J. Tracker and Petronics in Barkview. There are others around the country, but Barkview-manufactured products rule in this town," I said.

Uncle G stroked his jaw. "The paw print appears to be Cavalier sized."

"So, the thief unlocked the gate, inked a dog's paw, set up the collar without a noise from the dog or anyone seeing anything at morning rush hour downtown."

Russ summed it up well. At least there wasn't a Dior button this time. "We need to explore who the intended victim was," I said. "Somerset took Renny's appointment today. They are both Blenheim Cavaliers. The dognapper could've grabbed the wrong dog."

"Truth is I'm not sure if Char got lucky today or she should be the prime suspect," Uncle G said.

"You can't possibly think that she would..."

Uncle G cut me off. "A competitor is murdered, and two top contending Cavaliers are dognapped ten days before a career-cementing competition."

Put that way, it sounded bad. "The sheer boldness is scary. I can't help but wonder if the murder is the crime and the missing dogs a misdirect or the other way around. Wouldn't a normal dognapper run for cover after a murder?"

"A normal dognapper." Uncle G faced Russ. "What does the FBI handbook say about normal dognappers?"

I deserved his sarcasm. I'd stepped knee deep into that one.

Russ's deadpan seriousness helped me refocus. "We, uh, have a pattern." Not to mention a true PR nightmare for the Barkfest.

"Maybe." Uncle G remained unconvinced. "I've requested Lynda's financials and cell phone records. So far, nothing unusual pointing to a possible motive."

Except for the rumored high-profile mate Lynda had secured for Lady Mag to oust the Barklay Kennel. Lynda had all but guaranteed her buyers champion puppies. I needed to talk to Aunt Char about that.

"Any ransom demands?" I asked.

"Not yet. We are monitoring the mayor's phones, social media and texts." Uncle G checked his phone. "Olivia just arrived. Better get your report before the bloodhounds let loose." Uncle G's command could not be confused as a suggestion.

Better him than me dealing with Somerset's owner, Lady Olivia Austin-Worth. The daughter of the tenth earl of something or other, Olivia married Barkview's premier land developer, Richard Worth, back in the late eighties. Olivia's adjustment to the provincial lifestyle remained a work in progress.

I motioned for Sandy to follow. The old hot-story anticipation hummed through me. I smoothed my ponytail and jotted a few notes on a Post-it while Sandy set up the tripod and tested the lighting.

"Shoot above the waist."

"I know. Your left side is your best." To anyone else, Sandy's lip gnaw would indicate focus. I knew better. I ran my tongue over my front teeth. Errant coffee grounds or a cinnamon shadow filmed like Halloween macabre. When her lip chewing continued, I had to ask. "What?"

"OMG! Four o'clock. You're not going to believe this."

I pivoted clockwise, expecting who knew what, but definitely not expecting to catch Ricky Martinez skulking out of Barkview's most colorful dog psychic, Madame Orr's, draped doorway.

"Yuck." Sandy jabbed her forefinger in her mouth. "Talk about a hound dog." She adjusted the camera angle and took his picture. "Same pants and shirt he wore yesterday."

Not that that was so unusual. His absent-minded-professor persona made me question how well he'd fit in when I'd first interviewed him. No issue as it turned out. The man did a great job. A slimy-gross shiver still went straight down my spine. How had that flashy fifty-something séance queen even gotten on bird-watching Ricky's radar?

"His dog's loss really affected him," Sandy explained.

"Are you telling me he's trying to contact his dead bull-dog?" My dog insanity scale's scope just imploded.

"I know it sounds weird, but it's how they met. He said Madame Orr has a technique..."

No doubt. "I don't want to know." I really didn't. Sandy's acceptance bothered me more than I cared to admit.

"You asked." Sandy reset the camera. "Austin-Worth at eleven o'clock."

This day just got better and better. The distinctive stiletto tile-click confirmed Somerset's owner's approach. I yoga breathed. "Uncle G got rid of her quickly. She's coming our way, isn't she?"

Sandy ducked behind the camera. "I'd better get battle pay for this."

"I'm the one in the line of fire."

"I'm worried about the strays." Sandy's whisper sounded a lot like a moan.

I pivoted. Olivia modeled the best in coastal sun protection in a tan, wide-brimmed hat trimmed with a Cavalier hat band and face swamping, Jackie-O dark glasses not quite masking red-rimmed eyes. Although the British were internationally noted for their stiff upper lips, Olivia defined high maintenance.

"Cat Wright. Spinning another tale, I see." Although normally charming, Olivia's tea-and-crumpets elocution required a repeat for me to piece together what she'd said. Even then, still much remained open to interpretation.

"Spinning what?" My feigned innocence needed work.

Yet another dog master look-alike pair. Olivia's shoulder-skimming chestnut hair and Spaniel-brown eyes brought Somerset to mind. So did her rust-colored slacks and ruffled cream blouse.

Sandy stiffened.

"Not a word." Forefinger to my lips, I squelched any comment. I empathized with Olivia's helpless anger and opted for diplomacy. "Would you like to send a plea for Somerset's safe return?"

"Whatever for? We all know who has her."

I really tried to ignore Olivia's snotty jab. I knew better than to inflame an already rocky encounter. "We do?"

"Don't play innocent with me. Your aunt..."

"Was the intended victim today?"

Olivia's eyes flattened to slits. "Indeed. Coincidently, today of all days she cancels Renaissance's standing appointment."

Odd, but not unheard of. "And another Blenheim Cavalier was taken. How could my aunt possibly have known who would fill her time slot?"

Olivia's aristocratic disdain set my nerves on edge. "It is naturally a set up to make her appear innocent."

My patience fled. "Did she force you to take Renny's appointment?"

"Well, I..."

"Did she?" Hands on my hips, I held her gaze until she

flinched. "Didn't think so." Point made, I relented. "Look, I understand you're upset, but consider this. It should have been Renny taken today."

Olivia's hoity-toity harrumph offered no apology. "Charlotte was downtown this morning."

The small-town information super-highway certainly exceeded the speed limit today. "A Jeep was downtown along with twenty other SUV's."

"I saw the Barklay Jeep leaving the Smythes' at 5:45 yesterday."

"Impossible." So much for impartiality. "A car would've been a blurred blob in last night's fog. No way you could've identified a specific vehicle."

Half a dozen eavesdroppers suddenly looked anywhere but at me. Even Sandy's pressed lips implied one coincidence too many.

"Does it even matter? You and the chief will bury anything incriminating her."

I crossed my arms, refusing to even acknowledge that comment. "You know, Olivia, secrets have a nasty way of getting out anyway."

"Thankfully, the FBI is involved." Her queen's stare annoyed more than intimidated me.

Whatever she was hiding, I'd dig it out. "I have news for you. The FBI is not Scotland Yard for the privileged. It does not investigate theft." No need to set the record straight on Russ's job description. Someone would fill her in soon enough.

"Theft! Lady Margaret and Somerset were kidnapped."

"Maybe they were, maybe not. Doesn't matter. Both Lady Mag and Somerset are dogs. Legally, dogs are property. The charge is theft."

"But Somerset is my..."

"Dog." I hadn't meant to be quite so brutal. Okay, maybe I

had. A notch-or-two attitude adjustment could only help. "Look, Olivia, Aunt Char understands that Somerset is your daughter. Do you honestly believe she would hurt you like that?"

Olivia's eyes darkened. "For the Crown," she said, but her voice lacked total conviction. "All is fair in love and war."

Not that again. "You're letting emotion override your common sense. Someone else is doing this. You can help to find them or not. That's your choice. Blaming someone you know here..." I pointed to where I'd hoped to find her heart. "...is innocent is a waste of time and resources."

"Good heavens, this is utterly absurd. Lynda is dead."

"Yes, she is. Also not the FBI's jurisdiction." Harsh. But true.

"For argument's sake, you are correct. What can I possibly do?"

Olivia back down? Normally, I'd proceed carefully. In this case, I welcomed it. Maybe we could get down to the business of locating the killer and the dogs. "Make a plea for Somerset's safe return." The audience always loved real emotion.

"No! I'm a mess."

A mess did accurately describe Olivia's demeanor. Even still, I offered free press—any Cavalier contender's dream. Yet, she'd turned me down, instead addressing me. "You will find my baby. S-she is petrified of the dark."

Seriously? That was Olivia's number one worry? I didn't ask. Olivia deserved the benefit of the doubt. In her mind, she'd lost her daughter today, and I did understand loss. Shock affected people in peculiar ways.

"Did you see anyone when you dropped Somerset off this morning?" I asked.

"No one I recognized. No one who is anyone is out that early."

"You drove by the coffee shop. It opens at 5:30 a.m." Talk about self-absorbed. Downtown buzzed in the morning.

"Now that you mention it, the Barklay Jeep was parked in front of the bank."

Another witness. Great. "Who did you purchase your GPS collar from?"

"J. Tracker. For all the good it did."

I filed that one away. "Any idea who would want to murder Lynda?"

"Anyone with a champion Cavalier. Imagine, Lynda insisting she'd captured the Duke." No hesitation there.

"The what?" Surely, she didn't mean John Wayne.

"Duke Cathaway, the European champion Cavalier. That honor belongs to my Somerset. She did place in the Kensington Kennel Club show, you know. You reported on it." Confidence underscored Olivia's haughtiness.

"I did. As I recall, Duke won first and Lady Mag second at that show."

Olivia sniffed. "Somerset won second. She was…"

"Disqualified because of judge tampering," I remarked.

"It was all a misunderstanding. The Club apologized."

True, but Somerset's win had not been reinstated, resulting in Lady Mag's number two Cavalier title. Could there be more to this? Would Olivia kill Lynda over a show win and breeding rights? The vision of petite Olivia bashing Lynda with a Cavalier statue didn't play nearly as well as a stiletto stabbing. A botched dognapping might explain it. But why would Lynda accuse Aunt Char? I had to ask. "What's so special about Duke?"

Olivia's look branded me an idiot for sure. "Duke's lineage is as fine as Somerset's. Their puppies will be THE champions." No need to ask the champions of what. Anyone within earshot knew she'd just threatened the Barklay Kennel's reign.

Odd. Aunt Char had never mentioned Duke. Given both Olivia and Lynda's obsession, he sounded like the perfect match for Renny. Not that I followed the whole dog lineage thing, but I did understand rivalries and the extent some people will go to win.

Crazy as it sounded. Olivia had offered a plausible motive. Question was: did it incriminate Olivia or my aunt? Somerset was missing. Not Renny. I needed more info on Duke and to talk to Aunt Char.

I waited until Olivia left the area before I test counted into the mike, ready to tape. "Tighten the angle on the sign, Sandy. Then pan." My heart beat with that old familiar excitement. I loved TV.

"Good morning, Barkview. We are here at the Fluff and Buff on Maple to report that our local, two-time Cavalier King Charles champion, Somerset Austin-Worth, has disappeared." As if planned, Uncle G and Russ exited the building. I pointed the microphone at Uncle G's snowy beard. "Chief Schmidt, please tell us what you know so far."

"Somerset was last seen at 8:30 this morning. If you were on Maple between 3rd and 4th Street during the eight o'clock hour, I want to talk to you." Add a pipe and deerstalker hat and Uncle G could pass for a credible Sherlock Holmes.

"If anyone has any information on Somerset's where-abouts, please contact Chief Schmidt or our *On the Scent* tip line. Remember, the safety and security of our loved ones is a community effort. This is Cat Wright, on the scent."

Sandy lowered the camera. "You must get out more. That was perfect."

I smiled, couldn't help myself. It felt right. More right than anything had in ages. Russ's wink made me feel even better. "Pack it up, Sandy. We need to visit J. Tracker."

"Mind if I join you?" Russ's sandpaper voice practically

knocked my socks off. So, he was staying at least a bit longer. Having no official position here, I'd wondered. Would we have dinner? Or had that been Uncle G's suggestion? I hated to admit it, but I wanted to go. Truth was, I hadn't been that attracted to a man in ages. Considering my luck with the opposite sex, I could predict with Wright certainty that he had a psycho significant other somewhere. I did know that he didn't have a dog and that was a big keeper point. From a purely investigative standpoint, I liked having him around. Personally? Well, I'd already embarrassed the heck out of myself, blurting teenagisms. What else could go wrong?

"Uh, sure." My witty responses needed work. "My car's down the block." Sandy followed us toward my Jag.

Russ's gaze followed my finger point. "I'll drive. Mine is more comfortable."

My sleek Jag SUV versus his...? What did an FBI consultant drive anyway?

"I'll ride with the chief back to the station. Where should I pick you up?" Russ asked.

"At KDOG on Oak," I replied. The delay would give Sandy time to look into Duke and arrange an appointment with J. Tracker's founder.

"I'll find it. Thirty minutes then." His stride never broke as he caught up to Uncle G.

CHAPTER 5

Precisely twenty minutes later, Russ beat me to the passenger door of a black Land Rover parked in KDOG's passenger loading zone.

"I'm a little old fashioned." He offered his hand as I climbed in.

How about downright charming? I couldn't remember the last time a guy had opened a door for me. This one's keeper points continued to mount.

I followed his jog around the car in the rearview mirror, admiring his brains-meets-brawn good looks. His knowing half-smile screamed "caught" the moment he climbed into the driver's seat. Not again.

"You know, there's no way Olivia saw the Barklay Jeep last night," I blurted out.

"You don't waste a minute, do you?" He'd turned north onto First Street, the sandy coastline over his shoulder, as we headed to the Barkview Industrial Complex.

"That's what this is about, isn't it?"

"Maybe I just wanted to see you again."

"Sure." I wanted to believe it, really. Much as I liked his brash amusement, the something else I couldn't quite name troubled me.

"I filed my report with the FBI," Russ said.

"Is that what you normally do?"

"I assess a situation and report next steps."

"Like what? If you need to go in guns blazing?" Judging from Russ's reaction, I really needed to learn the art of "better left unsaid."

"Rarely blazing. Blue Diamond's mission is to assist law enforcement." Those bold blue eyes held mine captive in the rearview mirror. I wasn't sure what more to say. Had my reporter's need-to-know gone too far? A hardness tempered his words—the kind earned by experience.

The silence stretched between us, unnerving me until Russ parked in front of a concrete stand-up building with clear-day ocean views. A larger-than-life Jack Russell head above smoked glass doors made J. Tracker's world headquarters impossible to miss.

Naturally, the mania continued inside in Jack Russell pictures and statuary. The receptionist's expressive brown eyes and angular features even kind of resembled the oh-so-popular hunting dog. I didn't need to ask if she had a Jack Russell either. A photo dominated her computer screen.

"Hello." I extended my card. "I am—"

"Cat Wright." The receptionist rose with celebrity excitement. "It's a pleasure to meet you. I loved the story you did on Barking in Barkview. You were so right," she continued. "Those hounds can wail like a funeral procession."

She'd missed the point about the yappers, but so had fifty percent of our deaf-to-dog-barking viewers anyway. "Thank you, I appreciate—"

"I mean, my neighbor's Basset hound is a... barkful." The

receptionist's head-cocked smile mimicked my hokey closing report remarks so accurately I didn't know what to say.

Russ failed to hide his grin as well. "Barking in Barkview. What an original concept in a dog-centric community."

I elbowed him to silence or bruise his ribs. Either worked for me. "I'm here—"

"To see Sean. I mean, Mr. Riley," she said.

Was I ever going to finish a sentence? "Uh..."

"He's expecting you. Just follow the paws to the end of the hall on the right. Our prayers are with the mayor and Mrs. Austin-Worth. I couldn't survive if Jaybee was stolen."

I bit my lip with the sole purpose of keeping my mouth shut. The mayor's wife had been murdered. The focus needed to be on that.

"I'd advise against shooting the messenger." Russ's whisper cooled my temper. Of course, he was right. Scary how well he read me.

I flashed what I hoped passed as a smile. "Yes. Well, Sean is expecting us." I darted like a pouncing cat down the stone path. About half-way I regained perspective.

"Are these the same paw prints as at the crime scene?" I asked.

Unfazed, Russ replied. "We'll need exact measurements, but the form and size appear to be the same."

"They're also uniform. Stamped." No one would individually paint each print. Would they? Even my WDI scale couldn't visualize someone inking paws for the fifty-foot length of the walkway.

I recognized Russ's quiet contemplation mode right away as he took in the surroundings with computer-like precision. He processed and assessed details I couldn't begin to notice as we approached the appointed office.

Before Russ could share any insight, Sean Riley, a carrot-top marathon runner with leprechaun eyes hidden behind horn-rimmed, Cal-Techish glasses, met us at the door. "Cat, Agent Hawl." He shook our hands and gestured for us to take seats on a butter-soft leather sofa.

"Just Russ. I'm a contractor to the FBI. Not an agent."

"I see." Clearly, Sean didn't, but kept going anyway. "I apologize in advance, but I must catch a flight to San Francisco this afternoon. I wanted to help. I talked to the mayor. He is, well, I can't imagine. He tells me Lynda's murder might be linked to the dognapping. I can't believe this is happening in Barkview." He tossed aside a Jack Russell needlepoint pillow to join us on the sofa.

"We believe finding the dogs will help us catch the killer." I hoped I sounded reasonable. My senses spun like an out-of-control carnival ride. In addition to the portrait of his dog, JRu, in the place of honor behind his desk, the pedestal bronze, and a collection of working Jack Russell pen-and-inks lining the walls, every flat surface contained more Jack Russell trappings.

"We must find them. Sandy told me I could help," Sean said.

"Yes. We would like to ask you about your collars. Both Lady Mag's and Somerset's were removed," Russ said.

"Removed?" He leapt to his feet and paced with classic Jack Russell energy. "The locking devices on both collars are patented security deterrents. It takes special knowledge to unlatch them."

That, just about every Barkview resident knew. "Have you had issues before?" This kind of press could seriously affect his business.

"No." The flush creeping up his neck said otherwise. I shared a look with Russ and just sat back. Big issue or small.

Wasn't sure yet. "I mean, other than a few stones that need to be replaced, the collars have performed without issue. Dogs can be rough on collars. They roll around in the grass, run through brush. Jewels will fall out with constant abuse."

No doubt. "Is the collar guaranteed for life?"

"One year on the stones. The GPS function for ten years. We've had no problem with the collar's GPS integrity. None at all."

"How often is the GPS function used?"

"More often than you think. Dogs chase cars or rabbits all the time." Sean seemed calmer now.

Why did the stone issue bother him so much? "Do you replace the diamonds?"

"Gem's Palace handles our warrantee work."

Interesting comment. Somerset's collar was new, but Lady Mag had worn that collar for a few years. Had Lynda coerced Sean to replace the diamonds? Why? Money was not an issue in the mayor's trust fund world. A few replaced diamonds didn't explain Somerset's disappearance either.

Russ came to the same conclusion. "How difficult is it to unlock the collar?"

Sean checked the time and handed me a jeweled collar from his desk drawer. "Go ahead and try."

I examined the collar. No visible lock or clasp showed in the jewel-studded gold band. No luck bending it either. I handed it off to Russ. "Every Barklay Cavalier wears one. I know the secret."

Russ focused on the multicolored jeweled and gold circle. He squeezed the two edges and twisted. Nothing happened. He tried again. No luck.

"Let me show you," Sean said.

Russ's index finger stopped him. "Give me a minute."

Firm tone aside, I recognized the we'll-all-be-gray-before-he-quits glint in his eyes. Fortunately, the collar didn't last long under his full concentration. Two minutes later, it clicked open.

"Impressive," Sean said.

I knew that.

"Do all the locks have the same mechanism?" Russ asked.

"No. We have three models. Lady Mag and Somerset wore different models. The tracking device is randomly embedded beneath the jewels. The GPS codes are assigned at manufacture. They cannot be changed. The code masters are stored in my personal safe. Except for the owners, only I have access." Sean's glance flickered to the portrait of JRu, undoubtedly where we'd find the safe.

So, the dognapper had no choice but to remove the collar.

"Ingenious," Russ said. "Do you mind explaining how the tracking works?"

Mind? The red head lit up like a three-alarm fire. "Not at all. Our GPS is satellite driven. We can access the whereabouts of any collared dog within two feet anywhere in the world."

I shared a glance with Russ. Was this the connection?

"How do you access?" Russ asked.

"Each collar has a unique activation code that is known to the owner and is stored in our security firewalled system. We have not been hacked. Only I have master code access."

That made Sean an automatic suspect. The man was a total dog nut with a paw print fetish. If he was involved, how did the Dior button fit in? And what could he possibly hope to gain by dognapping champion Cavaliers?

"Subcutaneous implantable GPS trackers are fairly easy to come by these days. Why would someone purchase a collar instead?"

"The collar is both a statement and considered more reliable." I didn't get the chance to refute. Sean continued. "What I mean is, the current injectable GPS can have reliability issues."

I made a note to confirm info with Aunt Char.

"Ever consider government work?" Russ asked.

Sean's cheeks reddened as he laughed. "Bureaucracy isn't for me, but consulting.... I hate to admit it, but your dognapper must be familiar with the collar's locking mechanisms. Something else to consider. Even if you know what you're doing, it's not easy to take a collar off an unwilling dog." He swallowed hard.

I knew where he was going. "We think the dogs were drugged."

"That's a relief. The alternative is..." Spoken like a true dog lover. Or a really good actor. Sean checked his watch again. "I have a printout of our clients and a list of our employees and distributors for you. I can assure you that J. Tracker employees are screened to top secret government clearance protocols."

Now that was impressive. "Who else would have knowledge of the device?" I asked.

"Other than owners, over the years I've done shows and demos countrywide. Since we have three models with slightly different processes, it would take someone with intimate knowledge of all of the products to be proficient."

Not great news, but it could be helpful in eliminating suspects later on.

"Are there any circumstances where the tracking will not work?" Russ asked.

"The signal is spotty if the collar is underwater. It only activates when turned on remotely from our central system," Sean explained. "As long as the collar is serviced properly, the collar is guaranteed to perform."

"Anyone who might want to discredit J. Tracker?" Russ asked.

"Well." Sean's deep breath felt practiced. "Any successful company has their share of competitors and discontented employees."

I sensed, before I saw, Russ's tension. "Anyone in particular?"

"Howard Looc comes to mind," Sean suggested.

"He owns Petronics. They are competitors," I explained for Russ's benefit.

"Five years ago. Howard was terminated for insubordination. Off the record, his dog attacked a resident Jack Russell at our day care center. He was banned from the building."

"The dog or Mr. Looc?" Russ asked.

"The dog. Howard refused to come to work without his dog. No charges were filed."

"Mr. Looc owns a Border Collie." A genetic drover surrounded by a pack of Jack Russell Terriers. Talk about herding cats. This sounded like a case of dog discrimination to me. I squelched instant indignation. I needed to get a grip. "How did you get into Jack Russells, Sean? Your grandfather and father raised champion English Bulldogs."

Sean's proud papa grin fit the norm. Everyone liked to brag about their kids and pets, not necessarily in that order. "I was on track to do the same until a visit to County Clarke. I went exploring in the fey and broke my leg in a rut. My cousin's Jack Russell never left my side. His bark alerted the search party. He saved my life and started my career." Sean tapped his Rolex. This appointment was over.

Russ and I stood. "Thank you for your help, Mr.—"

"Sean. Please. We must find those dogs. I have a new product in development that makes the collar obsolete. It's an implantable chip that, in addition to providing all the current tracking and identity information, also tracks a dog's health and nutritional needs. Goal is to keep the dog safe and extend its life."

"Wow! That will sell well." Talk about a coup.

"My pet project," Sean said. "Get it? Pet."

We politely chuckled.

"One more thing. Do you still have your grandfather's original drawings for the Fluff and Buff building?" I asked.

"No. Your aunt received all of the drawings when she purchased the building. W-why do you ask?" If his suddenly beet-red ear tips didn't give him away, the pacing did. "It's the garden gate, isn't it?"

Russ motioned me to silence. Had to admire his technique.

"It's not in the drawings. The gate was, uh, added during prohibition to access the speakeasy."

"Who asked about the gate recently?" Russ asked.

The pacing picked up. "A lot of people. The Sunday Jack Pack discussed the *Sanctuarie*. One thing led to another..."

"It's his Jack Russell running group," I explained. Thank you, Sandy, for that intel. "You've seen the gate to the *Sancutarie*?"

He nodded. "I booked an appointment for JRu there once. Thought the spa would help him to relax. Don't know what she did to him, but Jack came out sluggish."

Maybe there was something to the chamomile biscuits after all. Renny always seemed relaxed.

"You saw the gate during your appointment?" Russ asked.

"No. It was some kind of big secret. I saw it for the first time on our run. We didn't enter though. Just looked through the bushes."

I wasn't buying it. Neither was Russ, judging from his sharp look. "How did you open the lock?"

"What lock? The door was ajar."

I believed him. Had to be the gardeners. Michelle was going to love this info.

"Is that how the dognappers got Somerset?" Sean asked.

"Can't talk about an ongoing investigation," Russ replied. "Who did you tell about the gate?"

Sean crossed the room to his desk. "Who I told isn't as important as who told me. It wasn't my grandfather. Howard Looc told me about it."

"Howard Looc?" I asked.

"Yes. He tried to buy the property. Howard had this crazy plan to buy up Barkview. He thought he had the Fluff and Buff property sewed up. His words, not mine. Last minute, your aunt bought it out from under him."

Aunt Char didn't deal in underhanded. That didn't make sense. I made a note to ask her.

"I really must be going to the airport. My assistant will show you anything you would like to see. I'll send you the list of people I told about the garden access."

We thanked Sean for his help and toured the building where Jack Russells ruled thirty employees. Although hovering in the seven to eight WDI Scale range, every employee expressed genuine concern for the missing dogs and Lynda. We returned to the car no closer to naming a suspect than when we arrived.

"What do you think?" I asked after we'd buckled in.

"That I'm starving. How about an early lunch?"

My stomach growled in agreement. "You're on. We can grab something in town."

He smiled. "In answer to your question, his transparency is commendable."

Russ's tone bothered me. "You think he's involved?"

"I don't know. Excessive helpfulness doesn't always equate

to innocence. The garden gate is bothering me. My gut tells me he's not telling us something."

"Your gut?" How archaic.

His nod was dead-dog serious.

"Isn't that called women's intuition?"

He eyed me over his sunglasses. "Call it what you want. Just trust it."

I inclined my head, bowing to his obvious experience. "What aren't you buying exactly?"

"The Howard Looc story is too convenient."

I agreed. Considering the gossip flow in this town, I should know more about it. Discovering who did might matter. "Time to run the Lexus-Nexus?"

"I see you've used the database."

"It's every investigative reporter's information stream." I left it at that. Uncle G would dig deeper since police access far exceeded Jane Reporters. "What about the diamonds?"

"Finding out why Sean covered the diamonds under warranty might be interesting."

Emphasis on might. "I'll call Ariana. She and her husband own Gem's Palace. She's a friend of my aunt's."

He nodded. "I suggest cross-referencing the list of people who know about the garden gate at the Fluff and Buff and those who have something to gain with Lynda dead and the dogs missing may net us some suspects."

Sounded reasonable. All that required a Post-it trail. My hand rattled around the bottom of my purse until Russ handed me a pen. I smiled my thanks, quickly jotted my notes and stuck the Post-its like an outdoor laundry line across the dashboard. Russ's you've-got-to-be-kidding-me look got right under my skin. Enough ribbing already. I had my way and he had his. "Don't even go there."

He didn't. He slammed on the brakes to miss running a stop sign.

My elbow bumped the dash, sending two Post-its fluttering to the floor mat. I retrieved them at the cost of my forehead. "Okay. Okay. Maybe I do need to organize better."

"A woman willing to change?" Dubious didn't begin to describe Russ's tone.

His new wave phone ring drowned out my not-so-flattering remark. He pressed his Bluetooth headset, leaving me to interpret the one-sided conversation. "I understand, sir. Time is not on our side" and I knew he had another case. The disappointment surprised me. Truth was, I didn't want him to leave.

He disconnected the call. "I'm afraid I'll have to take a rain check for lunch."

"I understand." I did. A murder and two missing dogs weren't his problem. "You can drop me at the corner. It's easy freeway access for you. Sandy can pick me up from there."

"I'll drop you at KDOG and be on my way." He turned left on 7th Street. We drove the next seven blocks in silence until he pulled into the KDOG parking lot.

"Well, then it's goodbye." I extended my hand, oddly bereft.

He reached across the center console and squeezed my hand. "How about dinner on Friday night?"

My pulse leapt. I couldn't help it. "Dinner?"

"You know, the meal after lunch."

And before bed, I thought wildly. I must've hesitated too long.

"I will get a hotel," he offered.

"That's not it. It's..."

"You have a boyfriend?" Inquisition under the guise of nonchalance.

"No! I-I'd like to have dinner with you."

He relaxed. "Great." He escorted me to the glass entry door. "I'll call you tomorrow and check on how the investigation is coming along."

He left me standing like an idiot in the foyer staring after him. I'd see him on Friday. Maybe. He didn't have my number. I relaxed. The man had connections. He'd figure it out. I needed to catch up with Aunt Char.

CHAPTER 6

Melodic music, halo lighting, the aroma of lavender fields and focused breathing, yet I still couldn't melt into the cushy massage table beneath me. As expected, the accusations and blame game all centered on my aunt.

"It's not time to make a statement." Cooling cucumber slices covered my eyes, so I heard rather then saw Aunt Char sheet-shrug.

"I know you mean well, but Lynda is dead and two champion dogs are missing. The mayor is floundering. I simply must do something." Her serenity had to be a façade.

I lifted a cucumber off one eye to be sure. Calming sea-blue walls melded with the cream linens. Renny sprawled between us on a satin pillow with cucumber slivers covering her eyes. A chamomile mask painted her furry snout. The gold chain anchoring her to Aunt Char twinkled in the incandescent lights. If that wasn't enough, José, Barklay Kennel's manager and Cavalier whisperer, stood guard outside the door.

To my surprise and admiration, Aunt Char lay in limp relaxation. Even draped in a soft cotton sheet with her platinum hair pulled back in a severe ponytail, she looked like royalty.

After all these years, my aunt remained an enigma. In addition to being a doctor, she'd been a Rose Parade princess, a lingerie model, and a TV reporter, who had tragically buried three husbands. Her combination of beauty, brains and street smarts made her exactly who I wanted to be when I grew up, minus the MD since I fainted at the sight of ketchup. Forget the pageant successes too. My good old American pie, sun-streaked hair and feline, sometimes blue, sometimes green, eyes couldn't compete with Aunt Char's striking beauty.

"I'm afraid you'll get pulled into a quagmire. You and Lynda weren't exactly besties."

"We sat on several boards together. Continuing Lynda's charity is going to be difficult."

"You were fierce competitors for the Crown. Trust me. That's all anyone remembers now. And as far as I know, there hasn't been a ransom request," I said.

"I do benefit the most from Lady Mag and Somerset's disappearances."

"True. That anyone would believe you could have anything to do with this makes me crazy."

"Olivia is broadcasting to anyone and everyone who will listen," Aunt Char said.

"A few facts weaved into supposition and innuendo makes for a good story, not a prosecutable case."

"That, my dear, does not matter in the court of public opinion."

True. Why it mattered to my free-spirit aunt made even less sense. "I still think the high road is the better choice. Playing defense only makes you look guilty. We need to focus on the facts."

"The facts don't exonerate me either."

Not completely. "By the way, is the jacket you wore the night Lynda died missing a button?" I didn't even care that Aunt Char's look said I'd lost my mind. Maybe I had. I needed an answer.

"I don't think so. Did you find a button?"

Too bad Uncle G had sworn me to secrecy. "Do you lose them a lot?" What else could I say?

"You'd be surprised. Those cuffs catch on everything." A gun struggle undoubtedly would qualify. "Just give it to Ria. She keeps the extras in the laundry room."

How many extra buttons did Aunt Char's housekeeper have access to? "You get extras with every jacket?" That made sense. Designer clothing came with extra buttons and thread. It also meant anyone with a Dior jacket or access to one had buttons to plant. That list had to be as daunting as the collar know-how list.

"Yes. Why...?"

I needed a redirect. "Do you have issues with the diamonds set in Renny's collar?"

"No. Lynda claimed Lady Mag's weren't set properly. She's taken it to Gem's Palace several times."

"Was she considering the Petronics version?"

"If so, she didn't confide in me. Lady Mag could be rough on collars. Renny is a lady." Renny stretched her neck to accommodate Aunt Char's affectionate scratch.

Had Lynda leveraged the Duke deal to force Sean to repair the collar?

"What happened when you bought the Fluff and Buff building?"

"Nothing notable. That was six years ago, dear. I renovated the building. I don't recall any issues. Zoning or otherwise."

"I heard you bought it out from underneath someone." My subtle interrogation skills needed work.

"Goodness, no. The property needed extensive remodeling. I submitted a closed envelope bid with my renovation plan per the instructions. I think there were three or four other bidders. Mine was chosen."

Hardly underhanded. "Why would Howard Looc feel slighted?"

"I didn't know he did. The process was the process. Did you know the house was a speakeasy during Prohibition? How exciting to need a password to slip through a secret door."

Exciting was a word for it. "You know about the gate?"

"Of course. JB's grandmother wrote about it in her journal. The woman liked her brandy."

Just like another woman I knew. I could picture Aunt Char and her late husband reading that journal in their library together. "Who else knows about it?"

"Anyone who is related to anyone who lived here in the 1920s, I imagine. It wasn't a take-to-your-grave secret."

Better to ask who didn't know. Why would Sean incriminate Howard over what amounted to common knowledge? Only a chat with Howard would answer that.

I needed another redirect. "Tell me about Duke."

Another delicate exhale I expected, not instant brow tension. "Duke Cathaway?"

"Yes. Have you ever competed against him?"

"Renny's sire competed against a two-year-old Cathaway male my first year with JB in New York. We won that year."

And eight consecutive years thereafter that Duke had not competed.

"Why would Lynda and Olivia consider it a coup to breed with him?"

"Duke is the European champion. Since all ranked US male Cavaliers have Barklay Kennel lineage, our breeding options are limited."

"So, Duke would strengthen the bloodline." Listen to me, a sudden expert on Cavalier breeding practices. Apparently, I had been listening all those years.

Aunt Char noticed too. "You never know. Good pedigree makes a handsome dog. A great show dog is about much, much more."

She had a point. Renny, Lady Mag and Somerset shared the same Barklay paternity, but Renny consistently topped the two, fueling the women's not-always-friendly competition. Was that grounds for murder? "Lynda hinted she'd made a deal to breed with Duke. Now Olivia claims she has. What do you think?"

"Bart Cathaway makes no secret he wants a Barklay champion for Duke." Her answer seemed too pat.

"He's contacted you, hasn't he?"

Her curt nod said a lot. None of it particularly good.

"Why don't you like him?"

"I didn't say I didn't like him."

But she kinda had. "Then what's the problem?"

"He is very, uh, persistent."

"You mean annoying?"

"No. Not exactly. He is a true Cavalier advocate. He funds rescue programs in Europe."

"You do the same here. I'd think that makes you compatriots. Renny is the natural choice. You've been looking for a male for her."

"A mate, Cat. Renny will choose her partner."

"You can't be serious. You intend to leave the future of Barklay Kennel to the whim of a dog?"

"Hardly a whim. I do know a thing or two about romance." Her speculative half-smile sent my imagination to a million possibilities all including sexy, oh-so-masculine Russ. She'd diverted me.

"A-are we talking about Renny or me?"

My aunt dodged a direct answer. "You need to concentrate on the problem at hand. I will take over your production duties so you can help the chief solve the case. Find the truth, my dear. The whole uncensored truth." Bombshell dropped, she swept out of the room with a regal swish of her sheet, Renny trailing behind.

I stood up, my sheet tight as a tourniquet around my hips, and my legs quivering beneath me. The whole uncensored truth? Last time, the truth had just about killed me.

CHAPTER 7

A mush burger combo that included two bones always worked best when asking for a favor from the chief, especially close to dinnertime. Some might call it a bribe. I preferred "buttering up the boss." Goodwill my goal, I proceeded east on Pine to Fifth Street and parked in the last visitor parking spot beside the police headquarters sign. Uncle G held open the glass door and smoothly relieved me of the brown paper bag.

"Char tells me she wants the truth," he said conversationally.

"She needs to be careful what she asks for."

"Amen to that." His frown would send small children crying to their mommies as he escorted me to his office and jerked the door closed. "This is a murder investigation. Best you remember that."

How could I forget? "With my aunt smack in the middle. This isn't my first rodeo, you know."

His sudden lazy manner failed on me. "No. It's not, is it? Thought you'd learned your lesson."

I had. Aunt Char's involvement changed everything.

Uncle G tossed the bones to Max and Maxine and bit into his burger. The biodegradable napkin shredded after his first mustache wipe. "Don't think our relationship entitles you to special treatment."

"Heaven forbid."

"I'm against this first amendment farce, but I can't stop you from researching the missing dogs. I will charge you if you interfere in my investigation or step over the line."

Nothing like open communication. "I'm not happy about this either."

He ketchup-dipped a fry. "Didn't think you were. Start your interview. What do you want to know?"

"Leads?"

He shook his head. "The usual channels are dry."

"What is your bottomless pool of information saying?"

He sat back. "Again nothing."

"Nothing you'll tell me, you mean."

"I mean nothing, period. Lady Mag and Somerset disappeared into thin air."

I sat back. I recognized dead-dog serious when saw it. "How is that even possible? Two fancy Cavaliers don't just vanish."

"No, they don't." Frustration showed in the tight line of his jaw.

"Find anything in Lynda's past?" I had to start somewhere.

"No. But there are rumblings that some of the mayor's campaign donors may be expecting favors."

That was interesting. "Anything prosecutable?"

"Just embarrassing."

Public opinion ruled Lynda's life. Only the welfare of Barkview's children riled her and, of course, Lady Mag.

"Not the woman you'd figure to be Cavaliered to death." At

least I got a sardonic brow lift out of Uncle G. "What about Lady Mag breeding with Duke Cathaway?"

"Mayor says it's true. Bart Cathaway claims otherwise. Mayor's looking for the contract."

Without a signed contract and Lynda dead, Bart could claim anything. "Why would Lynda lie about that?"

"Can't imagine she would. She was an attorney."

"Twenty years ago." Long before she encouraged a likable, trust fund frat boy to make a difference. "Could Lynda have had something on Bart?" Lynda did tend to gather favors.

"If she did, the mayor either doesn't know or isn't saying."

"What about Somerset?" I asked.

"Cathaway claims he has not signed a contract with anyone at this time."

"Begging the question, why Olivia would lie?"

"I don't doubt Olivia thinks she has a deal with Lynda dead. Bart Cathaway is a piece of work."

Which would incriminate Olivia if Somerset hadn't been dognapped. "He's contacted Aunt Char too."

"I'm sure he has. He intends to contract with the Crown winner."

"He said that?"

"Makes no bones about it. Renny's the odds-on favorite, especially with both Lady Mag and Somerset missing."

"Good luck with that." Little did Bart Cathaway know he targeted the wrong Barklay. "For argument's sake, say Lynda did have a contract. If the dog can't be found, the contract would be void."

"Reasonable assumption."

"What if Bart developed a case of buyer's remorse with Lady Mag and wanted out."

"If we can prove a contract existed. And that's a big if. Bart Cathaway's a renowned barrister. He freely admits to discussing the possibility with both Lynda and Olivia. I'm looking into other matches for Duke."

"What about the dog show accusations? Did Lynda really report the judge tampering?"

"No one at the Kensington Kennel Club will confirm the source nor why Somerset's second place win wasn't reinstated," Uncle G admitted.

"I'm guessing Olivia's family had something to do with this. She is English and her family raises champion Cavaliers."

"Her grandmother raised the dogs. Seems only Olivia has continued the hobby."

A dead end? "Anything in Olivia's financials?"

"Two cash withdrawals totaling $15,000 last week."

Suspicious timing for sure. "Is that enough to hire a dognapper? Where do you find one anyway? On Angie's List?"

It didn't take a medium to interpret Uncle G's get-a-grip-girl look. "Okay. Not funny." Actually, I thought I'd at least earned a mocking "clever." "Could easily be two Dior suits and matching shoes she didn't want her husband to know about." I caught myself chewing my lip. "So, this is about the Crown."

"The evidence is leading us there. AKC shows no other reported Cavalier-nappings in the US," Uncle G said. "No reported dognappings involving the J. Tracker collar either."

I didn't like his tone one bit. "Too convenient?"

"Something like that."

More intuition? Apparently, police investigations didn't focus solely on prosecutable facts. "It's the best lead we have to find Lynda's murderer. Have you spoken to the other Cavalier contenders?"

He handed me a highlighted, seven-name list. "The Crown committee sent the list this morning. They highlighted those requesting safety assurances for their dogs."

Bad news travelled fast in this dog-eat-dog world. Natu-

68

rally, the two other top five Cavalier owners, Barbara Chase and Andrew Windsor, had called.

"The financials on Chase and Windsor don't show anything unusual either." Uncle G refocused on the Crown contender list. "It is possible one of these folks hired someone to commit the dognappings."

"But you doubt it."

"Renny's top dog. The remaining dogs don't stand a chance against her." No need to verbalize the obvious, we both knew my aunt wasn't involved.

"We can't be sure Renny wasn't the target when Somerset was taken. That dognapping took planning."

"Point taken."

"What if Olivia took her own dog to make Aunt Char look guilty? There hasn't been a ransom request, right?"

Another get-real shrug. "No. But why dognap Lady Mag and kill Lynda?"

Granted, it was a stretch. "What about Howard Looc?"

"What about him?"

"He's J. Tracker's competition and possibly a disgruntled past employee."

"That's old news," Uncle G said.

"Sean brought it up."

"He did, did he? I'll have a chat with Howard."

"I've got the time. I'll do it." I volunteered.

"I said I would talk to him." No mistaking the end of this conversation; both dogs came to attention. Interesting. My long-dormant, investigative reporter's mind overloaded with possibilities. None Uncle G would acknowledge

A meditative breath helped. No sense shutting down his candor now. "What about the missing hour in Lynda's schedule?"

"The blood splatter on the patio indicates she was lying on

the travertine for some time. At some point she entered the downstairs bathroom, washed blood off her hands and brushed her hair. She was in the parlor, kitchen, and went halfway up the stairs. Security cameras have her car swerving downhill between 5:50 and 6:20 p.m."

"It's a miracle she made it down the road without crashing."

No comment from Uncle G. "She made two phone calls. First to the mayor's brother and the second to me."

No secrets there. "What about the housekeeper and gardeners?"

"Gardeners come Monday and Friday. Housekeeper leaves at 4:00 p.m."

"If Lynda had been at the studio as expected, Lady Mag would've been home alone. Whoever did this knew Lynda's schedule."

"Whole town knew Lynda was going to be on Char's show."

"Aunt Char pointed out that nothing would have stopped Lynda from bringing Lady Mag."

"I agree. This someone likely didn't know Lynda very well."

"That eliminates my aunt."

"Maybe." I had no idea how to read Uncle G's crossed arms. "Fourteen hours later, the dognapper grabs another dog from right under our noses during morning rush hour in front of hundreds of potential witnesses."

"No shortage of daring there," I added.

"Or a complete disassociation with consequences. The perpetrator thinks he's smarter than we are."

Psychoanalysis from Uncle G? I squelched the sudden flood of memories. Not fast enough. His calloused hand on mine stopped the shaking. "Castro's in San Quentin," he said so softly I almost didn't hear him.

70

I yoga-breathed for focus. "Y-you checked?" Why the dogfighting mastermind I'd helped to put behind bars even came to mind spoke to my trauma level.

"Let's just say I'm thorough."

There was more to it than that. Sheer relief surged through me. "You've been keeping an eye on him, haven't you?"

"I watch out for my girls."

I believed him, oddly touched. "I know it sounds paranoid, but Castro swore revenge and considering how this looks, I can't help but wonder if this could have something to do with him."

"Look, I know Char thinks this woo-woo crap works, but..."

I couldn't help myself. I tugged on my scarf. Physically, the bite marks had healed. Emotionally... "Dogs are everywhere. I have to deal with it. *I have dealt with it.*" Not a single big-dog-bark panic attack in years. I glanced sidelong at Max and Maxine. I hardly even noticed a big dog nowadays.

"If you say so. No matter this perp's original motive, he's now a murderer. I figure you want him as badly as I do."

I gulped. Couldn't help myself. I wanted the status quo. Once upon a time, I'd lived for adventure. Now, I liked Barkview familiar and predictable.

"Still too many questions. Any direction you suggest I start?"

"I'm looking further into Bart. He's Char's closest competitor."

"Something came up at J. Tracker's about the diamonds in the collar. I'll go to Gem's Palace and talk to Ariana after I visit the Crown Committee. I want to know more about the other contenders."

Uncle G glanced at his watch. "Ariana's at agility training. Have Char set up your appointment with the Crown Committee in the morning. They wouldn't dare stonewall their biggest sponsor," Uncle G said. "Have you spoken to Russ?"

"Not since he left."

"Before you bite my head off, he could be helpful. He said he'd try to be back on Friday."

Great. He might as well have taken out an ad announcing our date. I hadn't expected secrecy, but privacy would've been nice. "He'll be here."

That interference glimmer twinkled in his eye. "I've got an extra room at my place."

"So do I."

"Wouldn't be proper," Uncle G stated.

I bit back my mind-your-own-business remark. He meant well. Barkview's small town mentality could be inconvenient.

"The Salty Dog has the swordfish special Friday night."

My glare must've seared his beard, gauging how quickly he backed off. "Okay, okay. Do whatever you want. You always do, anyhow."

CHAPTER 8

Time was not on my side, I realized the next morning while stuck in bumper-to-bumper traffic on Oak Street on route to The Daily Wag. Although I knew the Crown Committee members, I followed Uncle G's advice and requested Aunt Char make the appointment. Good thing, too. Who knew the Crown Committee chairwoman, Jennifer Moore's, decaf mocha habit paid tribute to her twin ruby Cavaliers? Heaven help me if I showed doggie favoritism.

I parked at the corner Victorian. Built in 1907 as a private residence in the classic white-trimmed, gingerbread style, the building offered patio seating on the spindle porch fronting both Second and Maple Street. I trotted past the whispering gossips at the wrought iron tables to the period-restored counter.

"Not your usual time, Cat. Good thing I saw your car." A gifted barista, Gabby Turner's lanky, angular look pretty much brought to mind a strung-out caffeine junkie until I met her Saluki. Truthfully, I'd thought Saluki was a fancy word for 'God bless you' until I met the anorexic Sal permanently plastered to her calf.

Thank goodness for a recognizable car, I guess. She handed me my go-to tall, caramel cappuccino. Was I this predictable? "I'll need a mocha with cinnamon and nutmeg."

"Ah. Jennifer prefers soy milk." A multi generation Barkview native who'd left town to attend college, Gabby had found her calling lamenting over all-nighter caffeine options. She registered the town's pulse in her courtyard.

I nodded my thanks. "So, what's the word on Lynda's murder?"

Gabby's voice dropped an octave. "Most believe Mrs. Smythe died trying to protect Lady Mag. Can you imagine, killed by a head wound hours afterward?"

"Not very Hollywood. What about Lady Mag and Somerset's disappearances?"

"Mrs. B is the odds-on favorite Cruella De Vil."

I gnawed at my inner lip. Had Aunt Char been right about making that public statement? To address something so crazy felt wrong. Why give credence to the accusations at all? "What do you think?"

"That your aunt is much too nice a lady for all this cruel gossip." Gabby seemed sincere enough. Why wasn't I convinced?

"Are you trying to clear her?" Gabby asked.

"Clear her from what? She hasn't been charged with a crime."

Gabby's shrug spoke volumes. So, that's the way the Barkview breeze blew. "I see. Well, Aunt Char is a pillar in this community. I am stunned that anyone could believe she could even be involved." No sense letting Gabby's equal-opportunity gossiping go to waste.

"I agree. I mean, she is the first person to help the little league team and never mind all the rescue dogs and the new hospital wing. You know, I haven't had a chance to call the *On the Scent* line, but a client mentioned seeing a tan Jeep leaving the alley behind the Fluff and Buff around 8:30 this morning."

That fit the timetable perfectly. "Did this customer see the driver?"

"Yes. Grant said the driver was wearing a tan baseball cap and overalls and carrying a Toto."

I stilled my pulse. This could be the break we were waiting for. "Was there a logo on the Jeep?"

"Not that he remembered. I grilled him pretty good too. He also noticed the Jeep had a dog bone-shaped scratch on the bumper." She unfolded a Daily Bark printed napkin she'd removed from behind the counter. "He drew it."

I blinked twice. "That's a dog bone?"

Gabby chuckled. "The eye of the beholder."

Only in this dog-brained town could a curved line and squiggle be pooch related.

"I told Grant to call the chief. He's second year at Bark U. Just came off an all-nighter though. Why do doctors work 24-hour shifts anyway? They can't possibly be as sharp after all that time."

I'd wondered that myself. Hopefully, Uncle G could jog his memory. I thanked Gabby with a doubly generous tip and carried the coffees to my SUV. How many tan Jeeps could there possibly be in Barkview? The only two I knew were used by the Barklay Kennel, which had a distinctive swirled B logo on the door. Besides, José couldn't possibly be involved. The man lived for the Barklay Kennel and the prized Cavaliers.

I dialed Uncle G and updated him as I drove to the Crown Committee headquarters in the massive Victorian fronting Oak Street. A period masterpiece, the gingerbread exterior had been constructed with a true Covington flair in 1912 to house the first Crown judging. Every year, the Committee transformed the grassy yard into a tented ascot. My aunt had struggled to maintain the building's unique persona during the latest update and still meet all state-mandated earthquake safety standards.

Thanks to my Aunt Char, Jennifer Holt met me as I exited the manual Pullman elevator and escorted me to the Kennel Club conference room where a century of crowned Cavaliers lined the twenty-foot richly paneled walls. I sat in the five-slash mark seat where JB's grandfather had whittled his frustration over the never ending 1942 vote.

"I had no idea you broke that nasty dog fighting ring." Jennifer's reverence surprised me. Although she wore her bouncy, dark hair in a matronly bun, her melting-Spaniel eyes tugged at the heart, making it hard to believe she'd remained a fortyish spinster. Unless, like so many other Barkview ladies, she was married to her dogs.

"It was a long time ago." How could an incident I'd worked so hard to forget mean so much to her?

"Quite admirable. I talked to the mayor's secretary. He's, well, you can imagine."

I could. Brought back too many memories better left buried.

"I'll bring him my granny's pecan pie tomorrow afternoon. I don't know what more I can tell you that I haven't already shared with the chief, but ask away."

Had to love Jennifer's open-book helpfulness. Post-it in hand, I dug into my purse for a pen. Jennifer offered me hers. "I'm trying to understand what Lady Mag's and Somerset's loss from competition means."

"Well, there are five top contenders who share the Best in Show distinction on any given day. Without Lady Mag and

Somerset, the odds that either Renny, English Rose or Bella Chase will win improve to one in three.

Elementary math there. "Are there any other Cavaliers I should be looking at?" Uncle G's list had included seven dogs.

"Sunset Sky could get lucky, but she's young. Bart Cathaway's Duke could take the honors, but as of now he's not officially entered."

"Has he contacted you to enter?"

"Uh...Nothing official."

So he had called. "Politically it makes sense..." Talk about leading a witness.

"Yes, it does. But the dognappings are a serious concern. Both Barbara Chase and Andrew Windsor have requested extra security for their dogs."

Guards for dogs?

"How well did Lynda know Bart Cathaway?"

"I really couldn't say. The Cavalier show world is small. Olivia's grandmother owned Her Majesty." Jennifer must've seen my confusion. "She was an English champion in the 1980s. Duke is a descendant."

Wow. If Olivia bred Somerset with Duke, she could potentially recreate her grandmother's kennel. Why would Bart bypass a fellow countryman to breed his male? Unless the show controversy had changed the plan. Olivia had to be livid. Enough to eliminate Lady Mag? But why kidnap her own dog?

"I'm looking forward to the Barklay kickoff party," Jennifer said.

I refocused on her excited smile. "Uh... Me too." What else could I say? I made a note to swing by the cleaners to pick up my off-one-shoulder black dress. No escaping the Barklay Kennel's annual event at the Old Barkview Inn. "Any threats against the show?"

"No. Frankly, I can't imagine why anyone would do this.

Lynda was always so gracious and the Cavaliers... They are just little loves."

A sales pitch I did not need. I knew far more than I ever cared to know about the breed. "What about the Crown?"

"It's naturally an honor to win. The prize is mostly about bragging rights. The winner gets ten thousand dollars in cash. All the winners are in-demand."

For minor endorsements, breeding fees and puppy sales, I thought. Renny's upkeep cost significantly more than her two-time top Cavalier status brought in.

"What about the judges?"

"They are all qualified. The judging rounds are assigned on the day of competition."

The top-hat name draw had begun in 1952, amidst judge tampering allegations.

"Can you tell me anything else about Barbara and Andrew?"

"Their dogs have multiple BIS wins. Both dogs are Barklay Kennel descendants." Jennifer scratched the bridge of her nose. "These are good competitors. I simply can't believe they would be involved in anything underhanded."

Maybe they wouldn't, but someone was and we were running out of suspects. "Anyone else harassing you about the show?"

Jennifer chuckled. "Sean Riley is lobbying like a fiend for a specific Jack Russell category."

"You're kidding. Jack Russells have their own show in August." Who could forget the annual hyper Jack Russel infestation?

"I know. He claims it's discriminatory for the Cavalier to get special treatment."

I'd heard it all now. "It's a Cavalier show."

"That is what I explained."

"You're a better woman than I am. What's the verdict?" As if I didn't know.

"The current board is very traditional."

A good thing in my book. Now the bomb. "Tell me about Duke Cathaway. Is he 'the' dog to breed with?" I hand-quoted for effect.

It worked. Jennifer's long exhale reminded me of a filmed Elvis sighting. "He is a beauty. What I wouldn't give for my girls to be on his radar. I can dream," Jennifer said. "Renny is the natural choice for him."

"Really? According to Lynda, Lady Mag had snagged that honor," I said.

"She did say that. So has Olivia. Bart Cathaway is no fool. He'll wait until this year's winner is crowned before announcing."

"You know Bart?"

"You don't? The man's a legend supporting Cavalier rescue. His charity toward the breed is legendary."

"Why haven't I met him at shows?" More important, why hadn't Aunt Char mentioned him until today? The man sounded like her kind of dog lover.

"He shows mostly in Europe. His male lost to Renny's mom on his last trip to Westminster."

"That's like six years ago." Forever in dog show years.

"I suppose it is. Bart's mother passed away last year. The kennel was her passion. It's no secret Bart has been grooming an international Cavalier dynasty to rival the Barklay Kennel."

"Many have tried." And failed over the years. Just ask Olivia and Lynda.

"True, but the man is a meticulous planner. His last step would be breeding his champion sire with a Barklay champion."

"Hence an agreement with Lady Mag or Somerset. Why not Renny?"

"Indeed. Duke and Renaissance are Cavalier royalty." I heard her warning loud and clear.

Bart Cathaway's role added an interesting dimension. Would someone resort to murder to make their dog a champion?

CHAPTER 9

No missing the yellow police tape circling the Barkview dogwood as I drove past on my way to Gem's Palace on Fourth Street. The neon certainly served as a real reminder a killer lurked in our quaint town.

I parked in front of the emerald-trimmed Victorian framed by endless magenta bougainvillea. One of a dozen quaint houses on a block lined with colorful historic landmarks, Gem's Palace would be unremarkable except for a brilliant piece of marketing. At least that's how I saw the shiny chain-linked porch swing framed by potted blush roses. Called Aphrodite's Haven by a generation of Barkviewian romantics, legend claimed proposing on that swing portended a blissful marriage.

Truth, legend, or brilliance? Not for me to decide. Nor why Russ's boyish smile popped into my mind. His smile? Really? Why not his exceptional shoulders and abs?

Yet his smile remained on my mind as I opened the leaded glass door. Glittering prisms Swan-Lake-dipped-and-swayed before my eyes as Gem's Palace's jeweled rainbows drew me into fantasyland. Seven octagonal glass counters housed whimsical creations by world-class goldsmith, Christos Papas. Flanked by three buttery leather armchairs, the mini-islands invited delightful gawking. I plopped into the nearest chair, the scent of sugarplums bringing fanciful times to mind.

Too much? Maybe for some. I felt a warm hug. Far be it from me to question free enterprise at work.

"Prepared for the Barkfest, I see." From dangling pendants and pins to bracelets, jewel studded collars and dog tags, Cavaliers reigned in artful Victorian clutter.

Ariana shared a glance with Gem, her tan and black German Shepherd at her side. "If there is a Barkfest this year." A trace of her European heritage touched her vowels. Barely five-foot-two in heels, Ariana's enviable, lithe form made her polo shirt, slacks, and coordinating plaid sweater looped around her neck look both fashionable and timeless. While chasing Gem over, under, and around agility courses did qualify as exercise, only genetics could explain her youthful appearance. Or a skilled plastic surgeon. How else could a sixty-something-year-old woman pass for forty?

"I'm here for your help." No need to play coy. Ariana knew me too well.

"I see." She assessed my wandering eye. "Since you are here, you must see Chris's newest pin for your aunt's collection."

Talk about technique. Lightning-fast, an understated rose gold Cavalier pin accented with a slim pavé diamond collar swung with hypnotic grace before my eyes. I should've clamped my eyes shut and refused to even look, but, blingaholic that I am, I couldn't help myself. Of course, the chin-cocked likeness to Renny barked at me. Aunt Char would love it.

Ariana didn't say a word. She didn't have to. I just

handed over my credit card. If I was keeping score, I'd have to say: quintessential sales professional one, jewel-junkie zero.

I cleared my throat. "I wanted to talk to you about Lady Mag's collar. Sean tells me you replaced some diamonds."

"Sean is a foolish man." She focused on the credit card receipt, not meeting my eye. Straight-forward Ariana?

Maybe I hadn't been clear enough. I started again. "Was the collar defective?" Ariana's delayed response, like she was deciding what to and not to tell me, made me add, "Aunt Char wants the whole truth."

"I see."

Apparently, I didn't because Ariana's pressed lips stirred instant foreboding.

"Chris says the collar was not defective."

No reason to doubt Ariana's husband, the master gold-smith's, assessment. "Then how did the stones fall out?"

"Lady Mag was rolling in granite dust."

"Gravel?"

She stopped my follow up question. "Chris thought the same thing. Where would a prissy show dog find fine gravel? It was a puzzle. You know my husband and mysteries."

Everyone did. The man chaired the Barkview Holmes Society.

Ariana's furtive look had my full attention. I wasn't going to like where this lead. "The granite is the base for artificial turf."

That was specific. Did we even have artificial turf in Barkview? Odd since we lived in drought-ridden California.

"Not good to talk ill of the dead..." Another long pause hung between us.

"Lynda was complicated," I offered.

"Far more than any of us thought."

83

An odd statement. "Where did the gravel come from?" No way Chris had let that one go unsolved.

"Petronics office entrance."

Unexpected for sure. "No crime visiting Petronics."

"True, but when I asked Lynda why she'd been there she denied it." Ariana's brown eyes shimmered like rich, chocolate diamonds. "But I knew she lied. And she knew I knew. She finally begged me not to tell Sean. Told me she would tell him herself."

That made sense. Lynda had never run from confrontation in her life.

"She never told him. Came in for another diamond replacement."

"So, you told Sean." It wasn't a question. I already knew she had. Ariana's sense of fair play allowed nothing less. Question was, why would Lynda not tell Sean herself?

"Of course, I did. He brushed off my concern. Said Lynda would support the winning team. That's when he told me to charge him for the collar repairs."

A high-profile customer like Lynda jumping ship could be devastating for Sean, especially if Lynda had made the breeding deal with Bart. Could this really be about a cutthroat business rivalry? Bart Cathaway had seemed so plausible.

"You think Lynda was playing Howard against Sean and was killed for it?"

"Men and pride are a devil in the making." Said like a woman in the know. "What bothers Chris is why dognap Lady Mag and Somerset? Renny is the real prize. The only person to benefit is your aunt."

The recurring theme I couldn't quite escape.

She'd spoken her piece. Her genuine smile warmed me. "Is José's eye better?"

84

"What?" Aunt Char's kennel manager had seemed fine this morning. I shook my head, clearing my colliding thoughts.

"I was sweeping the porch when he drove by yesterday morning. Poor lamb was rubbing his eyes like he lost a contact. He didn't even wave to me."

"José doesn't wear contacts." The man had eagle eyes and the soul of a poet. He would never not return a wave to Ariana.

"It had to be José. Who else would be driving the Barklay Jeep?" But Ariana's frown seemed uncertain.

"Are you sure it was the Barklay Jeep?" The other Jeep sighting had been equally as puzzling.

"Only tan Jeep in Barkview."

I beat back my rising concern. Had she seen what she expected to see? "What time was it?"

"8:45. I told the chief."

Of course, she did. Ariana's story corroborated the Barkview vet student's and neatly put José at the scene of Somerset's abduction. Was the rivalry between Sean and Howard irrelevant after all? Granted, José fit the perp's profile all too well. He was definitely a Cavalier Crown insider. He knew how the J. Tracker collars worked. He'd lived just above Lynda Smythe's home for twenty years and had access to Dior buttons through his wife. The puzzle pieces fit way too neatly together. Except, I'd seen him earlier this morning at the spa and he'd been dressed Polo comfortable, not in a kennel uniform. And José kill Lynda? The man caught and released flies. Something wasn't adding up. I needed to talk to José.

I checked the time. Since he'd been tasked with guarding Renny, José should be at the station for tonight's show preparation.

CHAPTER 10

I found the tan Barklay Kennel Jeep parked alongside Aunt Char's Mercedes in the station parking lot. The air-conditioning-water-drip beneath indicated recent use

José's possible involvement plagued me. Although he had been a twenty-year Barklay Kennel employee, did that loyalty include Aunt Char, who'd only taken over after JB's death five years ago? José and Ria lived separate lives on the mansion property, seeing but never being part of the privileged lifestyle. Who was I kidding? José loved those dogs more than anything. Even Ria knew better than to put him to the test. He wouldn't hurt them. But could he be bought or coerced? What did we know about José and Ria before they came to Barkview?

I took the stairs to the second-floor suite I shared with Aunt Char and paused in the regal foyer. Lined with paintings of past Barklay Kennel champions separated by potted plants, the room cataloged the kennel's history. At the center stood a bronze of the Barklay matriarch, playfully called the Queen Mum. Aunt Char's closed door shouldn't have bothered me, but with all the craziness going on it did, big time.

I pressed my ear against the old-fashioned lock. Garble-garble, murmur-murmur. Eavesdropping worked better in the movies. I wanted to interrupt, but I needed to organize my kaleidoscoping thoughts. Besides, my aunt couldn't escape without me seeing her anyway.

Familiarity warmed me as I pivoted to my comfortably broken-in office and cozied up to my desk. I loved this bomb-hit-it space. Creativity flowed best here beneath the afternoon sun streaming through the panes. I found a yellow pad and a pen in my top drawer and started writing an update. No writer's block today. The words flowed easily for my normally adjective-challenged style.

With her usual uncanny timing, Aunt Char strolled in just as I hatcheted the last supercilious clause on my copy. Dressed in a classic navy knit suit and heels, her hair swept into a chignon, she looked like a St. John pin up. Proudly, I handed her the three pages. "This will fill two minutes."

Aunt Char adjusted her never-seen-in-public rhinestone-studded reading glasses. Halfway through page two, she motioned for my pen. She scratched out a line and pocketed the pen. "I'll return this to Jennifer for you."

My cheeks heated. "Uh, thanks." What else could I say? I really needed to get a handle on the pen thing.

"Have the morning team read this," Aunt Char said. "We need to talk." Her earnestness stirred trepidation. So did the fact that Renny was not attached to her hip.

"What's happened?"

"In my office, please." She gestured for me to follow.

I scrambled after her into a typical nineteenth century English-style country house library. From the book-lined walls to the leather, wing-backed chairs, the room screamed old money—Barklay money. Except for a small crystal vase filled with fresh sunflowers and a mystic crystal atop her desk,

JB's office remained as he had left it, as had his father before him.

I saw José half-hidden in the long shadows by the window. Dressed in the same generic polo shirt he'd worn to the spa, I knew he had not been by Ariana's. Then who had? Renny was there too in his arms, along with a kennel. "What's going on here?" It was a rhetorical question. I already had a good idea.

"I have a plan that I will need your help to execute." Not that telltale outside-of-the-box idea twinkle in my aunt's eyes, the one that promised ulcers.

I was definitely getting too old for this. José faded deeper into the dark shadows, taking a squirming Renny with him. Smart man. He knew when to let the women duke it out. I eyed the kennel again. Something moved inside. I'd swear it on bibles. That trepidation turned to real fear. What had Aunt Char gotten me into this time? "What kind of help exactly?"

My aunt's tinkling laughter disarmed me. "Oh Cat, you are funny, my dear. Do you honestly believe I would ask you to do something illegal?"

"To protect Renny, absolutely." Coming in second to a dog might challenge another's self-esteem, but I'd long since accepted my place in my aunt's pecking order.

Aunt Char turned serious. "Shame on you, Catalina. You are my favorite niece."

"I am your only niece." I'd still never put her to the test.

"My only family." Her sincerity seemed real, but that dog changed everything.

"I believe you." I did, but my eyes remained wide open for the pitfall because it was coming as sure as a dog barked. My gaze locked on the kennel. I couldn't look away if I had to. "Tell me that's not Lady Mag in there."

"That is not Lady Mag or Somerset." Aunt Char took a deep breath. "Considering recent events, I'm afraid the dognapper is targeting Crown contenders. Until he is caught, I must provide for Renny's safety."

No surprise there. My aunt worried about everything. "Who is in the kennel?"

"Renny," replied Aunt Char.

I noted the distinctive Blenheim spot atop the Cavalier's head in José's arms. "Who is that then?"

"Come here and meet Perfect Spot," she said.

José handed the dog to me. Aunt Char was funning me. This dog looked like Renny, smelled like Renny, and stuck her dainty nose in the air at me just like Renny, and the spot... My Aunt stopped me from scratching it.

"Not yet, my dear. It is still setting."

My hand froze. "You're serious? This isn't Renny."

"I am quite serious. She is a rescue dog. José picked her up yesterday morning by the bank."

"Around 8:30 a.m.?" I asked.

"Sí," the soft-spoken Mexican said. "I did not see the dognapper." His big hand fisted with heavy weight precision. "I'd like to go a round with him."

Watch out perp. "No violence yet. We must first get the ringleader." José nodded. Heck, I'd have agreed to anything under my aunt's blue-dagger gaze. "My point is that José cleaned her up and brought her here earlier this afternoon. We decided that if another Cavalier was taken that we would send Renny to safety."

"Great idea." What wasn't to like about that? No worries about Renny then. Why then did I suddenly feel like the proverbial sacrificial lamb?

"The issue is to whom do I entrust the safety of the living memory of my dear, late husband's legacy for the Barklay Kennel?"

I needed hip-waders to make it through that guilt pile. The

zinger was coming, and I already half-knew what it was going to be.

Aunt Char turned dead serious. "I want you to take her, Cat."

"Me!" The shriek just slipped out.

"Yes, you," Aunt Char said.

This couldn't be happening. "No way. I am not a dog person." Never mind if something happened to Renny on my watch, I'd be shot.

"You are responsible, trustworthy, and Renny loves you."

"Renny barely tolerates me." Between the snorts and her evil eyes, a person could develop a serious inferiority complex.

"Nonsense. You are imagining things. You've taken care of Renny before. And it worked out well."

Well, it was relative. We'd made it through the weekend. What I needed was a viable, undeniable excuse. "She won't be safe with me. I won't be home since I'm investigating the disappearances."

"Take her with you."

"You can't be serious. Everyone will see us together and know."

"I don't think so." Aunt Char opened the kennel and a ruby Cavalier delicately sniffed. "Meet Penny, the ruby Cavalier rescue that you are temporarily housing until a new home is found."

I stood there unblinking, stunned speechless. My mind flooded with a million objections I couldn't begin to verbalize.

"See José, I told you she'd think the idea brilliant." Aunt Char scooped up Penny. Even up close, the deep rust color looked natural. "I explained everything to Renny, and she understands. She will help you."

"Help me! She's a dog."

Aunt Char stiffened. "Yes, she's a dog. She's also my best friend and loyal companion."

I took a calming breath. I didn't want to hurt Aunt Char's feelings, but enough. "I know you adore Renny and want to protect her, but I'm not the right person. I don't even like dogs." There, I admitted it. I leaped out of the Barkview closet.

"You love dogs. Remember Snowball? That scrunched nose, fluffy thing you got when you were eight."

"Snowball was a cat," I said drily.

"No!" Aunt Char wasn't kidding either. "I thought it was a Pekinese, Keeshond, Lhasa Apso mix up. That explains why it looked so homely. The tailless black..."

"C.C. was a cat too. She lost her tail in a car accident."

"Poor darling. You have never owned a dog."

And I never would. This town cured any fence sitters.

"Now Cat, you can't let that evil Pit Bull attack jade you. Those dog fighters were bad people. They tortured those poor animals."

"Hundreds of stitches, three follow up surgeries, and a week in the hospital would jade anyone." I shuddered, remembering the Pit Bull's teeth tearing into my forearms as I protected my face. Aunt Char knew. She'd nursed me back to health.

Aunt Char crossed the room and wrapped me in a perfumed hug. "I'm so sorry. I wish I could change things for you." Her concern touched me. "Renny is different. She doesn't bite."

Tell that to my perpetually-nipped ankles.

"You remember Renny's mother refused to leave your side through your entire recovery."

More guilt. I glared.

"Renny just wants to make you happy," Aunt Char continued.

More like miserable, but who was counting? "Aunt Char, please don't ask me to do this."

Aunt Char chewed her lip. "The thing is that there is no other choice."

There was always another choice. Apparently just not one she was willing to explore. I was stuck and I knew it. "Sell job aside, answer me one question. Why is this so important to you?"

"Because when the time comes, you must be ready to take over the Barklay Kennel," she said without hesitation.

"What?" Talk about blind-sided. Me, in charge of a kennel? It had to be some cosmic joke. I barely differentiated between a Terrier and a Bassett Hound.

Except Aunt Char wasn't kidding. "You are my heir, Cat, the daughter I couldn't be prouder of."

Emotion clogged my chest. What a time for compliments. She was proud of me, I realized, and that made all the difference. "I'm overwhelmed."

"You shouldn't be. JB concurred. He believed you had the right stuff."

That certainly sounded like the down-to-earth entrepreneur. "You talked to him about this?" Five years ago, I was a snot-nosed brat.

"Of course. You know what a superb judge of character he was."

He'd married Aunt Char, hadn't he? "I don't know what to say." The idea of even trying to fill Aunt Char's size-ten shoes terrified me.

"It will take some getting used to. You will have a learning curve. Just like I did."

You think? "You aren't planning on going anywhere soon, are you?"

"Don't be silly. You know how I like to be prepared."

True. I still had no idea how I felt about this revelation, but suddenly, her plan made perfect sense. She wanted me to be the hero in adversity. In her own way, she was doing this all for my own good. I swallowed. "No one in this town is going to believe I willingly got a dog."

"Barkview is mighty forgiving of converts. You are only a temporary home until the dognapper is apprehended." Aunt Char gently scratched Renny's ear.

Which could well be forever the way the possibilities mounted.

"Besides, you need a dog to get the gossips off your back. What better cover than a new dog for your investigation? Everyone will go out of their way to speak to you."

"Offer advice you mean."

"There is that. You will be one of them."

Never. I was a perfect zero on the WDI scale. I'd agreed to investigate dog disappearances, not mull over walking schedules or organic food ingredients. Unfortunately, Aunt Char was right about the acceptance. I took a long look at the made-over Penny with the pet-store-variety leather collar. She did look like a different dog, at least to my untrained eye. "How are you going to get the color off? The Crown competition is in eight days."

"It's a rinse out. Don't get her wet," Aunt Char said.

"Aunt Char! I live at the beach." One accidental splash and we'd be outed.

"I'm kidding. Relax. It takes twenty or so shampoos with a special soap to lift the color. Frankly, the competition isn't important. Renny's safety is."

I knew that. I was glad she said it anyway. "What do I do with her while I'm investigating?"

"Take her with you, of course. She will follow you

anywhere. Renny, I mean Penny, may not be Maxine, but she can sniff out danger. She will protect you."

That dog has a nose for filet mignon. I'm not sure she'd recognize danger if it hit her square on her snooty nose. I took a long look at Penny. I already regretted this. "What do I need to know?"

"Penny is close enough to Renny for her to understand you." She read my confusion. "You do remember the behavior commands, don't you?"

"Uh. Yes." At least I thought I did. Every Barklay Cavalier was trained with the same word and corresponding hand signal I equated to dog sign language.

"Let's review anyway." She did. Sit, stay, come, go, quiet, speak, guard... The list went on. Penny obeyed perfectly. Of course, she did. Aunt Char had a way of making everything dog-related look effortless. "Just remember, dogs do not speak English. They will appear to disobey when they are confused."

Or want their way. I didn't say that out loud though.

Aunt Char handed me a blue nylon duffle. "Rescue issue. Feed her at seven a.m. and five p.m. You remember the Woof House kibble to rotisserie chicken ratio? She likes to walk directly after eating. The booties would be a giveaway, so just walk her on the concrete. She hates the creepy crawlies in the grass between her toes."

I didn't say a word about the toes comment. Aunt Char was on a roll.

"Since you don't have a doggie door, walk her right before bed. She prefers the right side of the bed. And..."

I tuned out the rest. Enough spoiled princess stuff. She was a dog. She'll get fed and walked. Period. When Aunt Char paused for a breath, I changed the subject. "I'll fill in Uncle G..."

Aunt Char's emphatic 'no' ended further discussion. "Trust me, Cat. Absolutely no one must know."

Trust her? Talk about a leap. Uncle G had known Renny since her inception. He'd sniff out this subterfuge in a heartbeat. "You are asking me to lie to Uncle G." Never a good thing in the best of times, infinitely worse when I had pertinent information.

"I'm not advocating lying. Knowing will put the chief in a compromising position."

Of course, it would. Uncle G's unwavering loyalty to Aunt Char could well appear preferential if this switcheroo became common knowledge. "I'm still going on record as saying that I think this is a bad idea."

"Noted. When the time is right, I will tell him." Aunt Char removed a frosted champagne bottle from her bar refrigerator and poured three glasses. She raised her crystal flute. "To your new companion, Cat. May the experience be rewarding."

I'd settle for surviving it. We clinked glasses and drank to success, each of us no doubt with very different ideas as to what that would be. Aunt Char said her tearful goodbye to Penny, and we were on our own. I have to admit, Penny behaved with dignity. After giving her the come command, she turned one long, woeful Spaniel look at Aunt Char and dutifully followed me into my office. She sat sphinx-style at my feet. How long it would last was anyone's guess.

At least I'd confirmed José's innocence in the dog's disappearances. Naturally, I couldn't tell Uncle G, who was going to flip when he eventually discovered this subterfuge. And he would, the minute he set eyes on Penny.

I couldn't think about that now. I had a dog to worry about. Not any old family puppy, but a prissy, self-indulged princess who looked down her pressed nose like I was the scrappy mutt, which I guess was true if you stacked her lineage up against mine.

Uncle G aside, I still wasn't convinced anyone was going to

believe this dog was a rescue. Except for the coloring, this high society dame could only be Renny. Aunt Char's confidence that my cover would hold wasn't working for me. A Penny test seemed in order, and who better to be my guinea pig than Sandy. She knew Renny and dogs in general. If Penny couldn't fool her...

I'd find Sandy no doubt pulling her hair out in the control room. Quickly, I checked the *On the Scent* line for any new leads. Except for a couple of people who reported seeing José, nothing new. I made note of the callers and stuffed the Post-Its into my briefcase. I'd bring them to Uncle G after the Penny test.

"Penny, come." She dutifully followed me to the staircase leading to the production cubicle. I got down two steps before the leash jerked my arm backward. It took me less than a second to realize that not only hadn't Penny followed, but she'd anchored her front paws on the top stair and held her ground. I tugged impatiently on the leash. "Penny, come. The exercise is good for you."

I swear she gave me a dirty look then her back. Of all the spoiled... Follow me anywhere, Aunt Char had said. Not exactly. I had a choice here. Pull her backward down the stairs or take the elevator like Aunt Char always did. I couldn't give in. This power struggle would set the tone for the rest of our time together.

"Penny, come." No confusion here. I tightened my hold on the leash and tugged harder. How hard could it be to force a fourteen-pound dog to follow? Harder than I thought, since she'd locked her front paws and held on as if the safety of the free world depended on her. So much for agreeability. She couldn't possibly think she'd win this battle.

I grabbed the leash in both hands, until she turned those melting chocolate eyes on me. Fear or manipulation? I wasn't

96

sure. In a single motion, I scooped the dog into my arms, her heart racing against my chest as I carried her unyielding body down the stairs. At the bottom, I placed her on the floor.

"Next time you walk." If a tail wag signified agreement, then I was in business. If not, I couldn't think about it. I had to solve this case. My sanity hung in the balance.

Penny followed a step behind me through the newsroom to the production cube. I found Sandy chomping a wad of bubble gum and pacing the cubicle. Two dozen Post-its obscured the console. Ha! Even computer savvy Sandy needed visual assistance. With three hours until air, she'd have a dozen more by then. I masked my I-told-you-so behind a grin as she clicked and pasted something on the screen and crumpled a note.

"I get it. I won't begrudge you your sticky notes ever again," she admitted.

Wait until she worked alongside memory-perfect Aunt Char for a few nights. Sandy would be totally confused on proper procedure.

"I'll be a little more computer savvy, I promise," I said. Penny squeezed her head through my legs.

Sandy blinked. "Am I hallucinating?"

"I don't know. What do you think you see?"

"A furry, four-legged d-o-g."

I kneeled to scratch Penny's ear. "You're not crazy." I was.

Sandy fell back into my swivel chair. "Are you feeling okay?"

"I know this is totally out of character..." Surprised I'd expected, flabbergasted I hadn't. I told Aunt Char no one was going to believe this.

"With everything going on, they don't have enough rescue homes. So, I agreed to take Penny until they can find a good home for her."

"Penny?" Sandy scooped the dog into her arms. "Well, aren't you a pretty little lady. Such expressive eyes."

Penny must've enjoyed Sandy's talking-to-a-five-year-old tone because she licked her nose. Ick. Other than a disdainful huff after our recent power struggle, she'd completely ignored me. Maybe Sandy should keep her. Her boyfriend could watch Penny with Jack. "Okay, so what gives? How did your aunt talk you into this?"

I tried innocence. "Talk me into what?"

"Keeping a rescue dog. You don't even like dogs." Sandy scratched Penny's ear. "Oh, you do like that, girl."

I swear Penny purred. That ham.

"Shush! Don't say that too loud. You'll start a riot."

Sandy chuckled. "Hardly. Coming out of the closet isn't the end of the world."

I might as well wear a scarlet letter. "I don't hate dogs," I repeated more firmly.

"Maybe hate is too strong a word."

It was. I didn't hate them. I rubbed my scarred forearm. Any animal with measurable bicuspids wasn't on my love-you-the-most list. "I just don't have time for one."

Sandy's reporter's scrutiny turned on me. I squirmed. I couldn't help myself. Fear did that to a person.

Sandy gave me a pass. "You caved to pressure, did you? I mean, no one seriously believes you took the Cavaliers."

"Me take the missing dogs?" A wind gust could've knocked me over.

"No one important anyway. Just because your name is Cat with a C and you hate dogs doesn't make you guilty." Sandy's persuasive skills needed tuning.

"I don't hate dogs," I repeated more softly. "Logically, why would I do that anyway?"

"To eliminate competitors."

I instantly regretted not muzzling Olivia when I had the chance. "So Renny would win a contest I don't care about. That makes sense."

"Or something like that. Speculation is that you are the heir apparent."

"Excuse me?" Maybe the walls did have ears. I'd only found out half an hour ago. "What do you think about me being involved?"

"It's a crock perpetuated by ignorance and desperation."

That was a mouthful of loyalty.

"I've told anyone who will listen that. Besides, you were in the control room with the entire news crew as witnesses when Lady Mag went missing."

"What about Lynda's murder?"

"Everyone thinks she got in the dognapper's way."

Of course. Everything was about the dog here. "What's the word on Aunt Char?"

"Overwhelming majority think she's somehow involved. And, that you, José and the chief are covering or will cover for her. This one isn't going to go away. The gossip keeps getting legs. I don't know how to squelch it."

"By finding the real dognapper," I said.

"That is probably the only way. Have you looked at what's coming in on the tip line?"

"Nothing noteworthy. We're going to need some serious luck."

"What about the José sightings in town when Somerset was taken?"

"It wasn't him," I said flatly.

"The man fit José's description and drove a tan Jeep. Know how many of those there are in Barkview?"

I was afraid to ask. "Two?"

"Three including the two Barklay Jeeps. A Bark U student drives a 2018."

"There have to be hundreds in the state." There better be.

"Think you might be a tad too close to this one?" Sandy asked.

No doubt. Too bad I couldn't spill the beans. "Maybe. Aunt Char wants the morning crew to do the update piece."

"I got it. Go home. I'll call you when I'm done."

"Thank you. Renny come. I mean Penny come." Forget the dog giving us away, looked like I would do it all alone and in record time. "Why would anyone name a dog Penny anyway?"

"Because she looks like a copper penny. Relax. You have Renny on the brain. I would too. She could well be next."

That I didn't dare consider. As usual, Aunt Char's clairvoyance had been right on. I needed a dog to complete this investigation. "Look, about the dog, Aunt Char is distracted with the competition coming up and all the dognappings. I'm just helping out."

"If you say so." Apparently, I needed persuasive training too. At least Penny had passed muster. I hated it when Aunt Char was right. Which it turned out she was most of the time.

CHAPTER 11

Penny may have passed the Sandy test, but my true believer status could only come from Uncle G. If he couldn't tell, no one could. I drove to police headquarters but did not stop when I discovered Uncle G's parking spot empty. Although we'd talked about meeting this evening, we'd never scheduled a time. I called his cell. No answer. He had been crazy busy since Lady Mag's disappearance. Maybe he just took the night off. Just as well. I could use a breather.

I changed direction and headed west to the beach. Penny rode shotgun, sitting sphinx on the seat beside me. Her size made her invisible to all except for semis and mondo-tired vehicles. A welcome reprieve in my mind. After Sandy's "you're-joking" response, I wasn't ready to announce my dog status change until I had a chance to digest it myself. I even drove into my garage and closed the door before exiting with Penny. We were home free. Once inside my two-story board-walk townhouse, she headed straight for the last rays of sunlight streaming through the picture window on the built-in jungle print seat, the only spot in the whole house with a direct view from the jogger's path. So much for secrecy. She'd effectively announced her queenly status in plenty of time to make the ten o'clock news. I could hear the trailers already. Barkview's number one dog hater converted. My phone would start ringing any minute now.

"Penny. Off!" She lifted one eyebrow then snorted with a mountain of attitude.

I flew across the room and snapped closed the dark wood shutters. Penny jerked backward into my chest. Guilt struck me hard. What was I thinking? She was a dog. How could she possibly know the ramifications of her actions? "I'm sorry." I rubbed her ears. She liked that a lot. When she lifted her chin for a scratch, I knew I was forgiven this time. This tightrope walk had a million obstacles.

"I'm about as pleased as you are in the witness protection program, but neither one of us can deny Aunt Char." Penny turned those melting, I'm-too-cute-for-words eyes on me. I crossed my arms, impervious to the blatant manipulation afoot.

I dumped the contents of the duffle onto the travertine floor. An assortment of fancy soft golf balls and squeak toys fell out. I emptied my Travel and Leisure magazines out of the rack and stacked the toys inside. Penny watched me, unblinking. I noticed she sat on the only non-leopard spot on the carpet. Come to think of it, every time Aunt Char visited, Penny never explored my jungle cat-decorated home. Did it bother her?

It took a full second for that thought to sink in. I had lost my mind. The real question wasn't about Penny. It was about me, the supposed voice of reason in this canine-crazed town. I'd just wondered if my décor bothered a dog!

I reached into the stainless-steel wine cooler and pulled

out the first bottle I touched. I'd walk the dog for exercise tonight, I promised myself as I topped off a goblet and took a long swallow. The dry chardonnay went down smoothly. Only ninety-proof would've been better. Penny's single sharp bark stopped me from taking the second swallow. She wanted to eat, I realized when she licked her mouth and nudged the bag of food still on the floor.

Not a word had been spoken, but I understood. It didn't prove anything about dog-human communication. I measured her dry food, added the tablespoon of warm water, sprinkled on the vitamin powder, ripped up a few pieces of roasted chicken I fortunately had in the refrigerator and fed her. Forget the ladylike façade. Penny attacked with last-meal-gusto that scattered kibble in a five-foot radius. I didn't get the dust-buster. The canine vacuum finished the job. I just sipped my wine, processing everything.

My cell phone rang as her radar-perfect tongue swept the floor. Leash in hand, I debated answering until the caller ID showed Russ's number. Instant electric shock took over. "Do you always do what you say you are going to do?"

"It's part of my charm." The sound of Russ's sandpaper-tough voice turned my stomach to mush. He'd said he would call today, and he had. Another keeper point.

"That's good to know." This juvenile tongue-tiedness had to stop. I was an adult. "Still at the office?"

"I don't have anything better to do. Hey, I heard you were tracking a murderer."

"You talked to Uncle G." Had Uncle G nudged him to call? That would be disappointing. "What did he want?"

"Information on a lawsuit involving J. Tracker."

Was Russ his new informer? "So, you know someone who works at the US Patent office?"

"I do. Turns out, Howard Looc is named on the original J. Tracker patent. He also holds an improvement patent."

"You made that call after our interview, didn't you?"

"You know me too well."

Not really, but it felt good to think so. "Petronics advertises that it sells a superior product. Go figure why J. Tracker's is the collar of choice in Barkview."

"Last month Petronics received a large cash settlement from J. Tracker. Because it settled out of court, the settlement documents are sealed."

That was significant. Penny nudged my leg. Walk time. I couldn't hang up now. "And?" He had more.

"Howard Looc was a former minority owner of J. Tracker."

That was news. "Why would Sean say he was an employee?" Was his Barkview Entrepreneur of the Year award a scam? Did it belong to Howard?

"Good question. Howard graduated from Cal Tech with a degree in engineering."

"The brains of J. Tracker's locking devices?" I wondered out loud.

"Possibly."

More like probably. Would all the hype surrounding Sean be enough to put Howard over the top? "Think this could be a high-profile way to discredit J. Tracker?"

"It is an angle. The collars are a link between the cases." Papers rustled on Russ's end. "Howard Looc emigrated from China. His legal name is Chunhua Looc."

The letter "C" tie-in. "Can it be that simple?"

"Revenge is a common motive." Russ wasn't convinced.

Neither was I. Targeting Cavaliers with the big dog show a little over a week away made some sense, but why impersonate a Barklay Kennel employee? And the Dior button? I was missing something.

"Howard Looc is a gambler. He has a line of credit at the Indian casino outside Barkview," Russ said.

That explained why he rarely ventured into town.

"He has motive and proximity. He lives down the street from Lynda. Petronics leases white Jeeps. Could've been dusty or a witness's mistake."

"I'm surprised you haven't mentioned the man's violent streak." Russ knew about Howard's knife-wielding argument with his soon-to-be ex-wife at her restaurant, Ciao Bella.

"It's not what you think. Tina's...uh... volatile. She has the knife skills." Although he'd married a long-time Barkview resident, Howard's status had changed after that incident.

"You know everyone's business, don't you?" Russ asked.

"It's a small town."

"Howard doesn't live in the Terrace house any longer."

I did know that. Just hadn't connected the dots. "So, he's homeless."

"A rich man is never homeless."

Good point. If he wasn't at the house, he'd probably be staying at the casino. "Does he own any other property?" Sean had said something about Howard wanting to own Barkview.

"The Petronics building and various retail spaces in town."

"Uncle G eliminated the Petronics building." Why hadn't Uncle G said a word about Howard staying at the casino? Could Uncle G be up there? It was outside Barkview's city limits on Indian land. Would anyone even report two dogs in a high roller's room?

"Your silence is scaring me, Cat. What exactly are you thinking?"

"Howard is a devoted dog person. I don't think he could hurt the Cavaliers. If he took them, hiding them in plain sight makes sense." A lot of sense actually. Who would ever look there for what amounted to grand theft? J. Tracker's collar's reputation would be destroyed, opening the door for Howard's reportedly superior product. It all added up aces for Howard.

"No judge will sign off on that weak theory," Russ said. "An Indian reservation brings up all kinds of jurisdiction issues."

"My point exactly." Maybe an outside-the-box idea would solve this one. "A reporter can..."

"Get into trouble taking the law into her own hands."

I twisted my neck scarf. No need to remind me. A simple look wouldn't hurt anything though if I could arrange it with relative safety.

"Promise me you won't go out there alone."

Russ's perception was downright uncanny. "I won't." I responded automatically. It wasn't a lie either. Penny was handcuffed to my side, figuratively speaking, and Sandy would be off in four hours. "Sounds like experience talking."

"Five years working with the CARD team makes you question humanity's evolution."

No doubt. "Want to talk about it?"

"Some day." I recognized the sudden tapping sound as keyboard typing. Conversation over. My reporter's mind still pressed for answers he wasn't ready to give. I had to respect his space for now.

The scratch by the door and Penny's tippy-toe polka drew my attention. Even I knew that meant she had to go out. Did I dare walk her and talk at the same time? Who was I kidding? She was a glamour dog, not a Great Dane. Penny ended my hesitation with one long out-or-the-floor bark that got me moving.

"That you barking at me?" Russ's surprise reminded me of Sandy's.

Another bark drowned out my no. The second I clipped on the leash, the Iditarod musher jerked me right out of the door. "Hang on a minute. Whoa. Slow down." I tripped down the two steps, teetered for five more before catching my balance just in time to open the gate before Penny dragged me onto the popular jogging trail. She walked a few feet, circled, and squatted. That was quick.

"I'm back. She had to go." I should've grabbed a sweater. The marine layer had come in quickly tonight, dropping the temperature and blanketing the shore in a London-like fog.

"She? What kind of dog is this?"

"A Cavalier. Aunt Char talked me into keeping one of her rescue dogs." I hadn't lied exactly. I was rescuing Renny. Hopefully, Russ would see it that way. I didn't dare tell him the truth. After all, I'd been sworn to absolute secrecy. "With everything going on, no one would take her. So, I volunteered."

"Volunteered?"

"Okay. I was coerced. The point is..."

I pictured him at attention at a metal desk and his sexy grin. "A fifteen-pound bird hunting dog just dragged you out of the house?"

More like fourteen pounds, but that sounded even worse. "Well, yes. I suppose..." I turned to leave, but Penny just sat there, staring at her own poop. "Furballs!"

"That didn't sound good."

"I forgot the poop bag." A double disaster in Barkview. That dog... but it wasn't her fault. Now what was I supposed to do?

Russ's laugh started mine. "Hey. Don't make me laugh. I can't just leave it here. The fine would bankrupt the US Treasury."

"That's already bankrupt," he replied. "Look for one of the free plastic bag cleanup stations. They're on every corner."

"They are?" Why would I notice? I'd never needed the plastic bags before. I glanced up and down the boardwalk. "No trash can, bag dispenser units in sight."

"Anything in your pants?"

"Besides my underwear?" I shot back.

His voice turned husky. "Tease."

I squelched the little devil stirring inside me. Why tempt fate? I patted the front and back of my slacks. "I found a gum wrapper."

"No Post-its?"

His keen observation and recall skills were kind of eerie. "If you could believe it?" I couldn't. What was wrong with me?

"The gum wrapper is something."

"Ick." I shuddered.

"Look around you. Any leaves or palm fronds?"

"Sand, surf, a seawall. A lot of people staring at me." I deserved it too, stressing over doggie doo like I'd never seen it before.

Suddenly, a plastic-covered hand swooped down and picked up the pile. "Hang on a sec."

"Get the bags that attach to the leash, Cat. You can't leave the house without them." Although the hand's owner's voice sounded familiar, I couldn't place it. The prancing, leaping, basically out of control Jack Russell did it.

"Thank you, Ford." I extended my hand to Sandy's Prince Charming. "You're a lifesaver."

"You're welcome."

He was polite. And cute in an All-American schoolboy kind of way. No wonder Sandy had fallen for him.

"Excuse me. Jack. Sit. Stay."

Sandy's tornado dog obeyed, quietly and completely. Unbelievable. That behavior demanded something equally as impressive from my exhaustively trained pooch. Naturally, Penny took that moment to take refuge from Ford's ear scratch behind my legs, practically tripping me in the process.

"A little shy, is she?" Ford chuckled.

Miss show-off dog? "I-I don't know what's come over her."

Ford smiled. "Happens all the time with Jack around. He's a little hyper."

"He looks sedated." The ADHD dog hadn't moved since Ford ordered him to sit.

"Looks can be deceiving. Welcome to the dog world."

"She's temporary until we can find her a new home."

Ford's orthodontic-perfect smile broadened. "That's what all rescuers say."

"I'm different."

Ford looked over his shoulder. "You're a good person, Cat Wright. I'm sorry for what's happening."

Me too. Before I could say more, Ford started jogging in place.

"Better get her inside. The Jack Pack is right behind me." He snapped his fingers and Jack blasted forward at full acceleration. Wow! In two strides, they both disappeared into the fog, taking the poop with them.

Ford was right about Jack's barely-suppressed energy. I followed his advice and scooped up Penny just in time. Ten Jack Russells erupted by, their owners huffing behind. Penny buried her face in the crook of my arm. A pack of German Shepherds running by would have made sense, but another equal-sized dog?

"Are you still there?" Go figure how I forgot about Russ.

"I am. Crisis averted?"

"This time. Barkview does have good Samaritans."

"That surprises you?"

It shouldn't, but it did. I had been an outcast for too long. "About tomorrow..."

My heart pitter-pattered. Was he going to cancel?

"Are you okay leaving the dog alone?" he asked.

I hadn't even thought about that until this moment. Oh sure, Penny wouldn't mess with my life. "Well, I..." Bringing the dog meant we'd be the center of attention. Leaving her alone wasn't an option either. Forget the babysitter. "How about I cook?"

"I was going to suggest that I cook," Russ said.

"You can cook?"

"That sounded like a sexist remark to me. I'm a good cook. It comes from liking to eat."

"I believe you. I'm just surprised. You actually do more than just grill?"

"You've been hanging out with the wrong crowd."

No doubt. "Okay. I'll make dessert."

"Fair enough. Sure you don't want me to come down tonight?"

"You're pushing your luck." Actually, I was. If he did arrive in two hours, he'd catch me red-handed. "See you tomorrow." I hung up before he could put together what I was up to.

My non-transparency was for the better good. No question philosophical holes in this theory loomed, but something didn't add up regarding Howard Looc. A casual look around his hotel room made too much sense.

I glanced at Penny, aka Double Door Snorer, sprawled out on my sofa. Sure, she wasn't going to get in the way. Just thinking about sneaking her into the casino turned my annoyance to amusement. Outside Barkview, there was only one way to get a dog legally inside and that meant Penny just graduated to a service dog. Not that anyone in the know would believe it, but legally no one could ask what service she performed. I even had a pile of snap-on-the-harness pirated patches after my story on how to turn your dog into a service dog for $25.

First things first, I called Sandy. "Yeah."

Unfair to bother her an hour before broadcast, but guilt still didn't stop me from asking. "Know anyone at the casino?"

"Uh...sure. What are you trying to do?"

"Access a guest room."

"With someone in it?"

"Not while I'm in it. I just want a quick look around."

"Let me think. Yeah. Bring a bag of your special blend."

"My Special Woofing Best Coffee?" That stuff was gold.

"You're asking for a big favor," Sandy said. "That place has cameras everywhere."

I heeded the warning. "Okay. Meet me at the buffet entrance at ten-thirty."

I'd need every bit of the three hours to prep. Quickly, I changed into black slacks and a dark, nondescript sweater that would blend in with the casino masses. Next, I dug beneath my workout clothes in my bottom dresser drawer until I found a stiff, black fanny pack. Not sure if the zipper stuck or my hand shook as I opened the faded nylon case. I'd vowed to destroy it, but never quite got around to it. Had I known deep down I'd need it again? I wondered as I tested the stun gun. Electric sparks flickered. I should keep this in my office desk. I stayed late often enough.

I checked the lock-picking and key-casting kit, pen and sunglass camera/recorders, and popcorn kernel-sized bugging devices. This set-up was ten years old. Imagine what I could buy today, no questions asked.

I fingered the blunt cut, dark wig, remembering the last time I'd worn it. The dark stained concrete walls and the smell of unwashed bodies and dog refuse. I breathed in and out. This time was different. Or was it? I was knee deep in dog crap all over again.

One glance at Penny blissfully snoring away on my super-soft throw and I knew I couldn't walk away. "Come on, Penny.

Time to earn your kibble." I smiled at her beat-it snort. "No kidding, lazy bones." I tapped her butt. She opened one eye and snorted again. I repeated my command. She took her sweet time, but finally stretched into a full body wiggle. I scooped her into the carry bag. Like it or not, we were in this together.

CHAPTER 12

Located in the middle of nowhere, the ten story Vegas-inspired casino lit the pitch-black backdrop in gold and red. The building itself rose like a ceremonial Indian headdress out of the sand. It was constructed mostly of glass with deer, hawk, and bear mosaics covering the exposed superstructure. An elaborate fountain greeted us at the five-lane entrance. I opted to self-park mostly to avoid the twenty-car valet drop-off line.

The crowd worked to my advantage. Penny and I slipped by the overwhelmed security guard, entering slot machine alley. What else would you call the red and gold carpeted path between four hundred feet of flashing, binging, popping chance machines and a dozen scantily-clad cocktail waitresses carrying overloaded trays?

I hurried past that mess to the blackjack tables. The crowd thinned out slightly there. The pit boss eyed me as I cruised around the horseshoe, following overhead signage to the high rollers' area located between two bronze totem poles. Howard was there all right, holding court in an extra-plush boardroom-style lounge. Two white-haired gentlemen sat on either side of him. The fourth player's back looked suspiciously like Uncle G dressed in civvies with a mountain of black chips and what had to be a two-finger scotch at arm's length. Two sparkling, scantily clad bombshells hung all over him like a regular sugar daddy. Sure, Uncle G liked the occasional Vegas jaunt, but this? Was he gathering intel or playing for real?

And if Uncle G saw me...

I skirted away, stepping behind a sweeping fern at the rendezvous place. Dressed in a nondescript Oxford and Dockers, Sandy met me there right on time. How she managed to look so fresh and put together after an evening of live TV, I'd never know.

"Uh, ingenious disguise," Sandy said.

"Don't ask."

Wrong thing to say to an inquisitive reporter type. Curiosity burned in her gaze. "If you say so. Howard's at the high roller table."

"So is Uncle G."

"The chief?" Her wide eyes made me feel marginally better.

I handed her the bag of my special blend coffee. Practical deniability overrode my curiosity.

Sandy passed me a key card. "Howard denied housekeeping for the past three days. First cleaning was this afternoon. No Cavaliers are in there now."

My pulse took notice. A three-day hiatus fit the timeline.

"Could be as simple as his regular housekeeper was off, and we all know how fastidious he is."

His ex-wife, Tina, had lamented about it often enough. I just had to know. "How do you...?"

"I ran a half marathon with the housekeeping manager last year. We bonded at the ten-mile mark." Trust Sandy to make the right contacts.

"I'd need oxygen."

"Not if you trained... Point is, I don't know anyone in security to see camera footage of Howard's activities. So you do need to look around."

I'd hoped, but deep down I'd known the dogs wouldn't be there. What I needed was a clue, something to incriminate or exonerate Howard and the collar angle.

Sandy handed me a grocery bag. "Uniform top should be good enough. Howard usually stays at the tables until two a.m. Take the service elevator to the twelfth floor. The maid's turn down cart will be in front of room 1200. Keep your head down. There are cameras at both ends of the hall."

Sandy's clandestine talents truly amazed me.

"You're seriously calm. How many times have you done this?" Sandy asked.

"Never. I'm a nervous wreck."

"Could've fooled me. I'll stay here and keep watch. Keep your phone handy. I'll call if he leaves the table."

"Stay clear of Uncle G." That man had world class up-to-no-good radar.

"You bet I will. Ever consider that he's already on it?"

"No lecture, okay?"

"You mean the one about taking unnecessary risks?"

My scowl worked. Sandy didn't say another word. At the end of the day, this was Uncle G's fault for keeping secrets. I nudged Penny toward the ladies' room.

"I'll keep Penny," Sandy said.

"Penny goes with me."

Talk about a pregnant pause. "Y-you can't. You'll stand out like a..."

She was right. I knew it. Indecision hit hard. Penny would be safer with Sandy. Except I'd given Aunt Char my word. Right or wrong, it was time to go. "I'll take her in the bag."

Sandy's you've-lost-your-mind look was easy enough to

115

read. No doubt. My heart pounded as I slipped into the ladies' room to don my wig and dark glasses and concealed Penny inside the shoulder bag.

"Penny, stay. Everything will be okay," I said more for my benefit than hers. The last time I'd played Rosa, the informant, I'd ended up in intensive care. At least there wasn't a pack of vicious dogs up there, just an empty hotel room with any luck containing actionable information.

I followed directions up the service elevator to the twelfth floor. The maid's cart obscured room 1200's door as expected. Not a soul occupied the hallway, so I ducked my head and tried the key. After a moment's panicked hesitation, the door opened. Penny growled as I stepped inside. "Shush. I mean quiet." Not a good time to confuse her.

The door clicked shut behind me. Another growl, deeper this time and far more menacing. The little hairs at my nape took notice. That wasn't Penny. What had I walked into? Frantically, I flipped on my LED light. Bolt, Howard's black and white overprotective Border Collie, couched directly in front of us. So much for no dogs allowed in the hotel. My breath caught. It was happening again!

Penny wiggled in the black leather bag until her head poked out and she barked a single, decisive command. She was snack-size to the ready-to-pounce Border Collie. Both of my arms closed around the tote, but Penny bucked and twisted until she broke free. She hit the floor in front of tooth-bared Bolt. With a dainty shake she assumed her royal stance and airily sniffed. Panic seized me. He'd chomp her for attitude alone.

Shockingly, he didn't. In fact, I'd never have believed it if I hadn't seen it with my own eyes. Bolt sat back on his haunches, his head cowered, aggression gone. That crazy little Cavalier had tamed a dog four times her size! I stared dumbfounded for a second before Penny, with queenly poise, permitted Bolt to sniff her.

Recovery took another second. My heart rabbit-skipped, but I could breathe again. I'd thank her later. I slipped on the latex gloves, prepared to explore the luxurious suite. Located on the top floor of the main tower, floor to ceiling windows showcased a twinkling skyline. Two sofas faced the view. A full wet bar and lacquered dining room table completed the living area. Howard's briefcase sat on the marble bar beside a sampled gin and tonic. He hadn't gotten far tonight. Fortunately, the fold-over flap was not locked.

Inside I found a fist full of documents. No time to assess relevance so I photographed everything. A confidential file holding technical drawings and a doodle of Petronics' logo superimposed over J. Tracker's caught my interest. So did the non-sequential page numbers. Where was the rest of it?

Hotel safes tended to be in bedroom closets. My soft-soled shoes didn't make a sound as I jogged across the marble floor to the opulently decorated bedroom. No expense had been spared making this Forbidden City vibe homey. Was Petronics a cash cow or did Howard have another lucrative income source?

I ignored my reflection in the full-length mirror and opened the closet. Sure enough, the locked safe was in there. Since safecracker was not one my talents, I tried a few familiar number sequences. No luck. Bolt's birthday would be on his license.

I returned to the entry. Of course, Bolt hadn't moved from the spot Penny had put him five minutes ago. I showed him my hand as I approached, tentatively at first. His tail wag helped. He wasn't going to take a bite out of me.

Sandy called before I could get to the tag. "He's in the elevator. Get out of there."

No chance to respond before I heard Uncle G's voice. "Sandy?"

Furballs! Disaster loomed now. I tapped my thigh. "Penny, come."

She nudged Bolt aside and leaped into my outstretched arms. I scooped her into the shoulder bag and beat feet out the door.

I looked right and left. Except for the maid's cart, the hall remained empty. Would Howard even recognize me in my Rosa attire if I boldly pushed the cart to the service elevator and escaped that way? Why chance it?

With Sandy in Uncle G's clutches, I hightailed it to the stairwell. The door clicked behind me just as the elevator's ding announced its arrival. That had been too close.

I walked down two flights and removed my disguise in the stairwell before riding the elevator the rest of the way to the lobby level. Sandy and Uncle G, in drill sergeant mode, met me at the elevator.

"Find everything okay, Rosa?"

This was bad. I needed to redirect. "Gamble much?"

"Every day I put my uniform on." He ushered me to a semi-private alcove.

I suppose that made sense. "Cleaned up already?"

"No. Howard had a call from China. We took a break."

Just my luck. "Well, then. No harm done."

"How did you get the key?" Uncle G asked.

I kept my gaze far away from Sandy. "What key?"

His glare radiated pure frustration.

Offense was my only escape. "You should've told me."

"Told you what? You've gone too far this time, Cat."

"What exactly have I done?"

"A B&E job at an Indian casino. Are you insane? This is federal jurisdiction. Do you even know the laws on the reser-

118

vation?" Sternness aside, Uncle G seemed genuinely concerned.

What had I done? Bravado was my only option. "Says who?" It took all my willpower, but my gaze didn't waver. Neither did Penny's. Good thing she chose that moment to add her censure.

"One look at the floor security tapes and... You brought the dog?" Uncle G's dagger gaze targeted Sandy. "And you let her?"

Sandy stepped back. Penny drew his attention to her service patch.

" A Cavalier blind assistance dog?" He shook his head. "You cost me fifty bucks."

"What?" I don't know what shocked me most, Uncle G's comment or him not beating a point to death.

"Never figured you'd fall for Char's plan," he said.

"You know?" Instant relief swamped me. One less worry. Aunt Char had seen the light.

"Of course. Think I wouldn't notice?"

"My argument exactly. Me with a dog? Who'd believe it?"

"You'd better hope the whole town. Let me see her."

Penny preened for him. He scratched her ear. She cuddled against him. He'd been caught. Uncle G's dumb grin said it all. That dog was unbelievable. "Maybe you should keep her."

"Keep her!" What had Aunt Char told him? Surely not that this was Renny.

"Now, Cat. Look how sweet she is."

"Give me a break." She had saved my butt earlier. I owed her that much.

"I have to go back to the game. We'll review what you found in the morning. No secrets."

"Works both ways."

"Yeah." He didn't mean it. I could tell. Well, two could play that game. "Go home and get some rest."

119

"What about you?"

"I'll be fine."

He would be too. He was enjoying this. I could tell by the silver-dollar-gleam in his eyes. "You don't think he did it, do you?"

"He didn't take the Cavaliers." Uncle G's emphatics aside, something still felt suspect with Howard Looc.

"Then what's going on between Howard and Sean?"

Frustration showed in Uncle G's shrug. "Focus on finding the dogs. I'll get Lynda's killer."

"Yeah, but... They could be connected."

"Three reporters called for interviews today."

"The onslaught begins." We'd gotten nowhere in three days. Despite Aunt Char's opinion, maybe the national news coverage would make a positive difference. That world wasn't about finding the dogs. It was about sensationalist headlines. I should know. I made a career out of writing them. Despite Uncle G's thoughts, just maybe I'd find something in the information gathered from Howard's hotel room.

I gestured for Sandy to follow. No sense pushing our luck. We'd gotten away easy—too easy.

"Wow! That was close," Sandy said. "I thought we were toast when the chief caught me. Still don't know how he found me. It's like he has radar or something."

"He does. No worries, we escaped." I opened my passenger door and motioned Penny. She jumped in and settled into the seat.

"Find anything?" Sandy asked.

I shook my head. "No evidence the Cavaliers were there. I took some pictures. Want to see them at my place?"

"I need to get home. Ford's on the red-eye to Boston tonight so Jack is home alone right now."

I understood. That dog digested chair legs regularly. "I saw Ford and Jack tonight on the boardwalk."

"Isn't he a dear, running Jack before he left?"

"He is a nice guy. He picked up my poop for me."

"Oh, no! You mean you didn't have a bag?"

"No. Give me a break! I'm new at this." I expected a litany of Ford's great qualities, not silence. "What's wrong?"

"Nothing."

But there was. I let the silence drag. Sandy hated that.

"Cat, is there such thing as too nice a guy?"

Too nice? She had to be kidding. "You're asking the wrong person." Between Dog Dumper, the Rugby Rogue, and Doctor Nightmare, I'd like to try too nice.

"Crazy, isn't it? He loves my dog. Enjoys all the same things I do. Cooks like a five-star chef. Puts the seat down. What more could a girl want?"

Passion came to mind, but this wasn't the time to share that novel idea.

"I keep asking myself that. I guess I'm glad he's gone. I need some time to think about us," Sandy said. "Want to take Penny for a run in the morning? The Jack Pack will be by around 7:30."

I glanced at Penny stretched out like a lounging lioness on the leather seat. Penny run? "We'll see."

"Sean will be there," Sandy said. "Quick trip to San Francisco I guess."

That made seeing him all the more interesting. I glanced at Sleeping Beauty snoring in oblivion. A prissy lapdog pacing a sleek speedster? That would be as amusing as me keeping stride with those diehards. "I'll call you in the morning."

Sandy disappeared back into the casino. I started my car and headed home. Watching Penny snore, I couldn't help but think about how she'd handled Bolt and put Uncle G in his place. Somehow, she seemed to know when I needed her help. It was as if she was human, but that wasn't possible. Penny was a furry, four-legged animal with good timing.

Despite my misgivings, Penny had still earned her queenly airs tonight. Once at home, I rewarded her with extra crunchies and chicken. When she jumped into my antique four-poster beside me and wiggled beneath my arm for an unobstructed view of the night's data, I didn't object either. Her warmth felt oddly comforting pressed against my pajama leg. I had to search for a magnifying glass to see the document details on the camera's observation screen, which was no bigger than an iPod screen. Despite Fifth Amendment protections, I didn't dare download sensitive information onto my computer.

"We did good, girl." I absently stroked her head and velvety soft Spaniel ears. I scrolled through the client bids. I couldn't make heads or tails of the technical data, but the description caught my eye. An injectable wellness checker. That was the same concept Sean had discussed. Had I just uncovered a classic case of industrial espionage? The first company to market with the technology would make millions. Who was the victim? From the looks of it, Howard was the brains of the pair. That gave Sean Riley a motive to discredit Howard. Lynda could've been passing J. Tracker info to Howard. But why target Cavaliers and the collars he designed? And why a Barklay Kennel employee look-alike?

It had certainly turned out to be an interesting evening. Uncle G would know what to do with the information. If I dared to give it to him. It was proof positive of my transgression. I couldn't tell Russ about it either, lest he figure out that I hadn't exactly told him the whole truth either. What a mess. I had to tell someone.

Aunt Char. I checked the clock before dialing. She tended to be a night owl and should be lounging in her silk jammies.

"Well, hello, my dear. What did you think of the show?" she asked.

"I haven't seen it yet." I had recorded it, but, oddly, hadn't even thought about watching it.

"You have trained Sandy well. Her process is very Catish."

Not sure if that was a compliment or not. Before I could ask, Penny jumped onto all fours and barked.

"Hello, my darling."

Penny heard her loud and clear; her tail batted me in the eye in rapid motion.

"How is it working out with you two?" Aunt Char asked.

"Fine." I picked fur out of my mouth. Penny's snort compelled me to add, "The little brat saved my butt tonight."

"Oh my, do I want to know?"

"No, you don't. Why I called was to tell you to put both Barklay Kennel Jeeps in the shop first thing in the morning."

"José needs to pick up the podium vases tomorrow morning for the opening ceremony."

"I'll get them. Make sure you get a time-stamped receipt and José gets a distinctive rental. Anything but a Jeep."

"Why, may I ask?"

"No, you may not. Just do it, Aunt Char. Don't argue. Trust me."

Without a moment's hesitation she said. "I do trust you, dear. 7 a.m. sharp, both tan Jeeps will be out of town. Anything else?"

"Yes. José needs to be with witnesses all day."

"Witnesses besides Ria or myself?" I pictured her knitted brow.

"Yes."

"I'll send him to the rescue for the day. He enjoys the

volunteer work and it's always good PR. Please collect the vases by ten."

"No problem. Thank you, Aunt Char."

"Did you hear that we have had a late entry for the Crown?" she asked.

"No." I sat tall, knocking Penny off my lap. This was significant. A definite number one suspect for the dognappings.

"Duke Cathaway from the Cathaway Kennel in Yorkshire. His UK wins qualify him under the 1922 ruling."

"Why did the Cathaway Kennel wait so late to enter?" It was right under the midnight entry deadline.

"Bart Cathaway is a bit eccentric. I imagine this is for the shock factor."

Or he'd manipulated the field to compete one-on-one against Renny.

I glanced at the now-snoring princess. She'd taken over the entire left side of my hand-stitched jungle motif quilt. I should wake her. I'd never sleep through the night with her in bed beside me, but I didn't have the heart to do it. She'd earned her place tonight. I dialed Sandy instead.

The call connected, but Jack's yapping made hearing her impossible. At least I hadn't woken her up.

"Sorry to bother you," I said. "Mind if I borrow your Jeep to pick up a couple of vases in the morning?"

"Will Ford's RAV work? Mine's in the shop. Someone backed into it at the hospital."

"Ugh. Did they leave a note?" Last time I borrowed her car I dropped the camera tripod on her bumper.

"No. Ford is taking care of it. Said it was his fault."

The guy knew his responsibilities, I'd give him that.

"See the broadcast yet?"

I'd only been home thirty minutes. "I spoke to Aunt Char. She says you are very Catish."

She chuckled. "Don't tell Jack. He'll have puppies." More seriously, she added, "That's a good thing, right?"

"If you want to emulate me. Yes. It is."

"Of course, I want to. You're an award-winning producer. So, what do I need to improve?" I loved her eagerness.

"Nothing." She was well on her way to finding her own voice. I just had to point her in the right direction.

CHAPTER 13

Me dressed and ready to run on the boardwalk at 7:27 a.m.? No self-respecting night-owl deserved this torture. Penny agreed. She growled at me from the gate. A chicken treat bribe got me a dirty look. A pull on the collar and the command to come did no good. No way, no how, was she moving. I didn't have time for this. Any minute now, the Jack Pack would be pounding down the pavement right by us. "Come on, Penny. We're supposed to be a team."

She wasn't buying any of it. In fact, she declared war when she turned tail and gave me her back. Apparently, dogs walked, and princesses preened.

Through the peek-a-boo sunlight, I glimpsed JRu tugging Sean way ahead of The Pack. Either I carried Penny or let this opportunity to question Sean jog right by. Like I'd waste donning running shorts and last year's Barkfest t-shirt. I scooped Penny into my arms and matched his stride. "Good morning," I said.

"Walking the dog generally means the dog walks," Sean remarked.

You think? I ignored his amusement. "A rookie mistake, but I'm learning." I exhaled fur from my mouth since Penny's paws wrapped my neck in a copper and white scarf, her heart racing against mine.

"I'm glad the rumors are true. It's about time Cat gets dog." Five miles down the trail and Sean wasn't the slightest bit winded. This guy had some great lungs. Twenty steps and I, on the other hand, needed pure oxygen. Come on, I wasn't in that bad of shape. Was I? It had to be the fourteen-pound dead weight bouncing on my chest, pressing against my diaphragm.

"Temporarily. Until a good home can be found for her," I said.

"That's what they all say."

"What does that mean?" Sudden irrational concern took hold.

"You know I support Jack Russell rescue, right?"

I didn't know, but it made sense.

"Every foster home gets one they can't part with. And you two look, uh, attached."

Relief washed over me. "I'm not one of them." Confidence brightened the day. No matter what I thought, or felt, Penny wasn't mine to keep. When it was all over, she'd go home to Aunt Char and my life would return to lonely, I realized quite suddenly.

Sean's I-told-you-so nod irked me. Before I could respond, he kicked up the pace. No way he'd escape on that note. I matched it. "So, was your San Francisco trip successful?"

He went from cocky to snarly in a blink. "No. Somerset's disappearance killed the deal."

"How could that..." I didn't get to finish.

"The client decided J. Tracker's collar wasn't secure enough and cancelled the contract. I can't begin to tell you how many more orders are on hold or cancelled."

Compassion wasn't in me over this. Regardless of who actually invented the technology, the collar had failed to protect the missing Cavaliers.

"We must find those dogs," he said.

I didn't like the sound of the desperation just beneath the surface at all. "Did Petronics get your contracts?" If J. Tracker was in trouble, Howard would have justice, not to mention a successful company of his own.

"What do you think? His new patent..." Sean trailed off. He'd said too much and knew it.

"What about the new patent?" Not another word from Sean. But I already knew, and I felt like the proverbial teasing cat on the fence top.

"I'm going to get Howard for this one," Sean muttered, only half under his breath.

I heard him loud and clear. "Is that a threat, Mr. Riley?" What was a little industrial espionage among capitalists anyway?

He stopped dead in his tracks, his fair complexion beet red. "No, Ms. Wright. It's called competition. Like every Barkview citizen, I am interested in the safe return of the dogs."

There was more to it than that. "Are you telling me that Howard killed Lynda and kidnapped the dogs?"

"No. I am not," he said defensively. "I have no idea who killed Lynda or took the dogs. Their disappearance is, however, crippling my business."

"I suppose you are insinuating that Howard has motive. Would you say it stems from patent infringement?"

Sean's lips pressed into a tight line, concluding whatever he'd been tempted to say and took off at a sprint.

I ended my pursuit after two strides. Not a chance I'd catch him with Penny plastered to my chest anyway. I'd learned that what divided Sean and Howard ran deep.

Whether it involved the Cavaliers remained to be seen. But I had another suspect.

Time to go see Uncle G after I played taxi to a couple of sacred hundred-year-old Cavalier painted vases.

The vase pickup and delivery took less time than anticipated so I arrived at the police station before Uncle G. I waved to the dispatcher as I passed two tablet-touting men with vulture-like regard pacing the ten-by-ten waiting area. Their slacks and button-down shirts pegged them as big city reporters. Penny didn't think much of them either. She tossed her nose in the air and sassy-pranced past their radar. My faith in her people judgment improved exponentially.

I smelled the rich Woofing Best roast before I saw Uncle G sneak in the back way. Max and Maxine trailed behind. He offered me one of the steaming cardboard-wrapped cups and took a long swallow from the other. His bleary eyes showed zero compassion.

"Win big?" I had to ask.

He growled.

I grinned. "Someone woke up on the wrong side of the bed this morning, I see."

Another growl confirmed everything.

"You're getting too old for...."

"Give it a rest." Uncle G plopped into the swivel chair and powered up his computer. No toothpick today. No energy to spare. "Should have Cathaway's report momentarily. What did you find in Howard's papers?"

"Possible industrial espionage between J. Tracker and Petronics." I handed him my camera. "I'm not sure who the victim is though. I ran into Sean this morning and he's borderline paranoid."

"With good reason," Uncle G's nose practically touched the screen. "You saw the reporters out front?"

"Hard to miss. Promise me you won't brutalize them. We don't want them messing up our investigation."

"You should know."

"Was I that bad?" Had I ever been that out of touch?

"Took you ten years, but you learned." As usual Uncle G spared me no humility.

Not exactly complimentary. Those boys were in for a ride. "J. Tracker is hurting from the collar failures. That points to Howard."

"Nothing unaccounted for in his financials," Uncle G said. "Howard was at the casino when the dogs were stolen."

No doubt on surveillance cameras too. "The man's a gambler. He could have cash stashed anywhere for a pay off."

"True. He didn't do it." Uncle G's conviction didn't waver.

"Okay. I'll bite. Why?"

"The J. Tracker failures are causing him to lose face too. He designed the collar. Petronics' version is better now, but the basic technology is the same."

I had to agree with that.

"Bart Cathaway's under-the-wire entry is noteworthy," Uncle G said.

True. "Does he use a J. Tracker collar?"

"No. One from Petronics."

That meant he knew the basic working of the J. Tracker version. It all sounded good—too good, to be honest.

"The José look-a-like is bothering me." Any casualness fell flat.

Uncle G didn't even look up from his computer screen. "Was wondering when you'd get around to telling me that."

So much for secrecy. "He didn't do it," I said flatly.

"José was reported on scene for the Somerset dognapping. He lives uphill from Lady Mag. He is familiar with the collar mechanism and has access to dog sedatives. He is also ex-military."

No need to remind me he knew his way around a gun. I didn't add that Ria had access to Aunt Char's *Dior* buttons. It looked bad for him. I didn't realize just how bad until now.

"He also has a vested interest in Renny winning the Crown since he gets a percentage of the puppy fees," Uncle G explained.

Apparently, there were many things about the Barklay Kennel that I didn't know. Not that it mattered. He hadn't done it. I'd known this would happen. How could I protect him without giving Penny away? "I'm telling you, he didn't do it. You have to trust me."

Uncle G sized me up. I held ground through his icy stare. "All right, Cat. Obviously, you know something you're not willing to share with me."

My because-I-said-so needed work. "I..."

"Don't deny the truth. I just hope this isn't loyalty talking. José isn't who you think he is." Uncle G pulled out a generic vanilla file. "His real name is Carlos Rodriguez."

Carlos with a C. My confidence dropped a notch. What did I know about José —Carlos? He and Ria kept mostly to themselves. I hadn't seen him personally. Aunt Char had corroborated his alibi. Could he have tricked Aunt Char? Or did she already know his true identity? "A lot of immigrants change their names."

"True. Ria's real name is Elena Amaya Rosas. She's legally married to Juan Rosas who currently resides in Mexico City."

José and Ria weren't married? They were the most devoted couple I'd ever seen—a Hollywood-quality love story. "Why not get a divorce?"

"Juan Rosas is a violent wife beater with multiple arrests."

"He beat Ria?"

"Don't know. His second wife had multiple hospital visits prior to her death."

"I thought you said Ria was his wife."

"Juan remarried. Apparently, Elena faked her death."

You go, girl. "That makes Juan a bigamist."

"Not his worst crime. His second wife's death was ruled suicide. He is on wife number three now."

"You think he killed his second wife?"

"Or drove her to it. I won't go into details."

"José is protecting her." He always protected the runt. He hand-fed puppies, nursed preemies, and coddled the bitches. What lengths would he go to protect the woman he loved?

"Everyone has secrets," Uncle G said. "Some bigger than others. They've lived among us for twenty years."

Russ had suggested that days ago. The thought gave me a chill. Not so much for the implications, but that I recognized his sneeze a split second before his rough-edged voice said, "Could be grounds for extortion."

I looked up sharply. An instant shiver shot down my spine. Dressed in jeans and a navy polo that emphasized his light blue eyes, I swallowed hard.

"You look lovely," he said.

So much for the flattering straight skirt and sweater set I'd planned to greet him in. Aunt Char's 'always look your best' mantra suddenly seemed right on. Too bad today wasn't one of those days. The sad part was that I'd actually rehearsed how I'd greet him. A hug and smile and then I'd say something coy. Forget it now. I just stood there like a simpleton, staring.

Uncle G spoke before I could untangle my tongue. "I asked him to come. We need an unbiased set of eyes." He handed Russ allergy pills and a water bottle.

I questioned the unbiased part. Russ's molten gaze screamed anything but an uninterested third party. Uncle G might discount it, but Penny didn't. She arched her back and stretched her front paws, her gaze fixed on Russ as if he were a meaty bone. He offered her his open hand. "Well, hello little lady."

One sniff later and his dog appeal struck gold. Penny licked his hand, her tail auto-dusting.

Russ scooped her into his arms. "I see why you couldn't say no to her. You won't have any trouble finding her a good home."

Penny preened, basking in the all-male attention and ear scratching. Jealousy took hold. I liked head scratching too.

"How did you find out about José?" Russ asked.

Uncle G cleared his throat. "Contacts."

He should've said spooks, since the information came from nowhere and disappeared as mysteriously. A lot like Uncle G's military service. No pictures, no phone calls, no visiting buddies. Kind of like it never happened.

Russ sidestepped the quagmire altogether. "Anyone from José's past could have recognized him and demanded payment."

"He didn't do it," I said flatly. "We're wasting our time pursuing this line of investigation."

Blue steel locked with my gaze. "What are you hiding, Cat?"

I couldn't lie. Not the way he stared me down. "Don't ask, Russ. I just know. You're going to have to trust me."

Faith, it seemed, didn't sit well with him either. His gaze probed further as if he could coax the truth right out of me. I bet it worked often too. I wanted to come clean, tell all, but I'd given my word. I didn't look away. I just bit my lip and said nothing. "Okay," he said finally. "For arguments' sake."

He got that right at least. "What other suspects do you have?" he asked.

"Other than Sean and Howard's feud, Lynda and Olivia's breeding agreement, and the man himself, Bart Cathaway. His late Crown entry makes him a natural suspect." Uncle G's printer suddenly spit out pages.

Russ took the top half of the stack I retrieved. "Bart Cathaway was born in London in 1960. Family money from Yorkshire. Graduated from Oxford. He's a solicitor."

"Grounds enough for suspicion." Uncle G leaned back in his chair.

I scanned my pages. "He's a Crufts judge. Donates heavily to Cavalier rescues in England."

"Here's something," Russ announced. "He withdrew twelve thousand pounds the day before Lady Mag went missing and another ten thousand two days later."

"It fits the timeline for a payoff," Uncle G said. "Since he only arrived this morning, he would have needed a local accomplice."

We had something. "Are you responsible for his security?"

"No. Bart insisted he will protect his own dog. He's staying at the Old Barkview Inn."

They'd been sold out since last year. "How did he get a room?"

"Not only a room. A suite." Uncle G frowned.

"That's not possible." Like football fifty-yard-line season tickets, longevity decided those assignments. Whose feathers had been ruffled?

"Sounds like he isn't worried about the dognapper," Russ said.

Possibly. Or was it that unfathomable male ego at work? I noticed Bart's ice-cold eyes the moment I looked at the photo of the burly, tweed-clothed fox hunter. If he had the same Englishmen's view of colonial incompetence as Olivia, that could be part of his reasoning.

"I have to ask myself, what would be worth chancing it?" Russ asked.

"Renny," Uncle G said. "Duke is the top Cavalier in England. Critics say Renny is the top Cavalier in the world. Char has refused all invitations to English shows."

"So, he is here about pride?" Insufferable English pride if you asked me. I glanced at Penny making nice with Russ and thought about Aunt Char allowing her to choose her mate. Power in the paws of a dog. Just wait until Bart discovered that the future of his kennel relied on the whim of a bitch. Both men would laugh me out of the room if they knew. "Any other secrets on Bart?"

"There are always secrets," Uncle G remarked. "The relevance is the question."

"We need to focus on possible insider help," Russ suggested. "Known acquaintances, beside Olivia? Links to any other Barkview residents?"

"Who would want to know a stodgy Englishman except Olivia?" What a scary team they would make with Olivia's intimate insider info and inherent dislike of Aunt Char.

"If she is involved then why steal her own dog?" Russ asked.

"Publicity. The media blitz if Somerset turned up the day before competition could seal victory," Uncle G said.

"She doesn't know where her dog is," Russ interjected. "I've worked with enough frantic parents to know the difference between those involved and those not."

I did trust him, I realized suddenly, despite the fact that he'd just disagreed with my opinion. I still refused to throw in the suspect towel on Olivia. "Let's not forget that Olivia dislikes Aunt Char."

"Beside Bart Cathaway, what else do you have?"

I laid a stack of multi-colored Post-its on Uncle G's desk

and started jotting down what we did know. Two dogs missing. All had the same security collar. All Crown-contending cavaliers. Two Barkview residents. One a regular visitor. The C shape of the collar and paw print. A single Dior button. No ransom. The José look-alike. I listed every Barkview resident in contact with the missing dogs and prioritized each note by possible links. The problem was, too many links pointed right back to José or Aunt Char. Yet, I knew they hadn't done it and I flat out couldn't tell why.

Finally, Russ pointed out the obvious. "I know you took José and your Aunt Char off the table, but the evidence doesn't lie. The José double makes them somehow involved."

I held my cool, despite my boiling frustration.

"Anything in Charlotte or José's financials?" Russ asked.

I shared a glance with Uncle G. He hadn't run them, I realized.

"Investigating family requires a neutral third party." Russ spoke from experience. I could tell.

"What did you do?"

"My job," he said flatly. "The truth came out."

I expected nothing else, I realized. Good or bad, Russ Hawl dealt in the truth.

Uncle G ended my questioning. "I'll take care of it."

"Someone is going to great lengths to make it appear that my aunt is involved." It had to be. How else could so much evidence point to them?

"And who might want to frame them?" Russ asked. "Renny is still in town."

"A very good question." Uncle G rose. "Speak with Char after you've seen Cathaway. Perhaps she will have a clue."

"Aunt Char doesn't have enemies. Except for an envious Olivia, I can't imagine someone disliking her enough to do this to her."

"Char is far from a saint. She has offended many people along the way." Uncle G waved to someone outside his office. "I need to talk to the reporters before they start fabricating evidence."

How well he read the situation. Those boys were in for it.

"Take Russ over to the Sit and Stay after you see Bart. Today is the meatloaf sandwich special. Have Nell's peach cobbler with it."

I frowned. A private meal at Aunt Char's beat out being the topic of conversation at gossip central. Was this the ultimate plan at work or Uncle G's stomach talking? "Is that a hint?"

"Sure would be nice being that I'm stuck in here doing damage control. Don't forget Max and Maxine."

"Bones, I know." Russ's hand brushed the small of my back as he escorted Penny and me out the door. He didn't say a word until we cleared the bustling lobby.

"I'm sorry I just showed up like that. The chief called this morning. He said he wanted to run some things by me."

I could hardly be mad at him for helping. Uncle G on the other hand deserved a piece of my mind. "Don't worry about it. Sorry I'm such a mess."

"You look sexy."

He sure knew exactly what to say to disarm me. Penny barked my objection for me.

"Sorry." He wasn't. He'd meant every word. His blue-fire gaze said so. "Walk or drive?"

"Walk. The parking is impossible this week." So was the traffic. "You're taking your life in your hands jaywalking."

"I noticed." Hard to miss the sheer number of people and dogs of all sizes and shapes, some decked out in frippery, others in flashy collars, all crowding the sidewalk. "All these people here for the dog show?"

"Twenty-five thousand. Every hotel is booked a year in advance."

"For a dog show?" He didn't believe it either. "No offense, Penny."

Penny's prance high-stepped. "She's shameless."

"Curious how Bart got that suite." Russ defined bull-dog tenacity.

"My thoughts exactly." Surely, Bart hadn't orchestrated the whole caper just for publicity for Duke. It seemed improbable, but you never knew with dog people.

CHAPTER 14

The stately Old Barkview Inn occupied several downtown blocks. Built in 1890, the charming sky-blue building accented by white gingerbread trim and twin towers surrounded by period widow's walks peeking through a slate blue gabled roof was the most photographed building in Barkview. In addition to serving as the setting for numerous Hollywood productions, the establishment had, over the years, hosted heads of state from around the globe. Inside the marble entry, the hand-carved mahogany ceilings and stained-glass masterpieces demanded admiration.

Today the crowd milled in the quaint parlors bordering the grand entrance, surrounded by the comforting smell of beeswax and fine wood. Good thing too, because as we entered the marble lobby, Penny broke free and beelined it to her life-like bust where she mimicked her regal stance.

I took off after her and scooped her into my arms, praying that no keen observer put two and two together.

Of course, Russ, Mister-Keen-Observer himself, stood there

and stroked his jaw. He'd noticed the resemblance. "Renaissance is your aunt's dog?"

Question or statement? I wasn't sure. I could kill Penny for this. "Uh, yes. Renny is her nickname."

"The resemblance is remarkable."

I had no choice but to brave this one out. "Not even close. Penny is a ruby Cavalier. Renny is a Blenheim."

"The facial structure and body shape is...."

"Champion Cavaliers are bred to look that way." I'd been saying that same thing for years.

"True, but there is an uncanny resemblance."

This could get ugly. Time to misdirect. I waved to the concierge, Franklin Duncan, dressed in a Victorian waistcoat and gentleman's ascot, behind the ornately carved mahogany counter.

He waved back, his normally stiff upper lip lifted. With Russ breathing down my neck, I closed the twenty or so feet between us in rapid strides.

"The vases are in place, Miss Wright. Would you care to inspect?" His Bostonian accent came off formally correct.

"Thank you, Franklin. That won't be necessary. I trust you." I did. Franklin the Magician took customer service to a level five-star pamper palace resorts could only aspire to. "I need to speak with Bart Cathaway."

"Mr. Cathaway is in the Windsor Suite." Not a blink or waver in his voice, but his sharp look gave away his true opinion.

"Where is our senior judge staying?" I asked, oddly put out. How dare he mess with Barkview tradition?

"The Cruft's judge opted for the Queen's Crossing suite."

Which set the domino effect in gear. I didn't want to know where this ended. Bart Cathaway had upset the barking order.

"Please tell him that Charlotte Barklay's niece is here to see him."

"Certainly, Miss Wright. Mr. Cathaway is popular this morning." He emphasized on the letter C.

"Really?" Mr. Cathaway hadn't won a friend in his concierge. I leaned across the counter and whispered. "Who has been visiting?"

"Jennifer Holt arrived at nine. The mayor left precisely forty-five minutes ago," he replied under his breath.

Interesting welcoming committee. Jennifer, the Crown Committee chairwoman's, greeting made sense, but the mayor had just lost his wife. Could he have been discussing the breeding contract with Bart Cathaway? "Thought you'd like a heads up that reporters will be arriving soon."

Franklin stood to attention. "Thank you for the warning." He picked up the phone and dialed. "This is the front desk. Mrs. Barklay's niece, Miss Wright, requests an audience with Mr. Cathaway." Although Franklin's expression remained impassive, I'm probably glad I wasn't privy to the other side of that conversation. Finally, he said, "Yes, sir, tea and scones. I will see to it." He took a deep breath and smiled. "Mr. Cathaway has asked that you join him in the Windsor Suite."

I smiled my thanks and directed Russ to the Centurion Otis 61 elevator. Installed in 1890-something, the wrought iron cage had transported presidents, dignitaries, and every Crown winner since the show's inception. Originally powered by steam, the industrial age masterpiece had been converted to electric during the inn's 1970's modernization.

As we waited for the cage to arrive, Russ pointed out the obvious. "Nice move, Ms. Behind-the-scenes-is-where-I-belong."

I refused to admit it, but just maybe he had a point. I'd

forgotten how much I liked that crazy thrill I felt when on the hunt.

The ornate gate slid open, and I greeted the ancient elevator operator. Dressed in starched dark tails and a Victorian striped waistcoat, Will Oldeman had the distinction of being the oldest employee at the Old Barkview Inn. "Hi, Will. This is Russ Hawl. He's a consultant to the FBI. We are here to..."

"Third floor," he said in a gravely, chain smoker kind of voice. "Renny will thump that British upstart."

I smiled. Will should know. He'd been up close with four decades of Crown winners. "I hear Duke is a looker."

"He is that. Attitude, Miss Wright. Renny was born to the Crown. Duke will be privy to her hindquarters. Be sure to tell Mrs. B that."

"Her hindquarters," I repeated as the old elevator chugged upward.

Will winked at Penny. "How are you today, pretty lady?"

I ignored Russ's renewed interest and placed Penny on the floor as far away from close inspection as I dared. "She's a rescue, Will."

"Yes, Miss."

Was he buying it? Or politely agreeing? I wasn't sure. This subterfuge was making me paranoid.

"Anyone else been up to see Mr. Cathaway?" Russ asked.

"The mayor and Miss Holt."

"Anything we should know?" I asked.

"The mayor wasn't pleased," Will replied. "He always remarks that 'progress will be the end of us, William.' He calls me William, Miss Wright. Today he said nothing. Not even goodbye."

Now, that was significant. The consummate politician, the mayor faced reelection in November. "The mayor isn't himself," I said. "Any idea what he spoke to Mr. Cathaway about?"

"No, ma'am."

Or wasn't saying since Butch the Bouncer, a freakishly large man arguably broader than an alpha gorilla with thigh-sized biceps, met us at the elevator door. "Follow me." His cockney accent negated the polished effect of the Alfred Dunhill suit and banker's haircut.

I found myself pressed up against Russ when another obviously ring-tested, heavyweight boxer-turned-bodyguard opened the double doors. No wonder Bart had declined protection. He'd brought his own dark-alley-crushing crew. This guy's crooked nose and pointed dark eyes sent a chill down my spine and made me question my tactics. Not enough to back down though. I felt safe with Russ. Why, I couldn't say. Physically, he didn't stand a chance against those two bruisers, but I knew he would protect me.

Inside the apple green and cream Eastlake parlor, I recognized the bull-like shoulders in the Hugh Hefner smoking jacket and slippers framed by the high-noon light from the riding photo in his file. Perched on a chair beside Bart Cathaway sat a seriously cocky Blenheim Cavalier. Déjà vu hit me square. Olivia's latest publicity photos depicted the same scene.

Penny trailed behind as I crossed the thick carpet. "Mr. Cathaway, thank you for seeing us," I said smoothly. His bear-like grip fell short of welcoming. "Let me introduce Russ Hawl. He's affiliated with the FBI. We are here to welcome you to Barkview and to offer you my aunt's personal invitation to the Crown opening." I hadn't exactly lied. Aunt Char would want me to be hospitable.

"Honored, Miss Wright. I look forward to seeing Mrs. Barklay again. Please join me for tea." He picked up Duke and gestured for Russ and me to sit on the dainty Queen Anne sofa.

I'd expected Bart's invitation. He couldn't afford to alienate my aunt. Duke's growl surprised me. Not at me but at Penny, who eyed him unblinkingly from behind the safety of my legs. "I shall convey your enthusiasm to my aunt. She is looking forward to meeting Duke." I offered my hand to Duke. That didn't help at all. He growled deep in his throat. I jerked back, startled. Penny responded with a Pit Bullish growl and lunged forward. Her leash snapped in my crotch, stopping her midair while I tumbled. Only Russ's quick reflexes prevented me from butt-planting at Bart's feet. He even caught Penny's leash too, ending her dramatic charge with a yelp. Furballs! What had come over her? Duke remained in Bart's arms, his teeth bared in Doberman-guard-dog style.

Hard as it was, I didn't dare laugh at the two fluff balls squaring off like welterweight contenders. I scooped up a quivering, tension-taut Penny. "I apologize for Penny. She's normally so easy going." Which was essentially true.

I ignored Russ's raised brow. Apology protocol format explained away my response. I couldn't know the dog's attitude after a single day. One thing was for sure, I wasn't taking odds on Bart's hope for a breeding alliance with Renny.

I expected a like apology from Bart. His dog had crossed the line too. "Penny, you say? I am not familiar with her lineage," he said.

"She's a rescue dog," I said quickly. Maybe too quickly the way Russ looked at me.

Bart's scrutiny didn't bode well either. The man had an eye for champions. The carpet suddenly turned to quicksand beneath me feet.

"Papers?" he asked.

"Not that I know of. She is my Aunt Char's charity case.

Needs obedience training as you can see."

"What I see is a spirited Barklay Cavalier." Bart placed Duke on the carpet. He sniffed regally then turned his nose up at Penny. The reigning Crown Cavalier snubbed like a mutt? I tightened my hold on her squirming, escape-intent body. It didn't help. The dog had a mountain of pride. Forget her cover. I had to get her out of here before the street fighter took over. If refined Aunt Char saw her now... I couldn't think about that and kept hold of Penny.

Bart took that moment to approach. Penny growled low in her throat—an intimidating, combat ready sound. Unfazed, Bart ignored her bravado and reached to her blind side behind her neck. He ran his finger over her ears and neck and opened her mouth in true judging style. "Shoulder balance and ear width are prime Barklay traits."

I knew where this was going. If he inspected her coat, biting would be the least of my worries. I placed Penny back on the ground, cognizant of that quicksand now creeping up my thigh. "Really? I never noticed that in Lady Mag or Somerset."

"Lady Margaret is equally well-proportioned. Temperament, now that marks a true champion. Lady Margaret and Somerset will always be second to Renaissance."

If Olivia knew that, there'd be no telling what she would do. "You've met Lady Mag and Somerset?"

"Judged them both at the Hyde Park Kennel Club Show."

So he knew both ladies. "Lady Mag won that one." Lynda had announced that in the *Daily Bark*.

"She was the best of the lot."

"Olivia must have been disappointed," I said.

"Olivia is accustomed to disappointment."

Spoken like someone in the know. I had to ask. "How long have you known Olivia?"

"Olivia showed an uppity bitch years ago. Never quite

made scratch." Bart's snobbish sniff got right under my skin.

Was he talking about more than dogs? I wondered. I couldn't fault Olivia for wanting to one-up him.

"Now, Renaissance is the prime specimen," Bart explained.

"You've met Renny?" I swear Penny understood. She crouched, teeth bared prepared to attack.

"I have never had the pleasure. Her video presence is impressive. I will know for certain the moment I see her personally."

Unless I intended to test our cover now, I needed to get Penny to safety fast. I scooped her up just in time. Penny lunged with the force of fourteen pounds of pure attack. Both hands on her torso, I barely held on as she barked like a mad woman. "Penny. No!" She barked a decibel higher.

Bart's pressed-lipped disdain matched Duke's. Retreat was absolutely the better part of valor here. "I am so sorry about this. I'll take her downstairs. Russ, please finish your tea."

I ran as if pursued directly out the door. Penny calmed at the elevator gate. One thing I'd learned today for sure, Bart wanted Renny and she wanted a piece of Duke. Not that I blamed her. Good looks meant nothing if he failed the attitude test and Duke went down with snobbish colors. The "why" bothered me. Penny had proven her ability to judge character. Was this a testament to guilt or just serious dislike? Was this about Bart Cathaway or Duke? I couldn't tell. Either way, Bart demanded further investigation.

The Otis's gate closed behind us before Will spoke in low tones. "Heard the barking downstairs. Is Miss Penny all right?"

"Seems to be now. She sure isn't a Duke fan."

"Proves she has good taste." Will's bushy, white brows narrowed.

Interesting development. "Excuse me?'

"Renny is too much of a lady to be fooled by that fraud."

"Duke is an English champion," I said.

Will's *harrumph* got me thinking. "You mean the dog upstairs isn't Duke?" Had Bart pulled the same scheme as Aunt Char and hid his champion? No wonder he wasn't fazed by a dognapper. Wouldn't that be a hoot? How could I prove that? Did I want to? The old adage about people living in glass houses came to mind.

"That dog is no champion." Will should know. Had the mayor figured that out too?

I had to ask again. "Any idea what the mayor came to see Mr. Cathaway about?"

"I imagine it was same reason as Mrs. Austin-Worth."

"Olivia was here?" The plot thickened.

"She arrived twenty-two minutes before the mayor. Skedaddled moments before he arrived."

Contract negotiations? "Was she pleased when she left?"

"No, ma'am. Snuck down the back stairs. Thought I wouldn't notice her."

So, Olivia hadn't taken the public elevator. "Nothing gets by you, my man." Everyone knew that. Olivia had to have been desperate. "How long did she stay?"

"Twenty-two minutes. The guards waited outside," he said. "Find those dogs, Miss Wright. This isn't right."

"I know. Here's my cell number. You're my eyes on Mr. Cathaway, Will."

His grin warmed me as he scratched Penny's ear. She nudged his hand. "You go, girl. Send that Brit home with his uppity tail between his legs."

Was he talking to me or Penny? More important, had he guessed Penny's secret? Will's wink didn't help either. An eagle-eyed old timer and a champion dog equaled a crazy situation. One thing was for certain, something about Bart Cathaway with a big letter C wasn't right.

CHAPTER 15

Russ met us in the lobby ten minutes later and ushered us out the stained-glass doors before speaking. "You two okay?"

We'd gotten out of there with our subterfuge intact. A win in my book. "I have no idea what got into Penny."

"Don't you?" He stopped dead in his tracks and stared me straight in the eye. "When are you going to start telling me the whole truth, Cat?"

I swallowed, suddenly afraid, not for myself, but for us. Testing trust was not the way to start any relationship. "It sounds crazy. I thought you'd think I was nuts."

"Try me." Utter calmness meant trouble.

"I don't think she liked Duke's attitude." I gauged his disbelief and quickly added, "See, I told you it was insane."

"It's not crazy. Dogs have a personality. It's been documented that people and dogs can have a symbiotic relationship."

"And you believe that?"

"I believe there is some level of communication between you and that dog," Russ said.

No sense denying that little truth. We did get along like the old acquaintances we were. Better than I'd thought possible. Too bad I couldn't share that info. "It just doesn't happen overnight, especially with a non-dog person. I'm losing my mind."

Russ's grin changed to laughter. "That's it? You found a dog you can relate to and it's scaring you?"

"It changes everything I've ever thought about dogs."

"I doubt that." He tucked my flyaway hair behind my ears. "Keep her, Cat."

I gaped at him, the effects of our physical contact slowing my reaction. Keep her! "I-I can't."

"Of course, you can. She needs a home and you two have something special."

Except Penny didn't exist. When this was all over, she'd go back to her pampered life and I'd return to mine. "Maybe." I couldn't think about that now.

He left it at that and changed the subject back to the case. "I don't blame Penny one bit. Those two are a pair."

A pair of what? I wondered. "Will saw Olivia sneak into Bart's room right before the mayor."

Russ shook his head, unsurprised. "And the saga continues. You were right leaving Olivia on the suspect list. We'll go see her after your aunt."

"And confront her about the visit?" I'd rather break up a catfight. "Considering Olivia and Bart's history, I wonder if Bart judged Olivia fairly. Lynda winning the prize Olivia coveted could be motive."

"What did Bart say after I left?" I asked after he alerted Uncle G.

"Nothing complimentary about Penny."

I should've told him that Will thought Duke was a fraud, but I hesitated. Would that idea open up too many questions about Penny? Questions I couldn't afford to answer? Another interesting idea came to mind. If the Duke I had met was an impostor, would Olivia know? And if she did, what would she do with the information? Misrepresenting a champion wasn't illegal around town. Showing them in competition was.

We arrived at the Sit and Stay before I decided what to do. The current-events-touting breakfast crowd mingled with the sunglass-ready lunch set and overflowed onto the gabled veranda, turning the sidewalk into a Marine Corps obstacle course. In all fairness, the twenty people weren't the problem. The small to extra-large dogs were. I picked Penny up. No sense giving that lip-smacking Newfoundland any ideas.

I squeezed past a standard Poodle, stepped over two Dachshunds, and avoided a Golden Retriever enroute to the reception desk. There I found Nell directing traffic with her usual angelic calm.

"Cat! Congrats. You've lost your virginity!" She skirted the podium and threw her arms around my neck.

Talk about a first date nightmare. Every eye in the place fixed on me, including Russ's. I would've made a break for it, but a stout Saint Bernard blocked the doorway.

"Are you going to introduce me?" Nell asked.

After that ice breaker? I ought to hang her. "Nell, this is Russ."

"Pleasure to meet you." She politely took his hand but focused on Penny. "The dog. Who is this gorgeous Cavalier?"

A compliment from a devoted Labrador Retriever fan? "This is Penny."

A short woof, followed by a tail wag, and practiced princess preening put Penny center stage. So much for subtlety.

"She's just adorable," Nell gushed.

"Thank you." I didn't know what else to say. I felt like an

idiot. I shot an apology in Russ's direction. No need to. His amusement made me choke.

"We'd like to have lunch. How long is the wait?" he asked.

Nell chuckled. "I'd given up hope of ever seeing this day. No wait. You know the rules. Follow me."

I cringed as we sidestepped a bone-gnawing Westie on our way to a café table in scrutiny-center of the dining room. "How about that one?" I pointed to a corner table half-hidden behind a ficus.

"But this is the best one in the house," Nell insisted.

"My choice. The rules are the rules."

Nell's frown promised retaliation, but I got my way.

"What rules?" Russ whispered.

"The new dog owner rule," Nell said.

She deferred the explanation to me. Of course, I knew the ordinance. I'd been railing about it for years. I hardly thought it would ever apply to me. "First available table in every restaurant in town goes to the new dog owner."

"Don't forget the parking," Nell said.

Now, that might come in handy this week. Too bad I was a fraud. "Any black and white spotted curb in town is reserved for thirty days."

"A spotted curb? I don't remember seeing that in the vehicle code," Russ remarked.

"It's a Barkview city ordinance." Which said it all as far as I was concerned.

Nell handed us each the doghouse-shaped plank menu and set a dog-stool at the head of the table. Penny took her to-be-seen pose, working the crowd like the pro she was.

"Hard to believe she's a stray," Russ remarked.

My weirdo-dog-reaction explanation wasn't holding up. If he didn't believe it, what avid dog lover would? I could only hoped his trained observation skills separated him from the masses.

"She's not a stray. She's a rescue. It doesn't matter how fancy she is. Penny doesn't have papers." All of which was true. I still cringed inwardly as his gaze held mine.

"Why didn't you want the center table? Was it me or Penny?"

"That's a loaded question."

"That demands an answer."

Forget evasion. Fortunately, no gag order covered that answer. Surely, he'd noticed all the eyes on us. "A little of both," I admitted, half under my breath.

He shook his head. "You are a bundle of contradictions, aren't you?"

Compliment or criticism? I wasn't sure. I could kill Aunt Char for putting me in this position. "Come on. I'm like a book."

"Sure you are. Sometimes you're direct, other times charmingly unassuming, still others reserved and sometimes verbose. You are not at all what I expected."

And that was good, right? I wondered as I eyed him over the flat edge of the menu. "Explain."

"Now, my loaded question. Here's my psychoanalysis. Part of you wants to fit in, but the other part likes that you are the talk of the town without a dog."

"I don't have a dog because I don't have time for one." Defensiveness snuck in despite my wish otherwise.

"What changed now?" That better-tell-the-truth look again. He was sure good at it.

Couldn't he let anything go? "The dognappings," I responded. "My aunt asked for help. I had to do it."

Russ chuckled, a deep belly laugh. I liked the sound of it and how it softened the hard planes of his face. "That must've

152

been some conversation. You can tell me how that went later. Right now...." He reached across the table and stroked my hand. "...I'd like to get to know Catalina Wright."

I nearly jumped out of my skin. How could this man I hardly knew have this effect on me?

"Know what?" Talk about another loaded question. Fortunately, Nell returned with two water glasses and a silver bowl for Penny.

"So, what can I get for you two lovebirds?" she asked.

I blushed to the roots of my hair. Russ remained cool. In fact, he never looked at the menu. "Cat?"

"I'll have the grilled chicken and pistachio salad with balsamic citrus."

"Meatloaf special for me and one to go," Russ said.

Penny snorted. Okay. I had forgotten her. "Bring me an extra plate. I'll share my chicken. Dressing on the side, Nell. The princess is a purist." Aunt Char would kill me if I let Penny eat greasy dressing.

I didn't need to see Nell and Russ's reaction to know I'd blown it big time. Unrecoverable? I wasn't sure yet. No telling how many ears had heard it. "What? The dog book states dogs shouldn't have..." I couldn't come up with anything they shouldn't have.

"Oil-based dressing," Nell suggested.

"Vinaigrette." The guest one table over proved my eaves-dropping theory. "I told you not to feed Misha that greasy salad junk."

And idiot me protected them. "Yes, exactly. It affects their digestive system."

"I've never heard that," Nell admitted. "Are you reading that New Wave dog crap? Dogs are carnivores, you know. A little olive oil..."

Heads turned all around us. "Just bring the chicken plain. I don't want to take any chances." Talk about a ticking time bomb. I pictured a total restaurant debate coming.

"Whatever you say." She collected the wood boards and scratched Penny.

"Where were we?" Anything to get the mood back.

"You were about to tell me all your life's secrets."

He'd probably settle for what was going on. Naturally, he suspected something besides my weird dog meltdown. That odd arch in his brow indicated as much. I'd have to brave this one out. "Like you didn't look me up?" FBI consultants had to have access to all kinds of personal information. He probably knew more about me than I did.

He smiled, the I'm-interested kind that could melt chocolate. "I did not. There are some things I like to find out on my own."

There was a compliment in there somewhere, I was sure of it. "I was an English major on the fast track to academia when the dogfighting story fell in my lap."

"A right place, right time situation?"

"Hardly. I mean, literally. My college roommate's brother was beaten up by the dogfighting ring. He died in my arms. The police called it gang related and weren't doing anything. I just got mad and started asking questions. My journalism professor recommended me for an internship at The LA Journal and the rest is history."

"It was your first story?"

"And last mainstream media report."

"You had no formal investigative training?" he asked.

"On-the-job training. A whole frightening lot of it that changed my life."

"You have great instincts. Why are you producing?"

It's safer, my mind screamed. "I'm where I belong," I said out loud.

"Behind the scenes? After that kind of adrenalin rush you have to be bored to death."

"Speaking from experience?" Was he a thrill junkie?

"I like a challenge," he said evasively.

"You mean like cliff climbing in your spare time?"

"Heck no. I scuba dive and water ski for fun."

A water fan. Big keeper points here.

"I catch bad guys for a living. They sometimes take issue with the rules."

Well stated. I'd already assessed a job-related dump 'em point. "Well, I like to sleep at night." With a little Tylenol PM and a Shiraz if necessary. "Contrary to your initial assessment, I'm not comfortable center stage."

"You had a bad experience, but that's not reason to hide forever."

"I like producing. I write copy all day."

"Telling someone else's story."

"Hardly. I decide what people see and don't see."

"I'm sure the FCC would love to know that," Russ said drily.

"I do human interest stories. There's a difference."

"Not really. I'm not buying the Cat transformation theory. You went from the frontlines to the home guard. What happened with Tomas Castro?"

Russ's intensity touched me. He wanted to know about the evil dogfighting ring. "Threats mostly. After my informer ended up in ICU, I knew I was next. Even after Castro was convicted and sentenced, I kept irrationally looking over my shoulder. It's over. He's been in prison for ten years and two months now."

"Three days and seven hours. But who's counting?" Russ asked. "Seriously, a traumatic experience like that is never over. Your reaction is normal."

He was part psychologist too. His understanding still felt good. "Aunt Char's my guardian angel. She picked me up and brought me here to heal both mentally and physically."

"Surrounded by dogs? That had to be hard after the attack."

"How did you know that?" Is it possible that a virtual stranger just gets you? Talk about an E-Harmony match.

"It would be for me." Russ Hawl ruffled by anything? "Okay. I understand the rehab, but why did you stay in Barkview?"

"My Aunt Char has that effect on people. You'll see." I actually couldn't wait for them to meet. I envied her uncanny ability to see beyond even the most complex defenses.

"What about your parents?"

"I lost my dad when I was twelve. My mom remarried. I have an eighteen-year-old stepsister who lives in Hawaii now. Aunt Char took me under her wing." It didn't feel like an interrogation per se, just his natural curiosity at play. A man who didn't want to talk about himself? "Enough about me. What's your story?"

"Not as interesting. I'm a genetic Fed. My dad was FBI. Rumor has it my grandfather broke in J Edgar, but if that was true, the evidence went to the grave with him."

"You're serious?" Talk about loyalty. "Those are some pretty big shoes to fill."

Amusement showed in the twinkle in his eye. "Not really. My grandfather was five-foot-ten in his boots. My dad swears to six-foot."

Russ towered over me. He had to be at least six-two. "Why aren't you FBI?"

I felt him withdraw. "I was. Before you ask, my niece was abducted."

I'd figured it was something like that. "I'm so sorry. Did you find her?"

"Yeah."

Suddenly, I knew. He'd been too late. I squeezed his hand. "How do you deal with the ones you can't save?"

"You focus on the ones you can."

His pat answer flopped. He'd said that there was always a clue. Maybe he was right. Fifteen years ago, DNA evidence didn't exist. Who knew what law enforcement would have fifteen years from now? "And you keep looking," I said. "There is no statute of limitations on murder." And no rules on a consultant.

He heard me. He stroked my hand. "My dad used to say that there was no such thing as unrealistic goals, just unrealistic time frames."

"An astute man," I said. "He kind of sounds like my dad."

Russ nodded.

"I admire you. I'm not the patient type. I want instant gratification."

"Don't we all? I just control it better."

A true poker face. I made a mental note not to play bulldog with him. "What happened to...?" I would've probed more except our lunch arrived. I split the butterflied chicken breast and cut it into Penny-sized bites. Her tail tapped the tabletop in true Spaniel fervor. "Here. Don't eat too fast. It gives you gas." Not that she listened. Penny virtually inhaled her meal like she hadn't eaten in weeks.

I frowned. Every eye in the placed was fixed on me. "What? Never seen anyone share their lunch before?" Russ's arched brow signaled another tactical failure--a very big mistake this time.

"Not with a dog." He inhaled deeply, sighed in contentment, and started eating. "You know, for a non-dog person you have Penny pretty well figured out."

I ignored his innuendo and forked my salad instead. Sherlock Holmes underfoot required caution. Clearly, I knew this dog and well. The Barkview gossips would be calling me a dog whisperer for sure. Wouldn't that be the irony of the century?

Russ attacked his sandwich with appreciative gusto. I picked out the fresh raspberries first then forked a few bites of the greens. Something wasn't right. Not the salad. It was fine. Something else that I couldn't exactly put my finger on. I lifted Penny into my lap and gave her another piece of chicken. She was safe. Russ eyed me yet again. It was unnerving.

"Don't tell me you're one of those females who don't eat in front of a man."

I nearly choked on my shock. "Does this body look like it has ever missed a meal?'

"Looks great from here." That devilish smile did it to me again. Good thing I was sitting. "What's bothering you?"

"I don't know. A feeling. I know it sounds crazy." I twisted my bandana knot a full three-sixty.

"Do you get them often?" He placed his fork on the table. At least he wasn't laughing.

"Not really. Hardly ever."

"When was the last time?" He drank his Coke.

I stressed my memory. "The night JB had his heart attack."

Russ carefully replaced his glass. "And before that?"

"The night Castro grabbed me."

"Premonitions or gut feelings aren't crazy. They save lives."

"You get them too?" I asked.

"I wish I did. I have seen people survive things they never should have because they moved one inch to the right or left. Embrace it, Cat, and learn from them."

That was practical advice. If only I could. The tension

played a jig in my stomach. Something was going to happen, and I was powerless to stop it. The waiting gnawed at me.

A moment later, my phone rang. Even Penny tensed tight as a bowstring. I swallowed, afraid to answer until Sandy's number showed in my caller ID. I exhaled in sheer relief. "Hi. Your car is at the police station."

"Don't worry about it. Meet me at Mrs. B's."

My heart went straight to my throat. "W-what's wrong?"

"A tip came in on the *On the Scent* line. It said that the missing dogs are in the Barklay Kennel. I erased it off the upload. Thought you'd want to investigate personally."

My fork clanked on the tabletop. No one else had seen it! "That's impossible."

"I know. That's why I called you."

OMG! If that was true... I couldn't think about that now. "I need a minute. I'm at lunch now."

"I know. With the consultant Fed. It's all over town."

So much for a quiet lunch. "We sat down twenty minutes ago. "

"Careful. Nell is text central."

Two taps on her phone and the whole town would know.

"This doesn't look good for Mrs. B," Sandy said.

Loyalty wouldn't allow me to agree. "Wait for me at the gate. I'll be right behind you." I hung up. "Sandy..."

Russ pressed his finger to his lips. "Not here." He flagged down Nell. "The chief was right about the sandwich. Just like my mom makes. Is it possible to have someone deliver one to him for me? And two bones for the kids?"

Like Nell could refuse that complimentary request. "Anything to help out." She beamed.

Russ tipped her well, I noticed. He had working gossip down to an art. We were out the door in a minute flat. I tucked Penny football-style beneath my arm. "The *On the Scent* tip line got a lead that the missing Cavaliers are at my aunt's kennel."

"Call your aunt. Tell her to stay away from the kennel. I'll call the chief."

"No!" My glass-cracking screech drew all kinds of looks. What was I thinking? "Please, Russ. I..." My thoughts scattered. The ramifications were too much to consider.

"What, Cat?"

The undivided attention from those penetrating blue orbs about did me in. I could hardly think. "I-I need to see this for myself."

"You can't hide this..."

"I know. I know. I won't. I just..."

"Just what? You're stalling."

He wasn't cutting me an inch of slack. I swallowed hard. "Exactly. I need time."

He wasn't letting that one go by either. "Time for what?"

"I don't know. Something is telling me this isn't right."

"Your instincts or loyalty?"

"I don't know."

"Okay. Call your aunt. Tell her to stay in the house. Assuming we find the dogs, if someone planted them in the kennel, they could still be in there."

"Or we might find evidence."

"Right," Russ replied.

"Thank you."

"Don't thank me. I may be a material witness for the prosecution," he said dryly. "I'll drive."

"I have Sandy's car."

"We're taking mine." No compromise there. I didn't fight it. Some battles just weren't worth it.

We speed walked the few blocks to his Land Rover with Penny double timing it just to keep up. She took the center

160

console, leading the charge until Russ hit the gas and I caught her before she tumbled into the back seat.

Good thing Russ had a GPS sense of direction and a lead foot. My head was everywhere but on the road. I squeezed Penny as tight as I dared.

"How are you going to get the dye off Renaissance in time for the competition?" Russ asked conversationally.

My jaw had to be on the seat. "W-what?" His eyes were on the road, safe from my scrutiny. Was he fishing?

"Your aunt gave her to you for safe keeping." It wasn't a question. He knew.

"H-how did you know?" No sense denying the truth.

"Your aunt and José were conspiring to hide Renny during the Somerset dognapping, weren't they?"

Another statement. He was good. Bad guys beware.

"Then finding the kidnapped dogs at your aunt's home is a set up."

"It has to be. I'm sorry, Russ. I couldn't tell you. I promised."

"You still haven't said a thing."

No, I hadn't. I just hadn't denied anything. My word remained technically intact. Was that enough for him? "What gave me away?"

He did meet my gaze then. I expected a cat-ate-the-canary look, not understanding the warm and penetrating kind. "The chief should be told."

"He can't know. He needs to have deniability."

"You are withholding information in a police investigation."

That did sound bad. "I'll talk to my aunt."

He didn't like my answer, but he didn't press. "Call her," he reminded me.

I obeyed despite my dread. She answered on the second

ring. "Hello my dear. How was your lunch with the FBI consultant?"

"How do you know?"

"You must learn to tweet, my dear."

Had Aunt Char embraced technology too? Was I the last hold out? "Russ and I are on our way."

"Wonderful, I'll steep the tea."

"Good. I mean, listen. Aunt Char..." I didn't dare explain it all. Aunt Char lived to push the *no* envelope. She just might run right out to the kennel no matter what I said. "You must trust me."

"I do, my dear. What's going on?"

"I will be there in ten minutes. Do not leave the house."

It didn't take an advanced degree to envision her confusion. "What is going on?"

"Nothing...."

"Nothing! Shame on you, Catalina Wright."

She'd cowed me good with that one. What could I say?

"Hold on, I smell something burning." I heard heels tapping on tile then a panicked, "There's smoke coming out of the kennel. The dogs!"

The line suddenly disconnected.

I dialed 911. The kennel was on fire with the kidnapped dogs inside!

CHAPTER 16

Russ stomped on the gas, plastering both Penny and me to the leather seat with what felt like Mach 1 force. I appreciated his Indy-speed as he tore up the switchbacks with admirable competence. Sirens roared in the distance. The acrid air already smelled like a dreaded California wildfire. Had the fire spread beyond the kennel to the surrounding brush? Although well maintained, the chaparral would ignite like kindling.

My heart hammered in sync with Penny's as Russ blasted around the last turn and through the open security gate. At first glance, the antebellum mansion appeared untouched. So did the garden fringe. The choking black smoke plumes only billowed from the single story, whitewashed kennel.

We skidded in alongside my abandoned SUV with the driver's side door ajar and the keys dinging in the ignition. I couldn't fault Sandy for going in without us. I'd have done the same. Penny and I hit the ground running before Russ's SUV came to a complete stop.

Not a moment to waste. Penny paced my stride with three

of her own as I sprinted toward the action. Didn't take a fire investigator to conclude the kennel was a goner. If the sheer volume of smoke didn't give it away, the angry flames licking the rooftop did.

Panic seized me. Not for the building and all the Barklay history, but the people. Where were they? On cue, the double doors burst open. Sandy, Ria and José stumbled onto the grass, coughing and choking. They each juggled an armload of whimpering puppies.

"Aunt Char?" I didn't wait for the answer. I knew she was still inside like any good captain on her sinking ship. I didn't think. I ignored the blistering heat and advanced on the inferno.

I reached the campfire-hot distance when a soot-smudged Aunt Char emerged gasping. Three full-sized dogs weighed down her arms.

"There are two more inside." She sagged into my outstretched arms in a half-wheezing/coughing fit. I managed to break her fall but stumbled to my knees as a result.

OMG! Blue-red flames shot out of the doorway, blocking the entry. Russ shot right by me and disappeared into the blaze with Penny barking wildly at his heels. I screamed. I couldn't do anything else pinned beneath Aunt Char and fifty or so pounds of Cavaliers. Five seconds ticked by, then ten. An eternity as the radiating heat toasted my cheeks, making each breath more labored. I pictured Russ and Penny overcome on the tile floor. I had to do something!

Finally, José lifted the dogs and Aunt Char. They were all breathing. Aunt Char, in short, asthmatic gasps. She needed her inhaler. Wherever that was. Fortunately, I didn't have to find it. An instant later, the paramedics cleared the front gate. Help had arrived.

A loud sizzle and pop refocused my attention to the fire. The roof buckled, portending collapse. Russ and Penny didn't have another couple of minutes for the firemen to get into position. I had no choice. I had to go in after them. Aunt Char stopped me with a weak touch of her hand. Good thing. Less than a heartbeat later, the doorway caved in, flaming beams crisscrossing the opening. They were trapped behind the firewall!

Adrenalin pounded through me. I don't remember how I got there or how I remembered that secondary dog run door, but I suddenly found myself sprinting down the brush side of the kennel and pounding on the oversized doggie door. It worked. The wood cracked and splintered, then gave way.

Penny darted through first, Russ following. He carried a ruby and another Blenheim Cavalier. Forget first date rules. I threw my arms around him and kissed him long and hard. I didn't even care that he tasted like an overused ashtray, or that his dark hair had an ashen tinge, or that he probably needed air more than me.

Another kind of fire ignited deep within me. Just as suddenly, he pulled back and coughed. "We have a problem, Cat."

Emotion rendered me speechless, if you could believe it. The swing from fear to relief and back, I guess. What was important was that everyone had survived, including the two missing Cavaliers. We'd figure out why Lady Mag and Somerset had been in the Barklay Kennel later.

"You're all right. That's all that matters," I finally managed. His arms tightened around me as the hose-bearing professionals took over.

"That's one fine dog you have there, Miss Wright," the white-shirted paramedic said.

"That's only the half of it. Penny led me right to the dogs," Russ said. "And out. She's earned a T-bone tonight."

Far more than that, I realized. I scooped Penny into my arms and kissed her forehead. It didn't matter that she looked like something an ill-mannered alley cat would drag in, caked in soot and matted beyond recognition. She still held her head like the princess she was deep down inside. Attitude, Bart Cathaway had said, was the mark of a true champion. He'd been only partly right. Courage was the true measure, and this dog had a heart full. Imagine charging into a burning building to save her competitors!

Russ kissed Penny and we walked arm-in-arm around the sizzling structure. Except for the fifteen dogs barking in migraine-inducing unison, a strange calm permeated what should have been chaos amidst the three fire trucks, two ambulances, and three police SUVs clustered on the lawn. I massaged my temples, barely able to think. How did everyone else go about their business with that racket? The thing was, no one else appeared bothered. The firemen hosed the hot spots. The police interviewed Sandy and Ria. José tended to the dogs alongside the Emergency Medical Vet or EMV, as noted on the Barkview City payroll. I'd always thought the expenditure another WDI scale-topper, but today I'd have signed the petition.

Uncle G, Max, and Maxine stood guard over the champion Cavaliers, who sat in relative quiet contentment. Despite an overcoat of soot and a chest of tangles a groomer would have nightmares over, the dogs appeared unhurt.

Aunt Char, on the other hand, lay on a gurney, her face obscured beneath an oxygen mask. The tips of her blonde hair ashen, Aunt Char still managed to look angelic in her color-unknown pant suit. For the first time, I noticed smudges hollowing her eyes and forehead lines that made her look every bit her fifty-six years. Penny wiggled out of my arms and landed on the gurney beside Aunt Char. She licked a pale line down my aunt's soot-streaked cheek and wiggled close to her side, prepared to defend.

Aunt Char ripped off the mask and struggled to sit up the moment she saw Russ. "Thank you." She had more to say, but Russ took her hand and pressed her gently back.

"My pleasure, Mrs. Barklay."

"Char..." A paramedic ended her coughing by replacing the oxygen mask. Gratitude glistened in her cobalt-blue eyes, making them appear violet. Beneath the mask, her lips formed one word. *Destiny.*

My destiny? Hers? I wasn't sure. He'd scared me to death when he'd raced into the burning kennel with no regard for his own safety, but that kiss. It had been pure, primal passion. I've always believed emergencies bring out one's true nature. Russ Hawl had hero written all over him. He was the kind of man you could count on.

The paramedic interrupted my thoughts. "Your aunt's asthma is acting up. She needs to go to the hospital."

I nipped Aunt Char's objection quickly. "Don't worry. I will stay here and take care of the dogs."

She visibly relaxed. No argument? She wasn't herself or she had a pretty good idea what was going down.

"I'll come to see you after we get everyone settled." I scooped up Penny. "She stays with me. So, does Renny," I added quickly.

I felt better when Penny rubbed her head against my neck and wiggled for release. Aunt Char would be okay. She'd never leave her otherwise.

Aunt Char motioned me closer and slipped the oxygen

mask aside. "The dogs weren't there at ten this morning when José and I fed them," she rasped. "Whoever did this knew our routine."

I'd expected instructions or praise, certainly not that revelation. "But who would want to hurt you?"

"I don't know. Someone has gone to great lengths to incriminate me."

No argument there. Might as well throw the criminal code at her. Conspiracy, murder one, possession of stolen property, grand theft, arson, and breaking and entering. No, wait. I'd done the B & E on an Indian reservation. "I will find them." I would, too. No one hurt my aunt and got away with it.

She patted my hand, the IV a stark reminder of frailty in a woman I'd always viewed as invincible. "It is your time, Cat."

"My time for what?"

To my chagrin, she didn't answer. On the lawn, the line of beleaguered formed, their eyes shock-glazed, expecting guidance. I was the go-to-gal now, the one responsible for the Barklay empire that included fifteen dogs, two caretakers, and three flourishing businesses. One glance at the stately, Grecian-columned mansion and I saw bars—the responsibility kind. My bandana about shredded as I twisted it round and round my neck. No rookie reliever could feel this much pressure at the bottom of the ninth.

I dealt with the immediate practical issues but waved away Sandy and her camera. My assistant had graduated to pro. Of course, locating the missing Cavaliers constituted breaking news. And we had the exclusive. Except the circumstantial evidence incriminated Aunt Char.

"Where is the chief? I need to talk to him first." My pulse quickened with another scary premonition.

"He and the fire marshal went into the kennel a half hour ago," Sandy said.

His absence bothered me a whole lot. The length of time made it even worse.

Sandy continued. "Max and Maxine are guarding Lady Mag and Somerset in his SUV. Renny is in the house. I checked to be sure she was all right."

"Thank you." Sandy had more to say. "Okay. Out with it."

"It's not important." Her frown told another story.

I took both of her hands. "Everything is important."

"It just doesn't make sense. And you know how that bothers me." She didn't wait for my answer. The comment had been rhetorical anyway. "Renny never leaves your aunt's side, right? Then why was she sitting on a pillow in the house when Mrs. B was out here injured?"

With the world crumbling around us, leave it to Sandy to remark on a dog's behavior. "Maybe she's just staying out of the way." I hated to lie. Since the missing dogs had been found, did Penny still need to exist? I'd have to ask Aunt Char that when I saw her.

"Maybe." Sandy wasn't convinced. "I'll go help Ria wash the dogs." She disappeared inside the house.

"You're going to have to make a statement eventually," Russ said.

"I'd like all the facts first."

"Careful what you ask for, Cat."

Talk about foreboding. I didn't always like the truth, but I did believe in it and reported it. He followed me toward the skeletal remains that had been the gold standard for breeding kennels. As we neared the once-proud building, the smell of burnt cinder, fabric, and heaven knew what else overwhelmed me and made me develop a real appreciation for a firefighter's stomach strength. I covered my nose with my tattered scarf.

Russ swore under his breath as we ducked beneath a still-smoldering black beam. The space brought a bombed-out shell

169

to mind. Not a single stick of recognizable furniture or wall space stood out in the open-air ruin. Only mounds of black and white charred debris glistened in fire retardant beneath the streaming afternoon sunlight.

We passed a fireman and two of Uncle G's officers carrying red lined evidence bags before locating Uncle G. "For the record, where were you between 11:00 and 1:00?" Uncle G's ever-present toothpick vibrated between his lips.

Me a suspect now? I pointed to Russ. "With him."

"You vouching for her, Hawl?"

"Yes, Chief. No way she could've come up here and met me for lunch. No way Bart Cathaway did it either."

"We need to bring in Olivia and the mayor." Contrary to the men's reaction, I wasn't reaching for straws. Someone was framing Aunt Char. I had to figure out who and why. "He was seen talking to Bart Cathaway before Olivia and reportedly left unhappy."

"Are you suggesting that our trust fund mayor or a millionaire developer's wife kidnapped the Cavaliers, including their own, planted them in your aunt's kennel and then set them on fire?" Uncle G asked.

Out loud it sounded absurd. "What if Olivia kidnapped the dogs and the mayor found out about it?"

"And burned down the kennel in what? Revenge for dognapping her own dog?" Uncle G wasn't buying it. Neither was I. Someone had done it, though.

"Aunt Char didn't do any of this," I announced. "Come on, Uncle G. Murder dogs? Russ stopped her from going in for the dogs herself."

"Which means that she knew they were here," Russ pointed out.

"The kennel housed rescue dogs. She obviously thought

they were rescue dogs." I had to make that clear. Despite her asthma, Aunt Char heroically risked her life to rescue the dogs in her care.

"You don't know that," Uncle G said.

"I do and so do you."

"I would've died in there if Penny hadn't led me to the dogs," Russ said.

"Okay. Then when did she do it? She was in the house when I called her?"

"She said she was in the house. You called her on her cell phone. She could've been anywhere."

I glared at Russ. Undermining my case wasn't ingratiating. "Where were Ria and José?"

Uncle G checked his notes. "Eating lunch in their kitchen. José had just returned from the rescue. They saw her run across the lawn from the house..."

I couldn't stop my *ah-hah*.

"The circumstantial evidence is significant."

"You don't really believe...?"

His hesitation scared me. "I don't want to believe it, but the evidence is damning," Uncle G said. "While you two were out, Char's financials came back. She's made one fifteen-thousand-dollar and one fifty-thousand-dollar cash withdrawal in the past week."

Talk about being blindsided. The timing and amounts suggested a payoff. No. She had to have had a reason. "I will ask her."

"How was the fire set?" Russ asked.

Uncle G held up a clear bag containing what appeared to be a charred and melted circuit board. "Cell activated incendiary packed in kerosene rags."

"Well planned. Fits our dognapper's M.O.," Russ stated.

"Possibly. This device could easily have been ignited from any location."

"Could Lynda's murder and the missing Cavaliers be unrelated to the fire?" I had to ask, although the idea seemed unlikely.

Both men shrugged.

"The arsonist had to have put Lady Mag and Somerset in the kennel after the dogs' regular morning exercise at 10 a.m. Aunt Char said she and José didn't see them this morning," I said. "Sandy could've passed him, driving down the hill."

Uncle G referred to his notes. "Sandy said no one passed her on the way up. Either the perp walked out or waited until the emergency vehicles arrived."

"Or is still hiding out up here." A chill shot up my spine.

"We'll search again," Uncle G assured me.

"Whoever stole Lady Mag knew the area well," Russ said. "It is not a stretch that he knew the Barklay Kennel schedule either."

"Check it out, Russ. I'll get the physical evidence to the lab. I have to return the Cavaliers and talk to the mayor. Start going through your aunt's files."

"What am I looking for?"

"Someone likely to hold a grudge against your aunt. We'll compare notes this evening," Uncle G said. "Don't look at me like I'm the bad guy. I don't want to believe Char did this any more than you do. But I am the police chief. Unless you want someone else to investigate, I have to at least give the appearance of following the evidence. If someone is setting her up, there has to be a reason. Find it."

Easier said than done. Although the deputies recanvassed the area, they found nothing. Somehow the murderer/dognapper/arsonist had escaped without leaving a trace.

Uncle G made a valid point about a suspect. It made no sense that Aunt Char had no clue who would do this to her. The perp's familiarity with everything to do with the Cavalier Crown suggested it was the most likely connection and made every past Crown contender a suspect.

CHAPTER 17

I stopped at the Barkview Hospital before I met Uncle G and Russ. Located at the northeast end of downtown at the entrance to the Industrial sector adjacent to our ivy-walled university, the hospital had been constructed with Barkview's Victorian past in mind. At least on the outside. Inside, Zen relaxation collided with Western medicine to create a restorative space envied in the profession. Thanks to generous corporate and individual grants, the hospital's concierge services included designer gowns, hotel-quality bedding, and gourmet food designed to encourage healing.

White as the sheet and surrounded by blinking, beeping machines, the woman I'd always thought of as invincible looked frighteningly frail. Even the cheery aster masterpieces scattered all over her private room did not lift a heaviness I couldn't explain hanging over us. Fortunately, I had a plan for that.

I closed the door, blocking the nosy police guard and duty nurse's view. As I approached the bed, I unlocked the boxy legal briefcase I'd just purchased on Oak Street. Penny's ruby head peeked right out of the paperwork file. She looked right, then left, hopped out onto the bed, and snuggled with Aunt Char.

"Oh, Sweetheart." Aunt Char readjusted her oxygen tubes, the light back in her eyes. "Cat, you shouldn't have. You know the rules."

Like I cared. Aunt Char's smile made the ruse worth any penalty. Besides, this was Barkview. Surely, Penny wasn't the first dog snuck in for a therapeutic visit.

A pang of something I didn't want to explore struck me as I watched Penny's tail thump beat against Aunt Char's heart when they hugged. Those two belonged together. Why had it taken me so long to understand that special bond? Maybe it just took a special dog. Or a willingness to try. My conscience added that possibility. Had I been so single-minded in my dog disdain?

"The other dogs are fine. So are José and Ria. Ricky will run a tape for tonight's show," I said quickly. "And Penny survived her bath."

"What about the arsonist?" Forget the pleasantries, Aunt Char cut right to the chase.

"Uncle G is working on a lead. Russ is checking the private surveillance videos leading from town to your house. We will meet later."

"How are Olivia and the mayor?" Aunt Char petted Penny with rhythmic, albeit slightly shaky, strokes.

Trust Aunt Char to be worried about the competition. "I don't know. I haven't spoken to Uncle G since the dogs were returned. I imagine they are relieved."

"You're not a very good liar, Catalina. The mayor is calling for my head. As I would be if JB had been murdered."

Penny huffed and buried her head beneath her ruby paws. I couldn't get away with anything these days.

"Gregory must follow the letter of the law. I will not allow him to jeopardize his position for me."

The position she'd essentially given him when the old chief retired. I wanted to shake her. Too nice was a thing too. I nodded to make her happy. Doing the "right thing" had new meaning in Aunt Char's world. I took my pile of colored Post-its from my bag and prepared to take notes. "Please think. Do you have any idea why anyone would want to frame you?"

Penny nudged her suddenly-still hand. "I have examined every possibility," she said so softly I had to strain to hear.

"And?"

Her long, ragged exhale couldn't be for real. "Nothing."

I sank into the soft leather barrel chair, shaken to my core. "Let's start with people you've annoyed. Surely, you've ticked off someone."

Her weak, yet tinkling laughter encouraged me. "Surely, I have. I do try to be fair, but it is impossible not to have a single enemy. That's what's bothering me. This set up involves something more than anger. It is..."

"Evil." I finished the sentence for her. I sensed it, too, a bone-chilling, psychopathic anger.

"Yes. Whoever did this wants to destroy me." Her matter-of-factness helped.

"Why not just kill you?" Fear about swamped me. Why else would I be asking for a Freudian evaluation?

"He must see death as an escape. He wants me to suffer a fate worse than death."

"What could be worse?" But I already knew. I got it the moment I watched her hug Penny. Locked up in prison without her dogs would be her hell. Panic wasn't the answer. I needed to go back to basics. "Please skip the psycho technical stuff, but tell me what traits to look for."

"I can't be one hundred percent sure, but he is likely a

loner. Has an above-average IQ. He is a meticulous planner. Deviating from his plan would cause mental chaos. He has a problem with authority figures. Likely abandoned as a child. He sees himself as above the law and does not fear capture. His boldness taunts, just daring you to stop him."

"Why is he targeting you?"

"*He* is rhetorical. It could be a woman."

A woman? Although the analysis offered insight, no immediate suspects came to mind. "Was Lynda supposed to die?"

"Lynda's death was sloppy. If he'd intended to murder it would have been swift and precise. She must have surprised him."

No argument from me. "Why did he double down on the dognappings? He'd get away with murder if he just went away."

"The power is going to his head right now."

So, I needed to find a narcissistic adrenalin junkie who hated Aunt Char. Time to concentrate on the facts. "Who did you give sixty-five grand to?"

I'd surprised her with that info. "I gave fifteen thousand dollars to help build a new rescue in South Hampton."

Not exactly a small donation. "New York?"

"England. Bart sent out an international plea. It seems their last building was destroyed by fire." Which explained Lynda and Bart's withdrawals at about the same time.

Another fire? "Arson?"

"As I understand it, lightning and century-old buildings don't mix. I'm sure Bart will be able to confirm."

I noted that. "Who did you send the money to?"

"I wired it to the name Bart gave me."

Her 'duh' shrug drove me to ask, "What was the other fifty thousand for?"

Aunt Char inspecting her manicure didn't bode well at all.

"Out with it," I said.

"It's nothing, really."

Maybe not, but her wavering gaze indicated otherwise.

"Please don't tell Sean, but Petronics' injectable health monitor is marvelous."

I perched on the edge of the chair. "You gave it to Howard Looc?" Did Sean know?

"I funded ten units. He will have a prototype shortly and it will change how we monitor animals." Always a supporter of innovation, her genuine excitement made it all believable. "If you go back a year, you will find cash withdrawals totaling two hundred and fifty thousand dollars."

Now that was significant. "All in cash?"

Aunt Char grimaced. "Howard's preference. I didn't want to hurt Sean's feelings."

"You had to know he would eventually find out."

"I hoped not. The Barkview Humane Society is the benefactor."

Talk about convoluted. "Explain."

"Eighteen months ago, Howard had just severed ties with J. Tracker and needed a test group for his units. I arranged for the testing and introduced him to a patent attorney. Ten percent of the profits for the *Looc Tracer* will go to Barkview's Humane Society for ten years. This technology will one day replace the current chipping. The unit stores all the same data as the chip but adds a tracker and monitors the animal's health."

That meant an animal could never be lost or unexpectedly ill again. "What do you get from this deal?"

"The knowledge that I helped less-fortunate dogs."

"That is quite a generous gift," I said, impressed as always by her giving spirit.

"Do not make this into more than it is."

I had a lot to learn about grace and courage. Right now, I

needed to focus on keeping her around for the lessons. Time to go off grid. "Tell me about Olivia."

She didn't look away as she patted my hand. "No one knows exactly how far anyone will go if pushed."

True. "Bart Cathaway may have awarded Lady Mag the win out of spite. There's some history there. What if she snapped?"

Aunt Char balanced her forehead on her steepled hands. "I've known Olivia for years. I can tell you, she's a lot of things including excessively prideful, but she would never jeopardize her family's good name."

On principle I agreed. "It could've started out as a simple dognapping that spun out of control."

Aunt Char shook her head. "Olivia understands consequences."

I couldn't help but agree. "What about Bart? He's an egomaniac on steroids."

"I don't know him well enough to offer an opinion. Do what you do best. You will figure this out. I believe in you."

Her confidence felt good, but it didn't last long. Murmurs from outside her door alerted me. The briefcase out of reach, I stuffed Penny beneath my jacket without a second to spare.

The duty nurse dressed in Scooby-doo scrubs entered. "Visiting hours are over, Miss Wright. Mrs. Barklay needs her beauty sleep."

I needed answers more, but Aunt Char looked tired and Penny's warm breath tickling my belly button wasn't helping my concentration any. The woman's gaze settled on my middle. Time to escape.

In the doorway, I turned and asked. "What about Renny's bath? She needs to keep up with the other Crown contenders."

I barely heard Aunt Char's winded reply. "Not yet, dear."

Penny kicked me in the rib twice as I hot-footed it out of

the building. No way she understood. Yet when I freed her on my front seat, she turned on the ferocious-guard-dog glare. I ignored her until I parked at the police station. Time for a woman-to-woman talk. "Don't blame me. You heard her. Suck it up, Buttercup. We have work to do."

My monologue worked. Penny dropped her head on her paws. I'd celebrate, except...I had just reasoned with a four-legged dog. No doubt about it. I'd completely lost my mind.

Penny couldn't have understood. Or could she? The way she'd protected me from Howard's Border Collie and how she'd led Russ to safety in the fire could be instinct, but what about her reaction to Bart Cathaway? Aunt Char swore Renny was an excellent judge of character. Could she be right?

CHAPTER 18

More questions than answers plaguing me, I entered Uncle G's office. Max and Maxine resembled foo dog statuary on either side of him behind his desk. Russ stood by the window. Dressed in a navy Polo shirt and Dockers with his hair damp at the ends, my fingers ached to smooth the style. Penny beat me to the first touch. She turned those melting Spaniel eyes on him until he scratched her head and curled up at his feet. That little turncoat.

"Thank you for joining us." Exhaustion showed in the ever-so-slight hunch in Uncle G's shoulders. He'd been front and center since Lady Mag's disappearance. Had it only been four days since serene Barkview had been turned upside down?

I laid out a string of color-coded Post-its.

"How is Char doing?" Uncle G asked.

"How do you think? She's in the hospital under police guard."

"Better than county lock up," Russ remarked.

True. I wasn't sure if the jumpsuit or the fact that it was orange would horrify her more. "How long can she stay there?"

"As long as Doc White deems prudent," Uncle G said. "I understand she's not in good shape. Something pulmonary."

Good thing JB's longtime friendship with the attending doctor mitigated the mayor's demand for swift justice. I relaxed. "What do you have?"

Uncle G handed me the coroner's report and a pen. "The Cavalier statue you, uh, found had traces of Lynda's blood and hair. Lynda never saw it coming. The downward angle indicates someone between six-foot and six-foot-two."

So, Lynda had been Cavaliered to death. Ouch. What a way to go. "Aunt Char is five-foot-nine." Finally, good news.

"Five-foot-eleven-inches tall in her heels. Six-foot if she stood on the step and aimed..." Uncle G demonstrated. "The angle and force indicate intent to kill."

"Like he was protecting his identity." I outlined Aunt Char's opinion of the killer's personality profile. Neither man seemed surprised by the revelations.

Uncle G continued. "In addition to yours, Char's fingerprints are all over the statue."

"That's not possible. Wait a minute. Aunt Char has the same statue in her garden. I bet you there are a dozen statues in Barkview. Sarah sold them at the Canine Carnival last year. José bought it for Aunt Char."

"She sold thirty-four. The statue at Char's house has Lynda's fingerprints on it."

"The dognapper swapped the statues? That indicates premeditation," Russ said.

"Or a clever set up." I turned to Russ. "Did you find any helpful video footage?"

"Footage, yes. Helpful?" He propped his tablet on the desk. I noted the contrast between my colorful sticky note system and his space age info. I did need one of those.

"This is from the mayor's security system." Russ scrolled down the screen.

A time stamped clip showed Olivia in cat-burglar-black, skulking by the mayor's kitchen door and scampering up the embankment at 6:30 a.m. and returning at 7 a.m.

"She's done that before." And often, judging from her sure-footedness. Were Olivia and the mayor romantically involved? Why else would she be at his home in the early morning? Had Lynda known? I really was reaching for glimmers.

"The mayor's security system automatically deletes in ten-day cycles."

"And?" I asked.

"This is her only recent visit," Russ said.

That cleared Olivia of planting the dogs at the Barklay Kennel. I doubted she planted the incendiary device with Somerset inside.

"The mayor left his driveway at 8:05 a.m. Witnesses put him at City Hall during the fire. The rest of his day is accounted for as well," Russ said.

Effectively eliminating the mayor as a suspect. "What was Olivia doing at the mayor's house and why did she to go up to the kennel?" I noted the question on a pink Post-it.

"I will ask her." Uncle G shuffled through some papers. "Her cell phone records show that she received a call at 6:15 a.m. originating from the Old Barkview Inn."

My pulse jumped. "Bart Cathaway's room?"

"The call routed through the main switchboard from a hall phone. Witnesses have Bart in his room all day."

Will would know for sure. I made a note to speak with him. "We know Olivia saw Bart today."

"Both Olivia and the mayor admit visiting to discuss breeding contracts."

"Who negotiates for missing dogs unless you know for sure they will be returned unharmed?" I had to point out.

"Valid point. Deputies are confirming both timelines on the hotel's surveillance footage. More importantly, Olivia received another call from an unregistered cell phone at 12:37."

"The same phone that triggered the fire?" An unregistered phone could well be everyday spam. I got my fair share daily.

Uncle G shrugged. "Maybe. Triangulating the cell signals looks easier on TV."

"The question is why did Olivia sneak into the Barklay Kennel in the first place?"

"She's behaving like a parent who lost their kid," Russ remarked. "Since the chief refused to search there, she needed to see for herself."

"She didn't care what the ramifications were?" That didn't fit Aunt Char's opinion.

"Frantic parents are not rational." Spoken like a man who'd seen too much.

Who was I to argue? I'd move mountains to protect Aunt Char. "Anything else?"

"The only other vehicle driving to your aunt's house before Sandy in your car was José in the Barkview Jeep," Russ said.

A ray of hope took hold. "Can you put the picture on the plasma screen?"

Two clicks later, he did. At 11:30, a Jeep passed the mayor's residence. I squinted at the grainy, shadowed picture. Who was this guy? The license plates were obscured too, caked in what looked like mud. "Can you focus the picture better?" I'd seen it done on TV. No doubt it could be done in the real world.

Russ zoomed in. The grainy black-and-white image could be anyone. "Can you identify the driver?"

"I can tell you it isn't José. The Barklay Jeeps were all turned in for service yesterday at the dealership."

Uncle G came to his feet. "Are you sure, Cat?"

"Call the dealership. The vehicles aren't due back until Tuesday."

Uncle G's half-smile reassured me. I'd made the right call getting the vehicles out of town. "I told you there was a look-alike. We need to identify him."

"Email that to me." Uncle G's half-smile indicated he had a friend who could help.

"This proves that the dognapper/arsonist isn't a Barkview insider," I said.

Russ scrolled through some files on his tablet computer. "The Jeep left at 1:37 p.m."

"During the chaos," Uncle G remarked. "I'll put out a BOLO."

"Isn't this good news?" I directed my question to Russ.

He exhaled. "Since your aunt has not been charged, the perp may not consider his job done."

Portending more violence.

"What about Char's withdrawals?" Uncle G asked.

As I reshuffled my Post-its, Penny snuggled in my lap. Oddly, her warmth comforted me. I explained the money trail and added Aunt Char's psychoanalysis. "She thinks whoever is doing this is toying with us." I couldn't completely mask my defeat. "Could this be about me or you?"

Uncle G sat slowly back in his swivel chair. He'd thought the same thing, I could tell. "Castro and his henchmen are in prison. There have been no recent visitors."

I exhaled in a rush, not realizing I'd held my breath. "Aunt Char said we should concentrate on the facts."

Like a clock's inner workings, I could see Russ's mind cranking. He resorted my Post-its twice before speaking. "Assuming the dognapper and murderer are one and the same, we know that he is familiar with the J. Tracker collar, has intimate knowledge of Crown contenders, as well as Barkview residents' daily habits. He also is familiar with Barkview architecture, has something against Charlotte Barklay and Lynda Smythe, knows arson techniques, and has access to burner phones."

"Can bypass an alarm system, has bought or rented a 2018 tan Jeep with California plates," I added. "And resembles José."

"I agree with Russ. The perpetrator walks among us," Uncle G said.

Russ's compassionate gaze bothered me. "Barkview does have its fair share of quirky personalities."

No kidding. On the surface, Barkview seemed so Pollyannaish. What could be more apple-pie than a town devoted to man's best friend? Between Howard and Sean's business rivalry, Olivia and Bart's personal issues and the mayor's sketchy reelection campaign, anyone could be responsible for the dognappings. Or none of them.

"You don't think anyone we've listed is guilty, do you?" It wasn't exactly what Russ had said, but how he said it that set off my trepidation.

"Guilty of something, undoubtedly. Not of killing Lynda or dognapping the Cavaliers. That fire was personal," Russ remarked.

"I don't understand." But I did and cold dread settled deep inside. "Then why return the dogs?" My voice sounded like a squeak.

Russ's hold tightened. "To incriminate your aunt."

"I concur," Uncle G interjected too quickly. "We need to look further into Char's past."

"There are no wronged relatives." Just harmless, jealous biddies, I added silently. "When JB married Aunt Char, he created the Barkview Trust. Aunt Char is the trustee."

Both men stared right at me. Even Penny snuggled close. It

had to be me. "You told me Castro is safely in prison. Nothing to worry about." Desperation crept into my tone. I couldn't help it.

Russ and Uncle G shared a glance I couldn't un-see. OMG! They concurred. "We need to look deeper," Uncle G said.

Fear swamped me, the debilitating kind that sucks the breath right out of you. "I-it can't be... They promised he couldn't hurt me anymore."

"I know." Russ stroked my hair. "What did he say to you?"

No need to define he. Castro's specter hung overhead. "He swore to destroy me." It added up too well. Tomas Castro would relish making my aunt pay for my crimes. "How could he possibly orchestrate something this complex from prison?"

Uncle G crossed his arms. "He'd need an outside man."

"Or woman," I squeaked.

"I'm sorry, Cat, but we need to go down this road," Uncle G said. "If this is true, you are in serious danger."

"Not me," I said. "Aunt Char is in danger."

"I will stay with you tonight," Russ offered.

Uncle G patted Russ's shoulder. "Thank you, Russ. I knew I could count on you. I'll fly up to San Quentin tonight and see Castro. Where is your car?"

"Outside." That small voice didn't sound like me at all.

"I'll have a deputy move it to the studio. Russ, drive her back to Char's. She'll be safer there."

I dreaded the conversation, but... "Aunt Char needs to know."

"Not yet. Right now, this is only a theory. I will double security and bring Max over tonight."

Russ's hand brushed the small of my back. No argument from me. I couldn't think anyway. Castro back? My worst nightmare had come true.

CHAPTER 19

"Tell me what happened." Russ's lips grazed my forehead, willing the truth from me. He'd asked because he wanted to help, not for a look at the macabre.

I'd traded my jeans for a cheetah-spotted cotton shirt, dark PJ bottoms, and a matching neck scarf. Firelight wrapped the Cavalier room in a comforting glow. Cocooned in familiarity with Penny pressed up against my side, I felt safe. I'd chosen this room on purpose. Crazy as it sounded, it felt like Aunt Char was there guiding me.

"I don't remember anything after the Pit Bull went for my throat and very little leading up to it. I woke up in the hospital with Aunt Char holding my hand and telling me I was safe."

My fingers wrapped around a steaming mug of double-seeped chamomile tea Russ had prepared for me. I eyed the chocolate chip biscotti piled on the tray with true emotional eater fascination. Calorie-wise they weren't too bad. I reached for two. Forget the healthy diet tonight.

I savored every satisfying crunch until Russ gently lifted my chin and untied my scarf. I swallowed hard as his fingers brushed the four-pronged scar. I should've stopped him, except delightful tingles spread to my toes.

"Besides hiding scars, scarves do have a few interesting uses." He tied one end of the silky fabric to my wrist.

A hundred squirm-worthy possibilities came to mind. Penny's low growl doused that flame as quickly as it started. Just as well. We both needed to focus.

"How did the police find you?" Russ asked.

"An anonymous call they traced to a burner phone. I tried to find the caller, but I never did. The LAPD decided a bystander called in. No one ever admitted to it or used it as a bargaining chip. Look at me. I'm shaking. I'm such a wuss."

"You survived a horrific experience. The mind heals in different ways."

"Survived, yes. Recovered, apparently not. Even now, there are so many blanks."

"Maybe it's time to remember."

"I don't want to." I more than didn't want to. Whoever said ignorance was bliss knew his stuff.

"I don't blame you, but you don't have a choice. Your aunt's safety relies on it."

I hated it when he was right. I just didn't want to accept it yet.

"Think back. Who was there?" Russ asked.

"Castro, Crusher, and Diseco. The three of them are in prison."

"What about the dogs' caretakers? Other members of the gang? Family members?"

"No. No. No. There were only the three of them." I remembered them all clear as if it had been yesterday in the caged arena. Castro's Machiavellian hiss, Crusher's twisted nose, Diseco's gold front tooth, and a shadow, a blur really, behind them all. Bad lighting? I'd let myself believe that.

189

"Are you sure?"

Good old too-perceptive Russ. Just once I'd like to sneak one by him. "I had this feeling there was a fourth, but I never found any supporting evidence, neither did LAPD. Crusher and Diseco did the dirty work. Castro was the brains. He came from the streets. He started running numbers then added dog fighting and drugs. By the time I got involved, the dog fighting had graduated to battery and murder. I still have my research at home in a file box in my garage." No doubt an inch of dust covered it. Why hadn't I tossed the boxes years ago?

"What about Rosa Delgado?" Russ asked. "She never testified, but could she know about a fourth conspirator?"

I stiffened. Of course, he'd read the case file. Rosa, the informant, had helped gather evidence for the case. Did I admit she was me?

"No," I said emphatically and gave it away.

"I see." He did. His *ah-ha* moments were as blinding as camera flashes and a reminder to never lie to him. I'd get caught every time.

He wanted to ask more but changed direction instead. "Castro's family?"

"Castro's trophy wife divorced him after the trial. She was a real piece of work. Claimed she hadn't known what he did for a living."

"Did you believe her?"

That he trusted my intuition helped. "The big house and diamonds made good blinders. Castro's fifteen-year-old son came to court once. Kid never looked up from his feet. I don't know what happened to him. I just wanted to forget the whole thing." I should've followed what happened to the kid.

"Your testimony closed the case." Statement or question? I wasn't sure.

"According to the DA, yes."

"We need to know who warned the police."

Task impossible ten years ago, or hadn't I tried hard enough? "Why?"

His hands cupped my face, his strong fingers splayed on my cheeks, drawing my gaze deep into his solemn one. I swallowed, suddenly parched. "You need to know to put closure to this."

I did, I realized. All those years hiding from the truth hadn't fixed a thing. This was still a case of unfinished business. "H-how did you know?"

"The same reason I need to find the guy who kidnapped my niece."

He would one day. Heaven help the guy when he did. We were frighteningly alike. Neither one of us could deal with loose ends. I suddenly yawned, unexplainably bone weary. I struggled to keep my eyes open. Maybe if I closed them for a minute. Russ's embrace felt so good—so safe in this sea of uncertainty.

A room-shaking woof woke me up with a head-pounding start. Max's, to be exact, with alarm clock precision right in my ear. My tongue ran over the socks on my teeth as I stretched the tweak out of my neck.

"Good morning." The streaks of light on the wood floor concurred with Russ's fresh-as-day tone.

A morning person! Serious dump 'em point. An IV espresso drip couldn't get me that perky for at least an hour. "I actually fell asleep?" It wasn't really a question. "I need to brush my teeth." He didn't need to know that.

"So do I." He looked great though. The five o'clock shadow roughing his chin begged my touch. On the other hand, I probably had raccoon-red eyes and lipstick bleed. Not to mention the lump in my throat that a bottle of chalky antacids wouldn't fix. Instant self-consciousness set in. Something had led to intimacy last night. Something I couldn't quite name.

We were still in the sitting room with Penny curled up at my feet and Max at attention at the door. "What time is it?" No hungry puppies yapped or whined. Only the steady tick-tock of the grandfather clock broke the silence. Had we missed breakfast? I was starving.

"7:30 a.m. José and Ria said they had something to do at church."

Of course they did. They were lighting every candle in town praying for Aunt Char's return. "We're alone?"

His chuckle about did me in. It took a repeat for me to finally comprehend. "You, me and sixteen dogs."

On cue, Penny kitty-stretched then settled in my lap, her timing impeccable as usual.

"Thank you," I said.

"For what?"

Were knightly actions everyday occurrences in his world? "Staying with me last night."

"You were tired. LAPD's case files should arrive within the hour. I'd like to see yours as well."

"You don't have to stay with me." Sudden uneasiness swamped me. It would be too easy to rely on him. Was I ready for that?

He crossed his arms, unmoving. "And why is that?"

"Castro's goal is to destroy what means the most to me. Killing me defeats the purpose."

"What do you think happens the moment he realizes that your aunt is still safe and his elaborate plan has failed?"

"Castro is a sadistic S.O.B. who lives for torture. Killing me takes all the sport out of it. Aunt Char needs protection. Not me."

His nod agreed. He'd read the psych evaluation. "I do not intend to take any chances with you either."

He meant it. Warmth pooled deep inside me. The rest didn't matter. I'd be safe. So would Aunt Char. He would see to it. I eyed him over Penny's rust-colored fur. Something so right was going on. All those years I'd struggled with one self-centered, Neanderthal man after another and the right one comes along in the middle of this mess. How does that happen? I'm not the lottery winner type. "So, what happened last night?"

"You snored."

Perfect? Who was I kidding? I hit him over the head with a tasseled pillow. He deserved it.

Thirty minutes later, Sandy arrived, dressed in nautical capris and a boat neck top, her normally neat ponytail askew as she struggled to not dump my case notes box and contain her ADHD dog at the same time.

I never should have agreed to Jack's presence. Not two steps inside the front door, the Jack Russell tore his leash out of her hands and took off in a barking frenzy through the house. Unlike Ford's admonishments, Sandy's did zip.

I motioned to Max. "Contain." In three strides the German Shepherd cornered the Jack Russell. One sharp, decisive bark and a growl brought Jack to his stomach with his paws covering his ears. And that was that. There was something to be said about well-trained dogs.

Sandy's jaw-dropping awe made me chuckle. "That dog is..."

"A police dog."

"Yeah. But how'd you know what commands to use?"

Good to know all the years around Max and Renny hadn't

193

been wasted. I motioned for her to follow me into Aunt Char's parlor. Midday sunlight cast magical prisms on the gleaming wood giving the room a fairytale charm I barely noticed. I quickly outlined Russ's assessment coupled with my own fears around a fourth conspirator.

"You think the goon you put in prison ten years ago is behind everything?" Sandy asked.

"It's a theory. The chief is at San Quentin now. I have to warn you that you could be in danger helping me at all."

"Oh." Sandy re-clipped her ponytail in a single twist.

Doubt assailed me. I was asking a lot. "Is that an 'oh, I'm out of here' or 'oh, we've got to catch this guy?'"

Her grin helped. "It's a 'what do you need me to do?'"

I hugged her tight. "We need to organize my notes and see what I missed ten years ago." I opened the first file. The Post-its fluttered every which way. "Case made for the computer super-highway."

She skipped the I-told-you-so finger shake I deserved. "Start dictating."

I did for an hour before Russ came in carrying an official-looking LAPD case file. How he'd gotten it, I didn't want to know. He took Sandy's hand. "Thank you for helping."

An attractive pink stained her high cheekbones, high-lighting her striking eyes. Russ didn't seem to notice. He winked at me.

"Up until last year, Castro's mother ran a rescue for abused dogs. She's a resident at a memory care facility in Brea now. His ex-wife remarried a Park Avenue plastic surgeon. She lives in Manhattan. His son is in medical school in Boston."

It all sounded so innocuous. "A dead end." Like all the other avenues we'd pursued on this case. I couldn't control the sheer relief. Why was Russ still so staid? "What?"

"It all looks good on paper. But..."

I never liked his but... "What are you suggesting?"

"I'm not suggesting anything," Russ said quickly. "We investigate. We confirm and validate. There are no judgments, no calls."

Spoken like a seasoned investigator. I swallowed hard. Dreading, but prepared for the case review.

Russ opened the file. "LAPD investigated the fourth conspirator theory but found nothing. They even offered the boys a plea deal to give him up. They also investigated all known associates and family members. Processed one hundred eleven prints from the scene. Traced priors on sixty-nine. Mostly gambling, prostitution and possession. Six petty thefts. No tie-ins to Castro's organization. Teresa Castro's church choir alibi checked out. Castro's wife alibied his fifteen-year-old son. Says the kid was terrified of his father." Russ paused. "Past MO is smash and run. No link to a meticulous dognapping and murder."

Verbalized, my whole fourth conspirator theory sounded absurd. "Wait a minute. My college friend's brother, Mark, was Castro's first victim. He was assaulted with a dog bone." My heart rate tripled. How had I missed the similarity to Lynda and the Cavalier statue? Both blows had been to the back of the head and caused mental impairment with deadly results.

"I thought your roommate's brother was hit by a car." Russ flipped through the file.

"He was. He stumbled from between two parked cars onto Gayle in front of the Sigma Chi house. The pickup floored it through the yellow light and hit him." I shuddered, remembering the incident with perfect clarity as if it had happened yesterday. "I held him in my arms as twenty half-naked frat boys tried to help. He kept saying 'boned to death.' I figured he was drunk. Coroner found rawhide fragments and dog saliva at the head wound site that happened before the car impact."

OMG! It was happening all over again. I didn't realize my hands shook until Penny licked my cheek. Normally, I'd beeline it to the sink, but this time her rough tongue just felt sweet.

"Ten years is a long time to hold a grudge," Sandy said.

"Ingraining a person in Barkview could take that long."

Russ nailed that one. Suspicion and newcomer went together like leash and collar in Barkview. We should be investigating anyone who'd moved to town less than ten years ago. Excluding the transitory veterinary students, the list wasn't that long. Michelle had arrived five years ago from parts unknown. Howard Looc had joined J. Tracker ten years ago. I'd hired Ricky five years ago, but he didn't live in town. Of course, Sandy had arrived only a year ago, but I'd headhunted her.

Russ taped aged photos to the white board he'd propped up. One showed the corner liquor store with the neon Budweiser sign in the storefront window and the phone booth beneath the streetlight on the corner. It had been foggy that night. The streetlight had been out. I remembered crunching glass beneath my tennis shoes.

I'd counted fifty steps before I'd ducked behind a Lincoln Town Car parked on the faded yellow loading zone in front of the tired-brick church all those years ago. I smelled something foul, like day-old chicken bones, as the tower clock bonged eleven times. That last bong vibrated in my head every time I saw a Pit Bull, leashed or not.

"What time did LAPD receive the anonymous call for help?" Russ asked.

No need to look that one up. I'd been over this a million times. "10:56 p.m. First car on scene was at 11:02."

No memory came to me. Only a black abyss the psychiatrist called Psychogenic Amnesia or Repressed Memory Syndrome. Wait a minute. I'd counted the clock strikes. I hadn't been attacked until after 11:00.

"The caller placed the call four minutes before the attack." My neck scar suddenly burned like a firecracker. The detective had walked me through the events at least a dozen times. Russ had been right. My perspective had changed years later.

I felt rather than saw Sandy and Russ's eyes on me, waiting for me to continue. "Only someone with a cellphone watching the liquor store could've seen me and made the call. The liquor store owner swore the store was empty." Had to have been a look out. Whoever it was had likely saved my life.

"It doesn't make any sense." I sat beside Russ hugging Penny tight. "Why would this unknown fourth give up his partners to save me?"

"It could be as simple as he wanted out and saw his chance," Russ suggested.

It's never that simple. "And take the chance those three miscreants wouldn't give him up? I don't believe it."

"Honor among thieves."

"Not these three. I'm missing something. Who would they protect?"

"Someone they feared more than a few more years in prison," Russ said.

"Castro was the big boss. Who would he protect?"

"The bigger question is why is this guy coming after your aunt now? What has changed?" Trust Russ to get right to the heart of the issue. "Sandy, can you find out which animal shelter Castro's son volunteered at?"

"I checked every dog shelter in LA County personally ten years ago. I never found a link between the any of the shelters and Castro's dogfighting ring." I said.

"Hang on. I remember something in the boy's high school commencement activities list."

A big thumbs up for Sandy's memory. The steady keyboard clicks reminded me exactly why I'd refused to take no for answer when I'd hired her. That list hadn't been available during my initial research. Tomas Jr. graduated two years after the trial, but Sandy had found it. "Here it is. The shelter was in Santa Ana."

"Fifty miles is a long way for a teenager to be driven to volunteer. He was only fifteen at the time. He didn't even have a driver's permit yet." Russ's half-smile confirmed my sudden optimism.

Sandy agreed. "You're right. It doesn't make sense. There are a dozen shelters closer. I'll call them and see if they had any missing dogs or odd adoptions when he volunteered there." Phone in her hand, she dialed as she skipped out of the room.

CHAPTER 20

Uncle G texted Russ to meet him at police HQ the same time Sandy bounced back into the sitting room, excitement bubbling.

"I spoke to the manager at the Santa Ana dog shelter. Castro's son worked two days a month for about six months. She said he had a way of sweet-talking the adopting families. The shelter's big dog adoptions beat the state average during his tenure. Wanna bet that's where the fresh fighting dogs came from? I'll go to the shelter tomorrow and find out who adopted the dogs. The records aren't computerized. I'll have to go through boxes."

In person always netted more complete results. "Welcome to good old-fashioned investigative groundwork."

"It's kinda fun in a dusty, historic way." Sandy gave me a Pekinese-scrunched nose.

I ignored the anti-computer dig and hugged her long and hard. I didn't know what to say.

"Mrs. B called. She asked me to bring her silk PJs and robe," Sandy said.

I glanced at my phone. No message. "Why...?"

"She didn't want to bother you. I'm happy she's feeling better. Ford just got back. He made Mrs. B some of his famous chocolate chip cookies."

Yummy. I could happily stress eat my way fat with those gooey delights.

"I'll take Jack to him." At the sound of his name, Jack sprung to his feet and barked. Max and Renny barked in perfect harmony, shutting him down with a whimper. Really, the dog hadn't been a problem all day.

I just agreed. No sense stating the obvious. The dog could behave with the proper training. "How do you feel about Ford returning?"

"I missed him," she said simply.

"That's good." Her silence made me question the code. "Right?"

"I guess. I have to go."

"Sure. Thanks for your help." I stole a look at Russ. I'd miss him when this was all over, I realized, more than a little.

Sandy gathered Aunt Char's night clothes and headed out with Jack in tow. I watched Sandy's taillights disappear into the dusk. "She amazes me sometimes."

"Her diligence or energy?" Russ tucked the white board under his arm.

"Both." I covered a yawn. I felt beat up.

"She has a good teacher. Let's see what the chief has."

Pure adrenalin kept me going as Russ parked at police HQ. Penny and I walked through the door he opened. I felt the excited energy the second I entered. Had to be good news. Uncle G's Cheshire cat grin offered real hope.

Still dressed in his travel-weary uniform, Uncle G smoothed a sleeve wrinkle. The minute I saw that he chewed on a toothpick, I said. "Don't even think about going good-old-boy on me."

"You take all the fun out of it. The BOLO hit from a car wash in Oceanside. We have a tan-colored Jeep pulling into the wash yesterday afternoon around 4:00 p.m."

The time certainly worked with when the dummy Jeep would have left the fire scene.

"After the car left, the drying rags had a tan residue on them," Uncle G said.

"Residue?" What was I missing?

"The paint washed off the Jeep," Russ explained.

That got my attention. "Temporary paint on a car?"

"It works like non permeant hair color," Russ said.

Self-consciously, I ran my hand through my neglected highlights. "Uh, do we have a license number?"

"Richardson is viewing the entry and exit camera video now. We will time match the vehicle. We should get a plate and photo."

That was good news. "What about your Castro visit?"

Uncle G's sudden bear hug scared me. "What? Can't I hug my favorite niece?"

It was worse than I thought. "Since favorite status comes with food and I'm empty handed, something's really bad."

"Respect is earned, Cat, and you earned it. Castro is dangerous."

You think? "And..."

"If he is involved, he's due an Oscar. You might like to know that he's dying of lung cancer."

"What?" Uncle G said it so nonchalantly, I thought I imagined it.

"You heard me. He weighs about a hundred pounds."

"He did smoke a pack or three a day."

"He's found religion."

"The man was Satan incarnated."

"He's a bible thumper now. He does harbor considerable resentment toward you though."

"It's mutual."

"He says he's not involved, but he knows or suspects something," Uncle G said.

I pictured Castro's cocky lip-lifting snarl. Getting even would please him.

Uncle G's computer bleeped. "Boston University student photo of Castro's son is here."

"He doesn't look much like Castro. Makes a man wonder about the milkman," Uncle G remarked. "He's currently doing his residency at UCSD."

"San Diego?" Less than twenty miles south.

"School records indicate he's been here for eight months," Uncle G said.

No way he'd infiltrated Barkview in eight months. It had to be a coincidence. Uncle G and Russ weren't buying it.

"Email me a copy." Russ powered up his tablet.

I peeked over his shoulder as he manipulated the image, changing the hair color to dark, eyes to brown and added a wide-rimmed baseball cap. The picture could well be José. Had we found the look alike? "Can you print it? I'll show that to Ariana and see if she recognizes him."

Uncle G put it up on the plasma screen. Suddenly, Penny leapt to all fours and barked. Not the I-want-attention bark, but a ferocious I-want-blood bark that even brought Max and Maxine to their feet.

I scooped the snack-sized dog into my arms. "What is it, girl?" Penny's heart beat a rockabilly solo. She knew him. That meant... "Aunt Char must know him," I said excitedly. So, Tomas Junior had been in Barkview. All I had to do was show her the picture and...

I took another long look at the image. Familiarity tugged at my consciousness. OMG! "That's Sandy's boyfriend, Ford." I said. "His full name is Clifford Tomas Castro Jr. CJ." No wonder Castro hadn't given him up.

Uncle G's computer beeped. "The Jeep we found belongs to Sandy."

I flopped into the chair, the pieces falling right into place. That bone-shaped dent on the bumper Gabby had told me about, I'd done it when I'd dropped the camera. How could I have not remembered that?

Sandy, my inquisitive assistant, who I'd trusted with vital, insider information. Sandy, my protégé and friend, who I'd opened every door in Barkview for, set up my aunt? The betrayal knifed me in the heart. How could I have been so blind, so...?

"The same Sandy's boyfriend who just made your aunt special cookies?" Russ asked.

She'd be delivering them this moment and Aunt Char would politely eat the one on top. Disillusionment changed to pure panic. I spun and I sprinted for the door, motioning Penny to follow. She beat me to it, moving with a greyhound speed previously unknown.

Pure adrenalin kept me going the three long blocks to the hospital, despite my mind-numbing berating. How could I have been so blind? I'd asked myself a hundred times how the perp had always been a step ahead and never once suspected.

Neither Penny nor I broke stride as we entered the hospital lobby and blew past the rotund guard shouting no dogs allowed and headed straight for the stairwell door. Just try to stop us on a mission. My heart pounded in my ears as we took the steps two at a time up the three flights to Aunt Char's room. Except for the officer guarding her doorway, the hallway was empty. Before he could object, Penny darted between his legs, unbalancing him. I finished the job with a side clip, sending him sprawling.

Felony assault charges registered somewhere in the back of my mind, but who cared. Only Aunt Char mattered. I would deal with the ramifications later.

Right now, Sandy hovered over Aunt Char like a ghostly specter.

"Renny, guard," I ordered. Penny leapt onto the bed, dislodging the cookie plate with a perfect head dive. The silver disk launched into an end over flip across the bed, landing in a crumbled heap on the fancy blanket beside Aunt Char. Penny planted all fours on Aunt Char's lap, her teeth bared at Sandy. I tackled her at the knees, dropping her like a blindsided quarterback. The echoing thud had to have hurt, especially with my full weight pinning her beneath me.

Guns drawn, the men arrived a split second later, Uncle G in the lead. "Char, did you eat any of the cookies?"

"Goodness, Gregory. You simply must learn to share." I had to admire Aunt Char's poise under duress.

"Did you eat any, Mrs. B?" Russ asked.

Both men towered menacingly over her, yet she didn't even flinch. "Heavens, no. Those cookies should be outlawed the way they inspire violence." Her hand gestured to the mess alongside her bed. "Please help Cat up, dear. I heard something crack."

So had I. I took inventory as Russ's warm hands pulled me to standing. Both wrists bent without pain. My knees shook but held me steady and there wasn't a single drop of blood on the floor. I'd pay for it tomorrow, but now I'd go on. Sandy wasn't so lucky. The red welt on her forehead looked surprisingly like a kitty treat.

Uncle G waved back the crowd filling the doorway and closed it behind him, leaving an impassable Max and Maxine on duty outside. The downstairs dog patrol had to be having puppies over not one, but three dogs inside. "Everyone okay?"

I nodded. So did Sandy. "Good." His gaze raked me up one side then down the other. "YOU are going to explain about Penny later."

I gnawed on my lower lip. The secret was out the way Penny guarded Aunt Char.

"Your issue is with me, Gregory," Aunt Char announced.

The you're-in-for-it-too look turned on Aunt Char. "She was party to this-this..."

Uncle G at a loss for words? Talk about trouble. "Subterfuge," I suggested.

"Exactly."

"She didn't have a choice," Aunt Char said.

"I always have a choice. Later, Chief." No excuse. I'd man up like the woman I was.

Uncle G's clipped nod portended true penance. I'd known this one would cost dividends.

Sandy rubbed the bump on her forehead. "I'm glad someone knows what's going on, because I don't."

She did have that deer-in-headlights look covered. Great acting? I wasn't sure. I mentally counted to ten. I had to handle this right. The ensuing ah-ha moment would define me as well as Sandy. She was my assistant, my responsibility. Had I been played? Just thinking about it felt like I'd been sucker punched.

"I don't want to believe you had anything to do with this," I said.

"With what?" Sandy demanded. "I delivered your aunt the clothes she requested."

She had. I eyed her long. She didn't flinch. I wasn't getting anywhere. Time to go for the jugular. "How long have you known Ford?"

"Ford? What does he have to do with anything?"

"Answer the question, please." Sandy's confusion seemed genuine, right down to her knitted brows.

"You've heard this a hundred times before."

I had. Question was, would the telling be the same this time?

"I met him the week before I met you. That was seven months ago."

Six months and three weeks, but who was counting. I took a page from Aunt Char's patience training guide and said nothing.

Chatty Sandy continued as expected. "We hit it off right away. I thought it was a 'sign.'" She quote-signed with her fingers. "That he worked near here. But you know all this. I-I have no secrets."

Up until fifteen minutes ago I would have believed her. Now, I wasn't sure. Aunt Char's expression remained maddeningly neutral. Was she letting me draw my own conclusion? Uncle G and Russ must've gotten the same memo because they had nothing to say either. "Russ, please show Sandy the picture?" He handed her the doctored photo. "This is Castro's son."

"No way." Sandy's jaw about hit the floor. "That's Ford. He's the sweetest, kindest guy. He couldn't. Wouldn't..." But her gaze was locked on the photo. A picture didn't lie. It was him. At the very least, he'd lied about his identity.

"OMG!" Sandy sank into the barrel chair. She jerked her hand though her hair. How a single strand remained in place said something about good hair products. "We talked about Barkview all the time. I thought it was cute that he was so interested in fitting in here and the Crown's history. I-I even asked you questions he asked me about the Crown that I couldn't find answers to. It was all for information, wasn't it?"

She didn't give anyone a chance to answer.

"I t-told him everything. Even things about the investigation. He's friends with Sean. No wonder he knew all about the collar." She buried her face in her hands. "How could I be so stupid?"

Not stupid. Played by an expert. Seriously, what won't we overlook for Mr. Right? My gaze traveled from Russ's linebacker shoulders to his sexy legs. Was he really as great as I thought?

"He used me. I was the inside person." Sobs broke the charged silence-heart felt, intense sobs that couldn't be feigned. At least I didn't think so. Could I even trust my own judgment? Don't ask me how, but suddenly I just knew she was telling the truth. It happened the same way I'd known about the dogs and that Aunt Char was going to be all right.

"You didn't know." I mimicked Aunt Char's matter-of-factness as best I could. My relief knew no bounds. She hadn't intentionally betrayed me or Aunt Char.

Russ and Uncle G seemed satisfied. "I should have known. He was TGTBT."

Uncle G scratched his Santa beard.

"To-good-to-be-true," I said automatically. Was it possible that techno-illiterate me spoke text after all? "He was a great actor."

Sandy blinked back tears. "I never suspected anything. What is it with me and rats?"

She didn't mean the rodent kind either. Gorgeous and skinny Sandy had problems with men? No way. She had to have them lined up Oak Street. My gaze strayed to seriously good-looking and honorable Russ. He was TGTBT too. Should I look for another agenda with him? Later. I couldn't deal with that right now.

"How did you find me, Cat?" Sudden determination replaced Sandy's poor-me attitude. "There had to be more qualified people for your assistant's job than a promising college graduate."

There had been. I turned to Aunt Char who sat regally up in bed, every hair in place, a golden glow haloing her. "Ricky Martinez recommended you. He said he saw you at the State Newscaster's Championships."

"I finished second. I don't remember..." Sandy chewed a nail. "Wait a minute, the judge with the slouchy hat."

I wasn't the only one lost by that statement. Every eye in the room locked on her, including Penny's. Sandy hurriedly explained. "I mean, he wore that worn Panama hat of his. I remember thinking he was weird."

Truthfully, so did I. Five years ago, I almost hadn't hired him because I doubted his ability to fit in. He'd proven me wrong about the fitting in part. Everyone seemed to work well with the strong, silent studio cameraman. I had been right about him marching to a different drummer, though.

"I met Ford a month later," Sandy said.

I didn't need to see Uncle G or Russ's eye roll to know their opinion on coincidence. The possibility alone gave me the creeps. I'd worked shoulder to shoulder with Ricky for five years, five days a week. He'd even ingratiated himself into Barkview's naturalist community. Sure, he could easily be the surveillance link we'd been looking for. No one would question a bird watcher hanging around outdoors, but he'd not slipped once. Only a full-on psychopath could be that covert.

Fortunately, Aunt Char stopped that line of inquiry in its tracks by pointing out, "Ricky was in the control booth with Cat when Lynda was killed."

"What's bothering you, Russ?" Uncle G asked. "Ford hit Lynda with the Cavalier statue trying to escape with Lady Mag."

"Motivation. Assuming Ford made the call to the police

that saved Cat ten years ago, why would he want revenge now?"

"His father is dying. Maybe he's trying to redeem himself."

Russ's frown dismissed Uncle G's line of thinking. "The kid wanted out."

"He feels guilty about his role putting his dad away and dying in prison."

It wasn't tracking for me either. The Ford I knew seemed like a genuinely kind-hearted family doctor. I borrowed a line from Uncle G. "What's your gut telling you, Sandy?"

Sandy chewed her lip. "I-I have no idea what was real and what wasn't anymore."

Could I ever relate? "Well, we need to focus on Ford. We know he was involved. Where is he now?"

"Waiting for me at home with Jack, a glass of milk, and warm chocolate chip cookies."

Talk about foreplay. I sneaked a peek at Russ's reaction. Add a tank top and running shorts and... Now I was hallucinating. I'd be happy with a warm body waiting for me when I arrived home. Food would be an added bonus.

"Are you going to arrest him?" Sandy asked.

Uncle G crushed her hopefulness. "Question him. It's not against the law to do a medical residency in San Diego and, uh, live in Barkview."

He caught himself before restating the rotten boyfriend angle. Good. Sandy's stricken expression told just how hard this betrayal had hit her. I changed the subject.

"I know it's a long shot, but if the cookies are tainted, they could be evidence."

Good thing Penny had destroyed them. She'd be forgiven. I, on the other hand, would have been hanged.

Uncle G agreed. "Even if I rush it, it will be a few days before we know anything."

"I can help expedite," Russ said.

"Ford doesn't deal with confrontation at all. He'll be gone if he thinks we are on to him." Sandy checked the time. "I need to go home as usual. I must keep up the façade."

I admired her grit. In fact, she even appeared taller than her normal five-foot eight-inches in flats. I couldn't be responsible for my actions the next time I saw Ford.

"It's too dangerous for you to go home tonight, Sandy. He has killed before," Aunt Char said.

"Accidentally. I'd bet Lynda recognized him when he stole Lady Mag." Sandy's shoulders squared.

Uncle G dialed his phone. "I will put surveillance on Ford."

Sandy's tone did not waver. "I have to do this. I caused the problems."

Nice as passing the blame was, I couldn't let her take it. "I caused the problem," I said. "Ten years ago, a boy took pity on me and I paid him back by putting his father in prison to die." Crazy as it sounded, I got it. This was a boy's revenge executed by a man, a very smart man who'd had years to plan. "This is between Ford and me. He gave me a second chance. Now, he wants payback."

I could hear my own heartbeat in the silence. I stopped Aunt Char's objection with my hand gesture. "This only ends with a confession. I need to confront Ford. Besides, we only have circumstantial evidence that he killed Lynda."

"A confession?" Aunt Char sat even more upright in bed. "This man is a psychopath, Catalina. You will not be bait for a trap. It is far too dangerous."

Did it matter? We had zero prosecutable evidence. Neither one of us nor Sandy would be safe until Ford was apprehended. I saw no choice but to defy her. I covered her cool hand with my warm one. "I love you and appreciate what you are saying, but there is no other way. He will continue to come after all those I love. If not now, then sometime later when I am not prepared. Maybe I'm being naive, but I know in my heart this must end now. Besides, Uncle G and Russ will protect me."

"Too risky. We can't control the outcome. I agree with Char," Uncle G said grimly.

"Confronting him gives us surprise on our side. He will make a mistake," I insisted.

"We'll be improvising as well," Uncle G pointed out.

"You have to agree, ours is the position of strength." I hoped anyway. "What do you think, Russ? Am I crazy?"

"No doubt. I agree with your aunt. If Ford did execute this elaborate scheme, he'll be unpredictable knowing he failed," Russ said.

"But you agree he needs to be stopped." No pussyfooting politically correct stuff allowed. I expected my man to support me.

"Yes."

"I'm open to better suggestions." The silence made my point for me. I didn't like putting my safety on the line either, but there was no other way. I looked deep into Aunt Char's troubled cobalt eyes. *"Courage is not the absence of fear, but the realization that other things are more important than fear.* Right, Aunt Char?"

"Nothing is more important than your safety," Aunt Char insisted.

Russ agreed. I could see it in his tight jaw line. That hurt badly. Why didn't even matter. Loyalty did. Not standing by me was an uncompromising dump 'em verdict. I turned away. I couldn't look at him. I felt like I'd been stabbed in the heart.

I nearly jumped a foot when he came up behind me. "Cat, we need another plan." He always read me so well.

I shook off his touch and the tingle. "There's nothing left to say."

"Yes, there is. Your safety is paramount."

I pivoted, my anger barely restrained in my whisper. "Supporting me is paramount."

"You're not being reasonable."

"Reasonable!" How dare a man who ran into a burning building to save dogs pass judgment on me? "This is the only way to protect Aunt Char and Sandy and get Lynda's killer."

He went stone-still. "Setting yourself up as bait is irresponsible. I will not support your death wish. We need another plan."

He'd made his choice and so had I. So much for Mister Perfect. I needed to run a few miles or cry my eyes out, but who had time now? I walked to Penny's side and scratched her ear. At least she agreed with me. Her head cocked smartly to one side, her melting dark eyes in perfect agreement. Protect Aunt Char at all costs. I would. No matter what anyone else said.

I inhaled deeply and mentally counted to ten before refocusing on the conversation going on around me.

"There is another option. We might be able to find evidence if Sandy will allow us to search her home," Uncle G suggested.

"You can search anywhere you like." Sandy's scorned-woman tone chilled the air. "I don't know what you'll find, but I hope it's incriminating."

So did I, but they wouldn't find enough. I knew as sure as the event had already happened. Uncle G's search would be legal, but fruitless and send Ford into hiding. I had to act now. "So, you gentlemen have a plan then. I need to get my head together." I motioned for Sandy to follow me.

My meek acceptance failed miserably. No one was buying it. Aunt Char glanced heavenward, undoubtedly asking for JB's divine intervention. No lightning. Not even a crack of thunder.

Just more oppressively tense silence. "Catalina Wright, promise me that you will let the chief do his job."

"Of course, just like I always do." Granted, my word choice could've been better. I still didn't deserve the collective stink eye, especially from Russ. He'd failed me.

"Penny stays with you," she announced.

Penny the vicious watch dog? "I'm going to the studio."

"It's Sunday," Uncle G said.

"My car is parked there. Remember?" It had been since yesterday. Had it only been two days since the world had turned upside down?

"Penny stays with you or I will walk right out of here with you." Aunt Char's chest-pounding cough belied that threat.

Aunt Char's adamancy always translated into my capitulation, so further objection admitted guilt. "Penny, come." I swear the fur ball nodded to Aunt Char before jumping off the bed and falling in step with Sandy and me. Penny might be a little fighter, but her bite couldn't stop a toddler brandishing a rattle.

"I'll drive you." For my ears only, Sandy whispered, "Whatever you need for me to do."

I had two allies. At this point, I needed all the help I could get.

CHAPTER 21

Knowing the role of Sandy's Jeep in the conspiracy made climbing in weird. Even Penny hesitated long enough to get Sandy's attention. "Okay. What's wrong?"

I didn't have the heart to tell her yet. Silence reigned as we drove the three blocks to 2nd Street and parked.

"Call Ford. Tell him there's a problem with your car and he needs to come to save you right away. That should get him out of the house before Uncle G gets there and sends him running. Wait until you see him drive up and call Uncle G for reinforcements."

"Your plan is to confront Ford here in the parking lot and hope the chief gets here in time?" Sandy didn't need to add her opinion. Her pressed-lip disapproval said it all.

"I would've preferred some guaranteed firepower back up, but..." Penny barked. I scratched her head. "Men are unreliable."

Sandy muttered something I knew I didn't want to hear but pressed for anyway. "What did you say?"

"This plan is insane. You can't seriously blame Russ or Uncle G for refusing to play along."

"It's Russ's job to support my decisions."

"Wow! I see your issue with men. You want a lap dog. Not a partner."

I did not. I preferred strong, decisive men. Just look at my last five failures.

Sandy's open palm stopped my denial. "Who am I to judge?" She made the call and left the urgent message.

"Now, we wait. I'll get the stun gun from my desk upstairs. Have your cellphone recorder ready. Don't worry. There are people all over. If something goes wrong, we can scream for help." I hoped I sounded more confident than I felt. Uber bravery did not enter the equation. Sanity preservation demanded that I choose the risky plan now rather than wait to be the whenever target later.

Sandy waved me away, regretting her part already, I was sure. Time to prepare for Ford's arrival. I left Sandy on lookout duty in the parking lot and headed inside, nearly tripping over Penny, her butt planted in front of the elevator door. Hadn't we gotten past this yet? I pressed the call button. "You win this time. Not because I'm a wimp, but because I'm too tired to fight you."

She wagged her tail. I scratched her head. Détente had merits.

The elevator groaned its age as it rumbled downward. Or was that the building requesting more work? Between the hundred-and-fifty-year-old structure and ninety-year-old plumbing, repair represented a significant monthly expenditure. I still wouldn't change it for anything. Funny, I'd never noticed just how spooky the place sounded at night all alone.

I stilled my breath. Ghosts weren't the problem. I followed

Penny into the elevator and rode it up to the second floor. As the door slid open, she poked only her nose out and sniffed. I followed suit. Orange wood polish and...

I swear Penny's look questioned my sanity. What was I thinking? I didn't bother to even answer that one. I just followed. She looked both ways as if crossing an intersection before exiting into the dimly lit hall. Except for the light streaming from beneath my office door, the hallway was inky-dark. Wait a minute. Why was my office door closed? Penny's nose cocked toward my door, sniffing I wished I knew what.

Her sudden ready-to-attack stance sent my heart rabbit-racing. Ford couldn't be here waiting for me. How could he possibly have known I'd come here tonight? My car, I realized in a rush. Monday was a workday. I'd have to pick it up some-time tonight.

Knowing this meeting had been inevitable didn't help at all. I just wished Russ were here. I pressed his preset call button on my phone. It connected to voicemail.

"Russ, I'm in trouble." No time to disconnect or run. Penny's deep, threatening growl came a split second before my office door flew open and a black and white blur, teeth-bared, leaped out at me!

OMG! Déjà vu! Dim light and an out-for-my-blood Pit Bull. I reacted instinctively. I threw my crossed forearms up in front of my face and waited for the teeth-into-flesh bite. I counted one, two. I tasted blood. Heard a guttural to-the-death bark. I braced myself. I was a goner now.

Another bark, equally as vicious, but different. Hope soared. Help! I peeked and about died on the spot. Separating me from the drooling-at-the-mouth, fight-ready Pit Bull stood Penny, every hair standing up on end, every tooth bared!

Freeze-frame the Pit Bull. It wasn't a Hollywood horror

flick either. Little prissy Penny had given me a nanosecond, maybe two, to escape before the vicious larger dog chomped her. Furballs! Frantically, I looked around. I needed a weapon —any weapon. The Queen Mum bust!

I'm not exactly sure how it all happened. But the next thing I remember is hearing Penny's agonizing cry and tripping over the Pit Bull sprawled unconscious at my feet with the bronze bust of Penny's great, great, great grandmother rolling from side to side on the floor beside him. Forget the Pit Bull. Penny lay on the floor in a ragdoll heap. Tears nearly blinded me as I kneeled beside her. She was hurt badly. Bright red blood stained the whole side of her body. That Pit Bull had vampired her good. I had to stop the bleeding fast. I untied my scarf and pressed it into the deep puncture wound. She raised her head and blinked at me, thanking me. No! She had to fight. Renaissance, the silly, pampered champion, had saved me from the Pit Bull.

Out of the corner of my eye I saw a shadow. Was it real or just a memory? I screamed anyway. "Call an ambulance. Renny is hurt badly."

"Tsk, tsk, Catalina the cat lover cares about a dog?" I recognized the voice right away. It wasn't Ford. Could the nightmare get any worse? "Ricky." I kept the pressure on Renny's wounds as I looked up. Although the hair and clothes hadn't changed, I hardly recognized the fiery madness burning in his hazel eyes. "Where is Ford?"

"Passed out on his sofa about now."

That made no sense. He'd gotten his revenge. Or was it his revenge after all? "You drugged him."

Ricky's smug half-smile said far more than words. I scrambled to my feet. I needed a way out. Seconds mattered to Renny right now. "Why are you doing this?"

His high-pitched laughter creeped me out. "The all-knowing Cat Wright without answers?" He was serious. Had Ford been a conspirator after all?

"Ford was there that night." I remembered now as clearly as if it had been yesterday. He'd been the wide-eyed boy chewing gum outside the liquor store, the shadow that I'd seen before the attack. He'd called the police.

"Ford wasn't involved. That sissy-boy couldn't stand the sight of blood." Another evil sneer. There was no love lost between the two men.

More like Ford couldn't stand to see the dogs suffer. "Forgive me. I was a little distracted that night. I don't remember you."

"Don't you, Cat? I'm disappointed. Very disappointed."

And annoyed, I realized, suddenly inexplicably calm. Think, Cat, this was the first exploitable break in his armor. Keep raining on his revenge. What good was a plan if your target didn't get it? I glanced at Renny's blood soaking through my scarf. I didn't have time for this. The question was, who was this guy and what did he want? "If Ford is Castro's son, then you are...."

"Ford is Christine's son."

Christine's son? What an odd thing to say. It hit me then. Christine was Castro's second wife. Apparently, Castro's first marriage shouldn't have technically ended in an annulment.

"You are so easy to read. I see you have it all figured out."

Suddenly, it all made perfect sense. Ricky was Castro's eldest son. "Why did you kill Lynda Smythe?"

"That stupid woman recognized me. Swore she'd make me pay. Me?" The madness came through his cackle loud and clear.

So, it had been an accident. Lynda hadn't come to the

station to confront Aunt Char. She'd come after Ricky. "The Dior button?"

"Your aunt snags them on her chair. I found that one on the stage a few weeks ago."

"What about Mark?"

"Who? Oh, that frat boy friend of yours? He shoulda stayed away. Enough. It's your turn, Cat." He leveled the gun to my chest.

OMG! I was going to die. "How did you do it? I mean, how did you get the dogs? You were in the control room with me when Lady Mag was taken."

"Delaying isn't going to change anything, but all right. Outsmarting you amuses me."

I counted to five before he continued. "I went on the coffee run."

I remembered the foot-tall frothy caramel cappuccino. I'd forgotten how he'd only returned minutes before the hard start. "Aunt Char always said my caffeine addiction would be the death of me."

"She was wrong."

"How did you know about Somerset?" Somerset's early appointment had been too last minute to be meticulously planned.

"Opportunity. I saw his early drop off from Madame Orr's and simply moved up the schedule."

Sandy and I'd even seen him walk down the street that day. "How did you know about the gate?" But I knew. Ford's running buddy, Sean Riley, had to have given him that info, as well as the intel on the collars. Ford was involved.

"You dressed up like José. The brown contacts gave you away." Ricky's narrowed gaze scared me. He didn't like mistakes. "Hiding the Cavaliers at Ford's grandmother's old rescue was a mistake. Dog drool leaves DNA." Whether it did

219

or not was irrelevant. Keeping him talking was my only chance.

Ricky's evil laugh chilled me to the bone. "Another Ford task. Kid did his job that time. Guess he wanted to protect his grandma's friends. I see you've answered the rest of your questions. You're too smart for your own good."

Not exactly. Or I would've figured this all out years ago. José and Ria's secret identities, the J. Tracker versus Petronics collar wars, the Crown rivalries, Olivia's spitefulness, and the cash donations had all been innocently unrelated. Talk about skeletons. Sleepy Barkview sure had a pack of them.

"Your father will be disappointed in you if you shoot me." I gulped down the lump in my throat. "He gets his kicks out of pain and suffering."

Ricky's sudden smile didn't track. There was more and I knew what it was. "Besides everyone will know you did it."

"Ford did it." He tossed a UCSD hat onto the floor. Presumably Ford's, with the DNA to tie this all neatly together.

"And what about you?" I asked desperately.

"I'll show up for work tomorrow as shocked as everyone else."

My eyes darted every which way. No escape. I envisioned leaping for the planter. I didn't think. I just reacted. I'd buy another second while he re-aimed, then I'd die in good company beside Renny.

Suddenly, Ricky screamed. A shot whizzed past my ear as my shoulder jammed into the floor. Pain blasted through me. More shots! Was I hit? I rolled onto my side, prepared for what, I had no idea.

I saw the rest through the large fern leaves in excruciatingly slow motion. Ford charging up the stairs. Ricky jerking backward then falling like a California Torrey Pine. And it was over. Ford had saved the day!

Or had he? I scrambled to my feet before I saw the whole truth. Renny lay crumpled beside Ricky, her teeth clamped to his ankle. Ford deserved my gratitude, but he hadn't saved me. That stubborn little princess had.

"No!" My scream greeted Russ, Uncle G and the paramedics who suddenly overran the room. "It's Renny. She's been bit."

The white-clad EMV beelined to her while the sandy-haired EMT caught me as my head started spinning. It's true you don't feel pain during a crisis. The minute it's over, watch out. My shoulder, heck my whole right side, felt like it had been hit by a tractor-trailer. Renny's blood all over me didn't help any either. It took forever to explain it wasn't mine.

"You need x-rays," the paramedic insisted.

"I'll be fine. Renny..." Russ stepped in before I could level the man. He held me against his unyielding chest.

"She's alive, Cat," he whispered, stroking my hair.

Blinding tears rolled down my cheeks unchecked. I didn't even care about my beach ball-sized shoulder or that he was all wrong for me. "She-she saved me."

"I know," he said.

"I need to tell her that..."

"She knows you love her."

I did, too. I, the quintessential cat lover, loved a persnick-ety, yappy, needy d-o-g.

Before I knew it, the EMV had Renny on the stainless-steel gurney. She looked so small and vulnerable lying motionless, her rust fur matted to her side and an IV poking in her paw. Her brown eyes stared blankly at me, unfocused. Was it the drugs or worse? "Is she...?"

"The U is ready for her," the bloodstained vet said. "I won't lie to you. She's lost a lot of blood."

I scratched Renny behind her ear. "Don't even think it. We're not done yet." She didn't move, didn't even blink, but I swear I saw a spark in her dark eyes as they rushed her out. Granted, it wasn't the usual fire, but I knew deep down she'd make it.

I hadn't lied to her. It wasn't over. In the chaos, Ford had escaped.

CHAPTER 22

While Uncle G and Russ took off after Ford, the doc reset my dislocated shoulder a floor below Aunt Char's room at the hospital. Why Ford ran I will never understand. He'd only been guilty of moving stolen property to protect his grandmother's friends.

Renny survived exactly like I knew she would. I'll never forget that long night at the University Animal Hospital waiting room with a pale but regal Aunt Char and drinking a gallon of that engine oil they passed off as coffee. She'd known that Renny would be fine, but had waited with Sandy and me against her doctor's orders. We alternated between pacing the tile floor and sitting on the hard-as-a-rock faux leather sofa, our hearts in our throats every moment the ER doors swung outward. Two hours into the wait, Sandy went on a caffeine-worthy run and I popped the question.

"How do you know Renny's going to be okay?" I had a lot more questions about the weird, inconsistent flashes of intuition, but figured this was the easiest place to start.

She smiled that frustrating, serene smile of hers and patted my hand. "Because I know."

"So do I, but how?"

Her smile seemed both pleased and sad at once. We shared something a little creepy. "Cat, you have survived a traumatic experience. Things happened that you can't explain. That doesn't make them any less real."

"I didn't say they weren't real."

"Didn't you? Western medicine doesn't have all the answers. Eastern philosophy says your mind went to another plane."

The explanation was even stranger than the experience itself. "How am I supposed to understand this?"

"You aren't. The key is to embrace these new feelings and learn from them."

"Learn what? How to deal with betrayal? I failed big time with Ricky. Did you suspect he was...?"

Aunt Char frowned. "I knew he was off. So did you. Certainly not to this extent. The man must have multiple personalities to keep up the façade for five years. Fascinating really."

"No. You are not making excuses. I refuse to feel sorry for him." I felt slightly better knowing I hadn't been the only one fooled. My faith in my ability to read people had been shaken to the core, though.

"Don't start questioning yourself, Cat. You didn't do anything wrong with Ricky," Aunt Char said. "Some good did come out of this. You conquered your fear of dogs today."

"I wasn't afraid..." Okay, maybe I was a little anxious around large dogs with big bicuspids. Who wasn't?

"All right. You had issues. In fact, your issues with dogs made you demand a dog's loyalty from people."

"That's insane." Or was it? My denial tasted all wrong.

Wasn't that the story of my love life? Did I really demand blind loyalty? All Russ had done was refuse to support my insane sitting-duck plan. I rubbed my shoulder in the sling as I thought about Russ storming into the hallway to save me. He'd been right. I'd taken an unnecessary risk. I owed him an apology, but he was gone. Destination unknown. Return uncertain. But I wanted another chance. I just needed to figure out how to make it happen.

Fortunately, he did return six days later with a triumphant Uncle G and Ford in custody. I found out with the rest of the national media at the police headquarters briefing. My reckless behavior had negated any insider points.

Although both men had cleaned up, they looked tired as they faced the cameras. Uncle G wore his Barkview dress blue uniform and Russ a dark suit and power tie. I couldn't help the little jump in my pulse just seeing him, nor my disappointment when Uncle G dismissed the entire press corps without allowing a single question. Not that I would've asked the one burning on my mind in a public forum. Heck yeah, I would've. *Can you forgive me, Russ?*

I waited around as long as I dared. Sure, I was late for the Barkfest, but I for one wanted more information—the personal kind that only Russ could answer. I finally cornered him in front of the building while the reporters packed up.

"Russ, can…" The words stuck in my suddenly-dry throat.

"Not right now, Cat."

I don't know exactly what I expected, but not his gruffness. My heart sank. I had blown it. "L-later then?" I tried for upbeat. Settled for hopeful.

"Sure." He disappeared into the building without another word. Sure what? Maybe my timing wasn't the best, but he'd never brushed me off like that before.

I played back every nuance from his board-stiff spine to his noncommittal answer as I headed to the Barkfest. I missed his smoldering looks and humor; even how well he read me. It couldn't end like this. I refused to let it. LA wasn't that far away. After the Barkfest, I'd drive up there, and sit on his doorstep until he listened to me

CHAPTER 23

I'd always considered the pomp and ceremony beneath the Barkfest big top to be a three-ring circus. This year's English garden theme felt comforting. Vibrantly blooming rose trellises framed the tiered aisles of the three-hundred-and-sixty-degree observation area, overlooking the manicured arena lawn. Ladies wearing rose-adorned Kentucky Derby hats sat beside bareheaded men toasting with bubbling champagne flutes, their every whim answered by Victorian uniformed wait staff carrying silver trays.

I stood on what amounted to the Rose Bowl's fifty-yard line in the Barklay observation box adjacent to the climbing rose-latticed judging dais. Surrounded by the familiar smell of freshly cut grass and fragrant teacup roses, I felt the warmth of tradition as Aunt Char opened the event. Elegantly dressed in a green and gold suit, wearing her signature stilettos, a mini rose entwined hat, and the Barklay Cavalier diamond necklace, she welcomed the competitors, guests and national media with grace and poise. She did belong in politics. She could do so much good for this town as mayor.

Oddly concerned by Renny's absence, I hightailed it behind the scenes to the dog prep area. Although she did not always accompany Aunt Char to the podium, I'd expected her and Aunt Char to present that impervious front they did so well. I wasn't worried about the Barklay Kennel's reputation. Three Kennel puppies and three two-year-olds had advanced to their divisional finals.

Renny was my concern. By special committee proclamation, she'd advanced to the Cavalier finals without competing in the prelims due to her reigning champion status. The Kennel Club had offered to postpone the Best of Breed competition until she had completely recovered, but Aunt Char had refused. Remarkably, the Pit Bull's teeth had missed all vital organs. Except for a few nasty bruises and a sprained right paw, the vet claimed she was good to go. I needed to see that to believe it.

I found Aunt Char and José deep in discussion just outside the Barklay Kennel's curtained staging area. "My dear, I'm glad you're here," Aunt Char said. "Please talk to Renny."

Talk to Renny? I peeked around José's dark-suited shoulders. Five dogs sat at attention outside Renny's kennel. This was not good. Renny usually reviewed the other dogs with military precision. "Is she okay?"

Aunt Char smiled sadly.

Tears threatened. She'd be the princess today if not for me. "Is she in pain?"

José shook his head. "It's in her head. She doesn't want to compete."

Anger took over. "After what she's been through. She..." I couldn't get the words out. I'd spoken louder than I'd thought. Bart peeked out of his prep room, so did the mayor. Wonderful, I'd just announced to the competition that Renny wasn't up to par.

"She must compete," José insisted. "It's like falling off a horse. She must get up."

For horses, I was all in, but a dog? The whole idea seemed ludicrous. "Aunt Char?" Surely, she would side with Renny.

Aunt Char's noncommittal 'talk to her' bothered me.

"Me?" What did I know about motivating a dog?

Aunt Char squeezed my hand. "Trust your instincts."

"Instincts?" Not intuition. I swallowed hard. "Go win some medals."

"We will, my dear." Aunt Char's wave disappeared in a cloud of young Cavalier fluff.

I stood at the doorway and rubbed my arm in the sling. "Renny, come. They're gone."

Renny's nose peeked out of her kennel first. Her head came next and then her front paws. Her Blenheim coloring stood out in fluffed and buffed perfection. Her eyes were the problem. Normally bright, spunky, and full of mischief, I saw only soulful brown. The two of us looked like an ad for the walking wounded.

We sat in silence for a long time. How did you pep talk a dog? Granted she was a special dog, but how? Speak from the heart, Aunt Char had said. Everyone believed that. Dogs, too, I hoped. "I don't care if you do this or not. You know that, don't you?"

With senior citizen speed, Renny exited the shadowed kennel, her weak paw cocked slightly to one side, not bearing her full weight. She'd been beat up and near death six days ago. How could anyone expect her to compete?

She flopped sphinx style at my feet, her exhausted exhale saying it all. I scratched her head. "I miss Penny."

I recognized her you've-lost-your-mind look. Maybe I had. I was talking to a dog. "Before we sit this one out, you need to know that physical beauty isn't everything." No kidding. Look at what sexy and gorgeous Sandy had just endured from a supposed boyfriend.

"It sure doesn't make a champion. That perfect spot on your head isn't the clincher either." I lifted her manicured good paw. "Or your clipped nails. Perfect teeth don't matter except for eating," I added. "Courage does."

Bart's clipped British accent interrupted me. "She is correct, my lady. Courage is paramount." He filled the doorway, Duke at his feet, his expressive Spaniel eyes concerned. Was that cocky Duke? Talk about an attitude change. Had it been the offensive dye odor turning him off all along? This proper English dog had Renny's attention. Her head cocked to the right as she gave him a coy once over.

Olivia chimed in next. "Compassion makes a champion." A fluffed Somerset slipped past Duke and nudged Renny with her nose.

"Heart defines a champion," the mayor added. Lady Mag, her Blenheim head high, squeezed in beside Duke.

Any question I had about dogs communicating dispensed at that moment. Renny's head was higher. I kneeled beside her. "I want to be just like you when I grow up."

All the attention worked. Renny stood, or at least tried to. She stumbled, teetered as if intoxicated, and sat again. Duke nudged her until she tried again. I am not sure if pride took over or simple grit, but she stood that time, unsteadily, but entirely on her own. Tears pricked my eyes and Olivia's at the picture of the four champion Cavaliers together helping one of their own.

Jennifer Holt wrecked the moment when she sashayed in wearing a flowing Victorian gown and announced the final best of breed line up. The competitors scattered with a hand-in-the-cookie-jar haste that made me laugh. Renny agreed. She licked my cheek. Forget my rush to antibacterial soap. I scratched her head. This was a proud momma moment.

Aunt Char's right-on timing didn't surprise me. "She's ready." I handed her Renny's gold lead. I didn't mention the other dogs' tribute. I didn't have to. Aunt Char knew.

She dabbed a tear. "This is your victory lap." She unclasped the Barklay Cavalier necklace.

I stepped back as if burned. "No way! I never..."

"Russ is out there."

Russ! He hadn't left after all. He'd made his feelings plain though. "I don't know what to do."

"Apologize, Cat. Give him a chance."

It wasn't that easy. "I-I don't mean that." The hell I didn't. I cleared my throat. "I don't know the show protocols. What if I do something to get Renny eliminated?"

Aunt Char's finger beckon drew me like a firefly to light. She untied my scarf and clipped the glittering, diamond necklace around my throat. "It's your time. Just focus. It will all come to you."

My time for what exactly? To make a complete fool of myself and Renny? The weight of the heirloom necklace felt oddly familiar.

"Just follow the Yellow Brick Road."

It was a cushy, light-as-air red carpet, but Aunt Char'd made her point. Russ deserved a plain old-fashioned apology. I didn't want to deliver it under the scrutiny of every gossip-hungry Barkviewian. Butterflies twittered in my stomach each step closer to the holding area adjacent to the show arena. Packed with waist-high vased roses, the sweet fragrance overpowered any lingering dog scents and brought an English garden to mind.

Russ was there. All unyielding six feet something of him lounging against a door jam, frowning. This was my chance.

Except he'd expected Aunt Char. Not me. He'd come to wish Renny luck, I realized, when he kneeled to scratch her ear. My flight instinct kicked in, but I couldn't run. Not this time.

My heart pounded instead. I should've known later did mean "later" to him. "I-I'm sorry."

"These were extraordinary circumstances," he said diplomatically.

"You're telling me. I still owe you..."

His forefinger pressed against his lips. No talking? He didn't want to hear my excuses. The knife jabbed my heart. It was over.

He swept to his feet, his expression serious. Tingles started in my toes as his hand closed over mine. "This isn't going to be easy between us. We're both strong-willed."

"Nothing worth having is easy."

"True. Trust is earned," he said.

Especially after you throw it away with both hands. Yet, his smile seemed genuine enough, so was the implication. He wanted to try to make us work. I didn't know if that was even possible, but I wanted to try.

"I..."

Jennifer Holt's interruption wrecked the moment. "Mr. Hawl, you can't be back here. You two can talk later."

"Yes, ma'am." Russ inclined his head. "I understand. Break a leg, ladies."

"Thanks a—"

"Don't be mad. He meant it as good luck," said Jennifer.

I squashed my smile at her rush to defend. "I know." He still deserved a taste of the riot act over that one. That left Jennifer, Renny, and me at the precipice of an arena full of looky-loos. I closed my eyes and focused.

I heard the murmurs and applause from the main stage, but I couldn't make out a single thing over my suddenly racing heart. It was time. I led Renny to the arched entrance. The ring was dark, except for the spotlight focused on Duke. He looked Cavalier-perfect the way his tail draped and his stance showed his broad chest. Beating him would take a miracle.

I unvelcroed my sling and tossed it aside. Forget doctor's orders, this was bigger than any injury. I reached down and unclipped the leash and motioned Renny into the ring. "Show them, Renny."

She tossed her head as the spotlight found us. The near-deafening applause did not deter her. Her weak leg did, and she stumbled. The crowd's gasp affected me too. So did Renny's melting brown eyes. The pain was too much for her.

A single clap and call for Renny, then another and another joined in until the chant replaced the applause. I tried to scoop her up, but she shook me off. I recognized the Barklay I'll-gut-it-out look. Forget the sore puncture wounds, the painful paw sprain, and the itchy belly shave. Leg quivering, Renny walked, one paw in front of the other, all the way around the arena, her head held champion high. We both did.

I thought about Russ's 'trust is earned' comment and I suddenly got it. Winning didn't matter today...moving on did.

The End

Join Cat on her quest for the perfect dog when she teams up with a German Shepherd to locate a stolen diamond and avenge the murder of an Olympic defector in *Shepherded to Death*.

Hope you enjoyed your adventure in the dog-friendliest

233

place in America. To learn more about Barkview and Cat's next adventure visit: www.cbwilsonauthor.com.

Sign up for **The Bark View** a monthly update all things Barkview including:

- *Friday Funnies,* pet related cartoons
- Recipes from *Bichon Bisquets Barkery's* canine kitchen
- Cool merchandise ideas from the *Bow Wow Boutique.*
- Not to mention Barkview news and fun contests.

Don't miss Cat's next adventure:

AVAILABLE NOW: BICHONED TO DEATH

What was once a simple rivalry turns into a deadly dog fight.

The award-winning, dog-loving chef should've been a perfect fit in the dog friendliest city in America, but no one is following the script. When murder strikes on the set of her hit cable show, *Fido's Food Fest,* executive producer Cat Wright wonders if this a competition gone wrong or something more?

With her star chef under arrest and her Bichon Frise a target, Cat realizes that far more than gold-ribbon dog treats are at stake.

Can Cat dig up enough evidence to bury the killer before he strikes again?

Bichoned to Death is the tasty second book in the Barkview Mysteries cozy mystery series. If you like characters living on the edge, surprising twists, and plenty of paw-inspired humor, then you'll love C.B. Wilson's bark worthy adventure.

Acknowledgments

When I started writing, I never knew it took a village to complete a book. From my writing cheerleaders, who endlessly listened to my ideas to serious editing, thank you: Pam Wright, Dee Kaler, Rebecca Boschee, Kathleen Givens, Bill Hubiak, Noel Mohberg, Donna Becker, Donna Belgram and Becky Witters.

For research and police procedure assistance, thank you Sergeant Steve Wolf, Irvine Police Department, retired and Richard R. Zitzke, Chief of Police, Whitehall, Ohio, retired. I assure you any errors are entirely my fault.

Thank you Jeremy Vilcheck and Rhys Davies. You took my vision and turned it into Barkview. Thank you Mary Ann and Greg Smith for my adventures with Dixie. She's the star of the show. Thanks to Laura Sciarrio and Rory.

You all have made a dream come true.

About the Author

The award winning author of Cozy Pet Mysteries, C.B. Wilson's love of writing was spurred by an early childhood encounter with a Nancy Drew book where she precociously wrote what she felt was a better ending. After studying at the Gemology Institute of America, she developed a passion for researching lost, stolen and missing diamonds—the big kind. Her fascination with dogs and their passionate owners inspired Barkview, California, the dog friendliest city in America.

C.B. lives in Peoria, AZ with her husband. She is an avid pickleball player who enjoys traveling to play tournaments. She admits to chocoholic tendencies and laughing out loud at dog comics.

To connect with C.B Wilson:
www.cbwilsonauthor.com
www.facebook.com/cbwilsonauthor

Made in the USA
Middletown, DE
19 June 2023

32811731R00154